MISSING
IN
FLIGHT

ALSO BY AUDREY J. COLE

Stand-Alones

The One
Only One Lie
The Pilot's Daughter

The Final Hunt Series

The Final Hunt
The Last Hunt

Emerald City Thrillers

The Recipient
Inspired by Murder
The Summer Nanny: A Novella
Viable Hostage
Fatal Deception

MISSING IN FLIGHT

AUDREY J. COLE

THOMAS & MERCER

Published by Thomas & Mercer, Seattle

www.apub.com

Amazon, the Amazon logo, and Thomas & Mercer are trademarks of Amazon.com, Inc., or its affiliates.

ISBN-13: 9781662520709 (paperback)
ISBN-13: 9781662520716 (digital)

Cover design by Ploy Siripant
Cover image: © zhihao / Getty; © Rocio S / Shutterstock

Printed in the United States of America

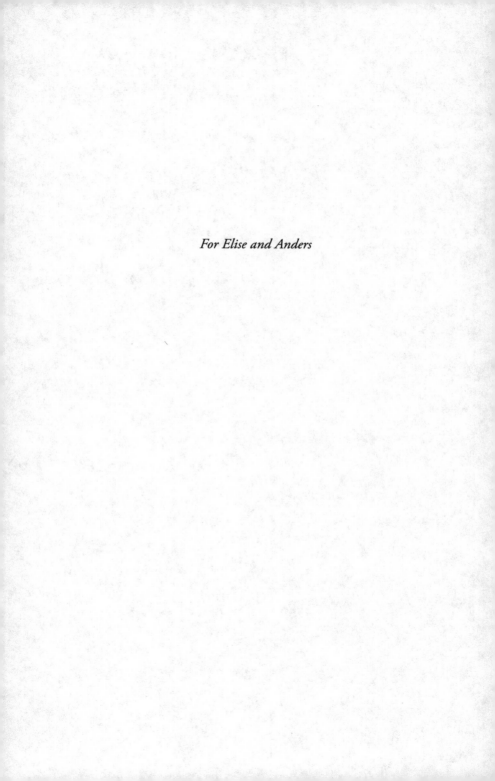

For Elise and Anders

CHAPTER ONE

MAKAYLA

Present

The weight of her head bobbing to the side jars Makayla awake. The cabin is dark. She tilts her head to stretch her neck, suddenly aware of the sharp ache in her bladder. She's still wearing her wrap, but when she looks down, Liam is no longer against her chest. Panic rises to her throat. Her gaze snaps to the bassinet against the bulkhead wall, and she remembers laying Liam down before drifting off to sleep.

She leans forward and exhales, seeing the outline of his sleeping form. He's hardly moved since she last checked on him. She sinks against her seat, still in its upright position, and unbuckles her seat belt.

A glance at her phone tells her there's nearly five hours to go. She bites her lip as she looks at Liam. There's no way she can hold it that long.

I should've gone before we boarded. Sitting forward, she considers putting Liam back into the wrap and taking him with her to the lavatory. His pacifier lies beside him. She can't imagine getting him back to sleep after waking him with the fluorescent lavatory lights and loud suction of the toilet flushing. Just yesterday, after she'd finally gotten Liam to sleep by taking him for a stroller walk along the downtown

Anchorage harbor, a tugboat blared its horn and woke him, and she had to deal with his screaming for the next twenty minutes. She hates to disturb him while he's adjusting to the time change in New York. Waking him now might even undo his new sleep pattern. If he sleeps through the rest of the flight, he'll be back on his New York schedule.

Makayla leans into the aisle and looks around the cabin, which is quiet aside from the drone of the engines. The few passengers around her are asleep, except for the college-aged girl across the aisle who's engrossed in what looks to be a thriller playing on the in-flight video screen. Makayla reaches up and presses the flight attendant call button. Surely, one of them wouldn't mind standing by Liam for the few minutes it takes her to use the bathroom.

The minutes feel like hours as she waits for someone to come. Makayla presses her lips together, trying to think of anything besides how bad she has to pee. Hearing voices in the cabin behind her, she peers down the aisle. A male and a female flight attendant are helping an elderly woman back to her seat. Makayla recognizes the petite, white-haired passenger as the woman an airline employee had to assist onto the plane when she and Liam boarded.

The plane bounces from a bout of turbulence. Makayla inhales a sharp breath from the jolt to her full bladder as the flight attendants struggle to keep the woman from falling over.

"Let go of me!" As the elderly passenger jerks away from one of the attendants, she loses her balance.

Makayla pities the woman, who, from the look of confusion and fear in her eyes, has some sort of dementia. She faces forward in her seat, knowing those two flight attendants won't be answering her call anytime soon. But maybe there is another in the rear galley that could watch over Liam for a few minutes. *Although,* she thinks, *by the time I find someone to come watch over Liam, I could just use the lavatory.*

After checking that Liam is still asleep, Makayla stands. She looks to the young woman across the aisle, who she recognizes from the boarding area, and taps her on the shoulder. The young woman lifts her head toward Makayla, making no effort to pull back her bright-pink headphones.

"Excuse me." Makayla leans toward her. "Would you mind listening for my baby while I use the bathroom?" She points to the bassinet, then the back of the plane. "He's asleep, and I'll be right back. There's a pacifier lying next to him if he wakes up."

The girl glances in the direction of the rear lavatory before nodding. "Yeah."

"Oh, thank you." Makayla offers a smile, and the girl returns to her in-flight entertainment.

After getting the elderly woman to her seat, the flight attendants retreat behind the lavatories as Makayla hurries down the aisle. A cold hand encircles her wrist when Makayla passes the older woman's row. Makayla gasps and yanks away, freeing her hand from the woman's grip.

The woman holds a trembling hand toward Makayla. "Sarah, is that you? They won't tell me where Roger is. Have you seen him?"

"I'm so sorry," a tall blond flight attendant says to Makayla before stepping in between her and the elderly woman. The small diamond stud in the side of her nose reminds Makayla of her friend Cori, a new mother Makayla met before the start of the summer.

The old woman unbuckles her seat belt and shakily stands.

"Rose, I need you to stay in your seat." The attendant's voice takes on a firm tone as Rose makes an unsteady attempt for the aisle.

Makayla continues toward the lavatory as a male flight attendant, short and slightly pudgy, strides down the aisle from the rear of the plane.

"You need some help there, Britt?" he asks.

Makayla steps to the side for him to pass by her, reading the name she heard him being called when he came by earlier with the drink cart. It was pinned to his navy sweater-vest: *Derek*. Before opening the door to the lavatory, Makayla looks beyond the two flight attendants to her seat at the front of the cabin. There's no movement or sound coming from Liam's bassinet. The girl with the pink headphones turns in his direction before looking back at her screen.

Makayla steps inside the small bathroom, feeling a pang of guilt for leaving her baby in the hands of a stranger.

Liam's fine, she reassures herself. Words from the therapist she saw after her mother died pop into her mind as she unzips her jeans. *You should never feel guilty for taking care of your own needs.*

When she sits on the toilet, she feels almost instant relief, knowing her therapist was right. *This will only take a minute. And Liam won't even know I was gone.*

After drying her hands, Makayla tucks a strand of hair that's fallen loose from her ponytail behind her ear and wipes away a small smear of mascara from beneath her eye. She unlocks the lavatory door and pushes on it. The lights flicker inside the small space, but the door doesn't budge. Stemming her impulse to panic, she uses both hands to press her weight into the door. It opens with an audible crack.

From his seat across the aisle, Derek, the flight attendant, meets Makayla's gaze when she steps out of the lavatory. She averts her eyes, shaking the uncomfortable sensation of the male attendant's stare as she emerges from the bathroom. Spotting the side of Liam's bassinet, she takes a deep breath, feeling the tension dissipate from her shoulders. *He's fine.*

Taking quick steps down the narrow aisle, keeping her arms close to her sides, Makayla passes the row where the elderly woman is eating from a tiny bag of pretzels and calmly watching an episode of *Friends* on the seat-back screen in front of her. Makayla contains a smile.

In the next row, a retirement-age couple appears to be asleep, the woman's head on the man's shoulder. Makayla thinks of Jack, wishing he could've come with them.

When she nears the bulkhead, her eyes are drawn to the screen of the young woman across from her, showing a car's headlights speeding down a gravel road at night. She touches the girl on the arm before sitting down.

"Thank you."

The girl looks up, keeping her headphones on. "Sure."

The girl refocuses on her screen as Makayla turns for her seat. She stops. Her heart somersaults. Mouth open and eyes wide, she steps toward Liam's bassinet.

An airplane pillow lies in the place of her son, tucked into his blanket. She snatches the pillow, lifting it into the air as she spins around. Her eyes dart to the young woman's lap as she lifts a pop can toward her mouth. Makayla yanks the pink headphones off the girl's head. Her clear soda sloshes out from the can.

"Where's my son?"

She lifts a startled gaze to Makayla. "Whoa! What are you doing?"

Makayla points to the empty bassinet. "My *son*. Where is he?"

The girl's eyes trail in the direction of Makayla's finger. Her brows knit together as she gapes at Makayla's actions. "I—I don't know."

Makayla scans the sleeping passengers around them. "I asked you to watch him."

The girl's confused expression melts into irritation. "I thought you were asking if the bathroom was in the back." She takes her headphones from Makayla's grip.

Makayla clutches the pillow to her chest. "But where is he? Who took him?"

The girl glances at the bassinet. "I . . . I don't know."

"Well, *someone* took him out of there." How could the girl not have seen a stranger plucking him out of the bassinet?

"I didn't see anyone." She stares blankly at Makayla. "I was watching a movie."

Makayla whips around, inspecting each sleeping passenger's lap for a sign of her baby.

"Excuse me," she calls, moving up the aisle. "Has anyone seen my son? My baby. I just went to the bathroom, and he's gone."

A few passengers open their eyes and shake their heads. Makayla is almost to the lavatories in the middle of the plane, and there's no sign of Liam. She hurries toward the crew seat behind the bathroom, only to find it empty. She scans the rear cabin for someone holding Liam, but the spaced-out passengers all look to be asleep or engrossed in their screens. And she can't see Derek anywhere.

Makayla turns. A few passengers have gotten up from their seats. Makayla recognizes two of them as the retirement-age couple she passed on her way back from the lavatory, and the other as the petite dark-haired woman who handed her Liam's pacifier when they boarded, after her husband bumped into Makayla from behind with their dog carrier. Now, the neatly dressed, muscular man remains seated.

"Did you see anyone come through here while I was in the bathroom?" Makayla asks.

"No," the man says.

The two women shake their heads. They each move up one of the aisleways, scanning the rows for a sign of Liam.

"I didn't notice anyone besides the flight attendants helping that woman across from me," the dark-haired woman says.

The older woman stops and turns to Makayla from the aisle on the other side of the cabin, her expression twisted in bewilderment. "Sorry, I was asleep."

Makayla stands still, feeling the woman's eyes on her as the other two passengers reach the rear of their cabin. Not finding Liam, they turn toward Makayla, the alarm on their faces causing a spike in her anxiety.

The blond flight attendant emerges from business class, making her way up the aisle on the other side of the plane. Makayla crosses through an empty middle row of seats and rushes toward the attendant, who stops close to Makayla's seat. When Makayla reaches her, the blond steps to the side, making room for Makayla to move past her.

"Excuse me." Makayla stops, aware of the panic in her voice. "I can't find my baby—my son. He's . . . he's not . . ." She exhales in frustration as her words fail to come out right. "Someone took him." She points to the empty bassinet affixed to the bulkhead wall.

Makayla thinks of Derek, now gone from his seat. *Please say that one of the crew has him. That he was crying while I was in the bathroom.* Instead, the attendant's eyebrows thread together beneath her bangs as she eyes the empty bassinet.

"Someone took him and put this in his place!" Makayla grabs the pillow and holds it inches from the attendant's face. *Why isn't she taking this more seriously?*

Pink Headphones gapes at Makayla, eyes wide.

"Okay, we'll find him. Try and stay calm." The attendant raises her hands, palms out, and Makayla recognizes it for what it is—an attempt to calm a difficult passenger. "I'll make an announcement. He can't be far."

"I don't understand. I was only gone for a couple of minutes."

"So, you weren't here?"

Makayla grips the top of the seat beside her and forces in a breath, but her lungs won't fully expand. "I just went to the bathroom. For like two minutes."

The woman's face relaxes. "Oh. Well, maybe someone tried to settle him while you were gone."

Makayla shakes her head. "He was asleep."

"Don't worry, I'll make an announcement."

"Can you turn on the lights?"

"Yes." The flight attendant turns and bumps into the woman who recovered Liam's pacifier when Makayla boarded.

The woman looks between Makayla and the attendant. "I moved up and down the cabin with another passenger. We didn't see your baby. Have you checked in first class?"

Makayla makes for the front of the aircraft, unsure if she responded to the woman trying to help her. The college-aged girl who was supposed to be watching Liam has resumed watching her movie beneath her pink headphones.

Makayla wants to shake her.

She flings the curtain open to business class, praying someone heard Liam crying and took him back to their seat when they couldn't find her. It's just as dark as the main cabin. In the three rows sectioned off by curtains at either end, Makayla spots only two passengers.

A middle-aged man wearing a suit sleeps with his head against the window. Makayla leans over and shakes him by the shoulder. His mouth closes with a snap as his eyes open.

"Hi, my baby . . . my baby, Liam, he was asleep in the bassinet right behind your seat in the main cabin. When I came back from the bathroom he was gone. Have you seen him?"

He shakes his head, eyes groggy. "No. Sorry."

A woman with a gray bob turns in her seat two rows in front of him. "Did you say you're looking for your baby?"

Makayla exhales with relief. She steps forward, hoping to find Liam in the older woman's lap. "Yes!"

Instead of Liam, the woman holds two knitting needles above a ball of yarn.

"I'm afraid there's been no baby up here, my dear," the woman says. "Did you check in the back?"

Makayla stares at the woman's lap and the empty seat beside her before yanking open the curtain to first class, scanning the few sleeping passengers and empty seats for a sign of Liam as she moves between the leather chairs.

Liam couldn't have been taken far—it's a plane. Plus, she wasn't in the lavatory for more than a few minutes. *How is this even possible?* Her lungs stiffen with fear, making it impossible to draw in a deep breath.

Where could he be? And why can't I find him?

CHAPTER TWO

ANNA

Three Hours Earlier

Anna reaches forward and presses the number two autopilot button as Miguel finishes his announcement and replaces the PA handset in its holder.

"Nice job. That was a bit of a rough climb out," he says through the interphone.

"Thanks."

"So, the captain you flew out here with called in sick?"

The radio breaks in before she can answer. "Pacific Air 7038, contact Edmonton Center one three four decimal one five. Good day."

Miguel keys the microphone button on his side-stick controller. "One three four decimal one five, roger, Pacific Air 7038." His right hand moves down to the radio panel and spins the knobs to the new frequency.

"Yeah," Anna says. "I could tell he wasn't feeling good during the flight. He had a bad cough and kept blowing his nose. We had a forty-eight-hour layover, so I thought maybe he would've felt better by the time we left. Although, to be honest, I'm kind of relieved not to have to sit next to him for another seven hours." She thinks of her plans for after they land in LaGuardia. She has no desire to get sick. "Were you on call?"

"Yep. I deadheaded to Anchorage last night after getting called in. You live in the city?"

She nods. "My husband's a trauma surgeon at Manhattan General. We live a few blocks from the hospital."

"Ah. That's impressive. That kind of job must be so intense. I pass out from the sight of blood." He flashes her a half smile. "Get woozy from even a paper cut."

"He loves it." She can almost taste the resentment as she says the words. "You live in Manhattan?"

Miguel lifts his index finger as a time-out signal and presses the transmit button on his control stick. "Edmonton Center, Pacific Air 7038 checking in. Flight level three six zero."

"Pacific Air 7038, Edmonton Center, roger. What is your estimate for Fort Laird?"

Anna assesses their nav screen as Miguel responds, remembering they don't have radar as they fly over the Yukon. "Ah, we estimate Fort Laird at zero two three seven," he says, then looks up from the radio panel to meet her eyes again. "What was the question again?"

"Do you live in Manhattan?" Anna repeats.

"Hoboken. We love it there. My wife is a third-grade teacher." He pulls out his phone, ignoring the airline's policy against pilots using their cell phones in flight, and flips the screen toward Anna. "This is Teresa and our twin daughters, Mia and Zoe." Miguel uses two fingers to zoom in on the photo of a blond woman standing in front of the Hudson River, flanked by two brown-haired girls who look to be about ten.

"Beautiful family."

Miguel beams. "Thank you. I think so too. Teresa's pregnant with our third. Due next week." His smile grows wider as he slips his phone into his shirt pocket.

"Oh, congratulations."

Miguel looks out the windshield at the snowcapped mountain peaks protruding above the cloud layer. "It wasn't exactly planned, but we're ecstatic. And the twins can't wait to meet their baby sister."

Anna follows his gaze to the white cloud layer below them.

"You got kids?"

"No." She swallows the tinge of regret that rises to the back of her throat. She and Carter had planned on starting a family once he finished his residency and fellowship, but his work never seemed to slow down. After his fellowship, he only worked harder. Both focused on their careers, and their thirties passed in a blur. They finally started trying for a baby a few weeks before her fortieth birthday. After several months of no success, Anna went to a fertility specialist to learn she'd gone into early menopause, extinguishing her chance of having a child of her own. That was six months ago.

Devasted, she inwardly blamed Carter for them not trying earlier—ruining her chances of getting pregnant. Carter coped with the news by burying himself even deeper in his work. Now he practically lived at the hospital, which only deepened Anna's resentment.

They'd briefly discussed adoption, and Anna had managed to get an appointment last month with New York's top adoption agency, after waiting months to get in. Carter missed the meeting, forgetting to tell her he'd taken an extra shift at the hospital. Without both prospective parents present, Anna was forced to reschedule their meeting for two months later.

She worries about what the state of her and Carter's relationship will be by then. They already feel like strangers.

"How long you been married?"

She chides herself for the last thought that crept into her head. "Almost eight years." Feeling Miguel's eyes on hers, she feigns a smile.

"Fifteen years," Miguel says. "Today, actually." He flips the seat belt sign switch to "Off."

"Oh. Happy anniversary." Hers is at the end of the month. Carter has already told her he'll be working.

"Thank you. We celebrated last week, knowing I'd be on call today. Last year, we were . . . going through some crap and were separated around this time, and I wasn't sure we would make it to this one." The side of his mouth lifts into a half smile. "But we did."

"What changed?"

He hesitates. She worries her question was too personal for having just met.

Miguel lifts his eyes from scanning the engine gauges on the center display panel and stares out the forward windscreen. "Somehow, being together, we'd forgotten what we had. We let life get in the way of what really matters, I guess. After we separated, I realized I didn't ever want to be without her." He shrugs. "Hard to see what's right in front of you sometimes. And now," he adds, "we couldn't be happier."

They hit a bump, and Miguel unbuckles his shoulder straps. "I better use the bathroom before we hit any more turbulence. Coffee's catching up with me."

With his right hand he presses the "FWD" button on the calls panel. "Hey, Miguel here. I need to use the lav. Could one of you come up here?"

Anna notes the fuel remaining and the time at a checkpoint on the navigation log.

He turns to Anna before he climbs out of his seat. "I guess this new policy of having two people on the flight deck at all times is a good idea, but it sure is a pain sometimes."

"Yes, it is," she agrees, sliding one of her headphones behind her ear so she can hear the flight attendant come into the cockpit.

As Miguel moves toward the cockpit door, she thinks about his fifteen-year marriage. Until recently, she always thought she and Carter would be together forever. When they were dating, she'd fallen hard for his humor, his intelligence, his drive. How Carter could be such a hopeless romantic at times. He used to leave notes around the house when they were first married, like *Good morning, beautiful* and *I love your smile.*

But over the years, their spark had dimmed. Hearing Miguel's story makes her both happy for him and sick to her stomach. *Is it hard to see what's right in front of you sometimes? Maybe. But it's also impossible not to notice when the life has gone completely out of something.* She doubts she and Carter can recover from this. Unless something changes. Drastically.

Miguel peers through the glass peephole in the flight deck door. "Here she is. You need anything when I come back?"

"No, I'm good," Anna replies.

Hearing the cockpit door open, she reaches for her phone, remembering she forgot to put it on airplane mode before takeoff.

On the screen is a new text, and her stomach flutters with nervous tension. Despite Miguel's open use of his phone, she lowers hers before opening the message. She bites her lip, fighting the guilt that surfaces at the thought of what she's about to do.

"Thanks, Aubrey," Miguel says to the flight attendant at the door. "I won't be long."

"No problem," Aubrey, the flight attendant assigned as the cabin supervisor, says from the doorway.

Anna's pulse quickens, and she uses the in-flight Wi-Fi to send a reply before Aubrey steps inside.

CHAPTER THREE

MAKAYLA

"Folks, this is your captain speaking. We have reached our cruising altitude of thirty-six thousand feet. We've smoothed out sooner than we expected, so I've turned off the fasten seat belt sign. But just a reminder, it is our policy here at Pacific Air that you keep your seat belt fastened anytime you are seated, just in case we encounter some unexpected turbulence."

Makayla shifts in her seat. Spending two weeks with her dad in Anchorage, where everything seemed to slow down, left her relaxed. Already, the thought of returning to New York and its streets—filled with all those people—makes her lungs seize up. Soon, she'll go back to spending her days alone with Liam in their condo, with Jack's early-morning promises to "see you tonight" followed by his return from the Financial District almost inevitably after she and Liam are asleep.

Makayla eyes the small blanket she tucked around Liam after laying him in the bassinet, cocooning his lower half. Sweet Liam didn't fuss at all during takeoff, when she held him against her chest, despite having been jolted awake by the man with the dog carrier when they boarded. Now, beneath the blanket, his body is still.

A female voice comes through the overhead speakers, announcing the variety of drink options for the first in-flight beverage service.

Makayla's eyes drift to a screen flashing across the aisle. The young woman wearing bright-pink headphones searches through the in-flight entertainment options.

When Makayla's mother's face pops up on the girl's screen, Makayla's breath catches. The girl lingers on the Netflix documentary that recounted Lydia's life and death, particularly her infamous TV interview on *Mornings with Sally*. Makayla didn't realize the airline was showing it. She swallows the bitterness that rises to the back of her throat, wondering if the mention of her mother in Jack's *Forbes* article prompted the airline to acquire the eight-year-old documentary.

She's glad that she's let her hair return to its natural color since her documentary interviews. Her being nearly a decade older, and no longer being blond, should help keep anyone who watches the documentary on the flight from recognizing her.

As Pink Headphones swipes right and selects the latest Reese Witherspoon movie, Makayla relaxes against her seat. She doesn't like how the documentary portrays her mother, highlighting her memory lapse and sensationalizing the home invasion by a fan turned stalker. That incident had traumatized her mother for years afterward.

Even worse, she hates to think of her mother being remembered—and defined—by her final moments. The media circus surrounding her death was everything her mother had worked so hard to escape. It's what spurred Makayla to create an awareness campaign after it happened. In the years following her mother's death, the campaign garnered a substantial following—thanks to her mom's fame and an interview Makayla did on *True Investigations*.

The rom-com begins to play, and Makayla watches a jean-jacketed Reese Witherspoon drag her suitcase down the streets of New York, gaping at her surroundings like a tourist. Makayla turns away and leans her head back, surprised to still feel the tender spot on the back of her head from her fall yesterday. She hopes it doesn't bring on a headache. She hasn't had one in a while, but the last one she had, while she was pregnant with Liam, kept her in bed for a whole day.

She's well aware that migraines are also a precursor to developing her mother's amnesia disorder. Her mom had them for years before it happened. Initially, it frightened Makayla when she started getting headaches, but she didn't get them often—not like her mother. She attributed the last one to her pregnancy.

Makayla closes her eyes, recalling the scared look in her dad's eyes when she tripped on their hike, losing her balance from the weight of her backpack and bumping her head against a large rock on her way to the ground. Thankfully, her dad had been carrying Liam. She had to assure him more than once that she was fine, refusing his suggestion that she see a doctor. For the rest of their hike, Makayla downplayed the throb at the back of her head, knowing her dad's overconcern stemmed from losing her mother so suddenly.

"Anything to drink?"

Makayla opens her eyes, surprised to see the blond flight attendant who offered her headphones before takeoff standing behind the drink cart, waiting eagerly for her answer. She couldn't have had her eyes closed for more than ten minutes.

"Um. I'll take a ginger ale." Makayla glances behind the blond, past the male flight attendant standing on the opposite end of the cart, remembering most of the seats on the flight were open.

"I meant to ask you earlier about your mom, Derek. How is she?" the attendant asks her male counterpart as she pours Makayla's soda from the can.

Derek sighs. "Not good. Her latest treatments haven't been working. There's a new immunotherapy drug that her doctors are hopeful could put her in remission, but because it's still considered experimental, her insurance won't cover it. It's why I picked up the extra trip."

The blond attendant places a hand over her heart. "I'm sorry; that's so tough."

"I'm fine. I'm just worried about *her*. Thankfully, there's been a ton of overtime shifts available lately. I'm trying to help however I can."

She hands Makayla a plastic cup with a napkin underneath. "Here you go. Would you like the can?"

"No, thanks." Makayla takes the cup. Her eyes fall to the attendant's name pin. *Britt.*

Makayla turns around to see the male attendant, her heart going out to the stranger faced with losing his mom. A pain she knows all too well. Britt turns to Pink Headphones across the aisle while Makayla reaches across the seat beside her and manages to pull the tray table out of the armrest without waking Liam. She takes a few sips before setting her half-full cup on the tray table.

Makayla reaches inside the diaper bag for her phone. She connects to the in-flight Wi-Fi, hoping to have gotten a good-night text from Jack. Instead, she has a new text from her friend Cori. Are we still on for coffee tomorrow? Excited to see you!

She met Cori at a Tribeca mother's group before most of its members flocked to their summer homes during the city's hottest months. The group's park day was the biggest outing she'd attended with Liam since his birth. It was windy. She remembers having to chase after his blanket several times after it blew off his stroller. Toward the end, Liam spit up all over her shirt, and she discovered she'd only packed one burp cloth. She felt like a mess compared to all the other put-together Tribeca mothers and had come home exhausted.

Afterward, she and Cori connected through the group's social media page while Cori summered in the Hamptons. Through texts and a few phone calls, they'd grown close over the last few months, discovering several things they had in common.

Makayla types a reply. Yes. Can't wait to see you too!

Dots appear below her message seconds before a new text pops up. I have some exciting news about that preschool close to your condo!

A month ago, Cori asked which preschool waiting lists Liam was on. Makayla laughed and told her none, reminding Cori that her baby was only two months old. Cori warned her that if she waited any longer, Liam's only options would be preschools in New Jersey. After Makayla got over her shock that she needed to start so early, Cori offered to help her navigate through the best preschools in their neighborhood.

Unlike Makayla, Cori had lived in Manhattan her whole life and was well connected. Over the last few weeks, she had managed to get Liam added to three waiting lists after the schools turned Makayla down. With Cori home from the Hamptons, maybe Makayla will feel less alone.

Being an only child, Makayla always dreamed of one day having a big family. But losing her mom so suddenly took a toll on her, and it was several years before she felt ready to become a parent. Then it took a few years of trying before she finally became pregnant with Liam. Jack practically living at the office hadn't helped.

The cabin is now quiet, and Makayla's gaze falls to Liam's sleeping form. The plane hits a bump, lurching upward. Makayla is pulled against her seat belt, instinctively extending her arms toward Liam as his pacifier rolls to the top of the bassinet.

She prepares to give it back to him if he cries, but he remains quiet. She sits back, and her attention drifts to the white clouds floating outside the half-shaded window.

She thinks of her dad, back at home on Lake Anchorage, and tears spring to her eyes. How long will it be before she sees him again? She closes the window shade, wondering why it's hitting her so hard.

She hasn't seen him more than a few times a year since she moved to New York, when she was eighteen, back when her parents still lived in Seattle. While she wishes he lived closer, she can't remember the last time she got this emotional about it.

She tells herself it's the hormones and lack of sleep causing her overreaction, but the sight of Liam's peaceful, sleeping face in the bassinet consoles her. Her dad promised to try to visit for Christmas. She swallows back the lump that forms in her throat, reminding herself the holiday is less than five months away.

She retrieves her phone and scrolls through the photos she took on her trip. She pauses, smiling at a photo of Liam asleep in her dad's arms. She opens the cloud storage on her phone and swipes through the nature photos she took with her Nikon, debating which ones to post on her blog. The moss-covered evergreens in Chugach State Park and driftwood-lined shores of Kincaid Beach remind her of the countless photos she took while growing up on Bainbridge Island.

Her childhood home offered views of Seattle beyond Elliott Bay. After getting a Kodak for her third birthday, Makayla started capturing images of the beach. By high school, her bedroom walls were covered in photos she'd taken on the island. That little camera was why she moved to New York to major in photography at Columbia. She remembers her younger self standing in the darkroom on campus over a chemical bath, dreaming of having her work on display in photography galleries around the city.

Instead, she put her photography on hold after her mother died to raise awareness about the condition that killed her mother. All these years later, it is still hardly more than a hobby. She hopes that someday, maybe, it will be more.

Her gaze travels out the window. It's still daylight, but all she can see is a layer of clouds beneath them. She wishes Jack could slow down and realize all that he's missing. He works so hard for them, and she's grateful. But she doesn't need all the things Jack feels so compelled to give them.

She and Liam need him to be present. *Part* of their lives. Not just providing for the life they're living mostly without him.

Jack has already missed so much of Liam's first few months, small everyday moments that she'll have forever. Time he'll never get back. She thinks of her mom. You never know when your time with someone could be your last.

She rests her head against her seat, careful not to put pressure on the tender spot from her fall. Someday, Liam will be grown and living his own life. She worries for Jack. And Liam, too, as she knows the resentment Jack holds for his own father's absence—and why he feels so bonded to Lionel.

She feels a spark of sadness at the realization that she doesn't know Jack well enough to guess what he's thinking anymore. All the years he's spent working around the clock have taken a toll on their relationship. They are starting to feel like strangers. Even when she does see Jack lately, he seems preoccupied, consumed by his work. Or someone he works *with*.

A sinking feeling forms in her gut at the thought of Sabrina, his boss Lionel Rothman's daughter and Jack's childhood best friend, who serves as the firm's managing director. Jack and Sabrina dated briefly in college before Makayla met him. While Makayla has always suspected Sabrina still has a thing for Jack, she never worried about it being reciprocated. Until lately.

Years ago, Jack told her that he and Sabrina had a falling out after Sabrina gave one of his client accounts to someone else at the firm. The image of Sabrina and Lionel in the recent *Forbes* article, each with a hand on Jack's shoulder, flashes in her mind. *It's all in the family,* the article said. Like Jack and Sabrina were some power couple both working for her father. Her cheeks flush with anger just thinking about it.

Then, there was the other photo of Jack and Sabrina laughing together, and the article's mention of how they grew up as next-door neighbors. From the way Sabrina beamed at Jack in the photo, it was hard to imagine a rift between them. If not impossible.

When Makayla commented on it to Jack, he was quick to dismiss her misgivings. *It's not real, just a publicity stunt for the firm. We were only doing what we were told by the photographer.*

But she couldn't help but wonder if Jack and Sabrina's falling out was over something personal. And now, had they rekindled?

She thinks of all the late nights when she believed he was at work. Has she been a fool to trust her husband so blindly? She cringes inwardly, recalling Jack's menacing tone when she asked him how things were at work a few days before she and Liam left for Alaska.

He was so defensive. So *mean*. He'd never snapped at her like that before.

Her phone vibrates in her hand, tearing her from her thoughts. Makayla opens the text from Cori. As usual, her friend is reading her mind.

Are you going to confront Jack when you get home?

Makayla bites her lip before sending her reply. I haven't decided.

She's sure Jack is hiding something, but what she's not sure of is whether she's ready to handle the truth.

Cori's response appears less than a minute later. You have to! You deserve so much better. I think you're being way too passive about it. If I thought Fletcher was cheating on me, I'd chop him up into tiny pieces and dump every last bit of him into the East River.

Makayla stifles a laugh at the three knife emojis that appear below Cori's message. She smiles as she sends her reply. You're sick.

It's why you love me.

That I do. Makayla rests her phone on her lap after sending the text, remembering the moment she and Jack first met at Columbia.

It had taken her a few moments to dial in the settings on her newly purchased Nikon in order to imbue the campus's lion statue with a negative emotion. A group of laughing students entered her frame, and she waited for them to move past. She took the photo right as more movement entered her lens.

"Oh. Sorry."

She lowered her camera to find an athletic-looking guy blocking her view of the statue, his shaggy brown hair reminding her of Zac Efron's.

"That's okay," she said, but when she lifted her camera in front of her eye, the guy didn't move.

Instead, he stepped toward her.

"I'm Jack."

She lowered her camera a second time. "I'm Makayla."

He gestured to her Nikon. "You a photography major?"

"What gave me away?" A flush of red appeared on his cheeks, and she smiled. "What about you?"

"Business." He flashed a crooked smile. "Your degree sounds more fun."

A tingle ran down her spine. Jack was decidedly hotter than Zac Efron. He pointed toward the statue. "This an assignment?"

"Yeah."

Jack made no effort to continue wherever he was going.

Makayla tucked a strand of hair behind her ear that blew forward in the wind. "We're learning how to manipulate lighting to evoke emotion in the viewer."

He came a little closer. "Can I see?"

"Oh. Sure."

When his eyes locked with hers, she noted the yellow flecks in his hazel irises. He stood beside her, and she held up the camera, clicking through the photos she'd taken earlier that morning.

"Here." She paused on a bright photo of the lion statue. "This should evoke a positive emotion. Where this"—she flipped to the image she took right after the laughing students walked by, where she'd reduced the exposure—"conveys a gloomier feeling."

"Amazing."

She looked up from the small screen on her camera and found him staring at her. Her pulse quickened.

He cleared his throat. "Would you want to get a coffee with me later? Or something?"

"Oh."

His face faltered, reading her surprise as disinterest. She immediately berated herself for being at such a loss for words.

"Sorry." He put up his hand. "I know we just met."

"I'd love to."

His grin reappeared. "Okay." He stepped backward, keeping his eyes on her as he grabbed the straps on his backpack. "You free at three?"

Her last class ended at two. "Yeah."

"Cool. Meet you here?"

She nodded. "Okay."

"See you then." He turned, and she watched him stride away until he disappeared around the corner of a building.

She flipped back through the photos she'd taken, trying to refocus on her assignment that was due in less than an hour. She'd gotten the assignment last week but left it to the last minute, knowing the lighting would be best today.

When she got to the last photo, she stopped and found herself zooming in. She'd gone too far in reducing the exposure, trying to evoke negative emotions in the image. The image was underexposed, making the lion statue behind Jack appear as a dark blob. Despite the shadows, she could clearly see the startled expression on Jack's face. She stared at Jack's open-mouthed realization of being in her photo. Biting her lip, she felt a smile reach the sides of her mouth.

She keeps the photo on her phone to this day. She lifts the device, still in her hand. After finding the photo, she studies the image she's seen a thousand times, wondering if they'll ever get back what they had.

Makayla yawns. For the last month, she's been trying the sleep training method Cori used to get her daughter to sleep through the night at only ten weeks. Liam finally started sleeping through most of the night this week.

She sends Cori one last message before closing her eyes. **Liam is already out. Fingers crossed he'll stick to his new sleep schedule after we get home. Looks like I might get to sleep on the flight!**

Aware for the first time how tired she is, she feels the tension fade from her shoulders. She relaxes against her seat, succumbing to sleep.

CHAPTER FOUR

MAKAYLA

Present

God, help me find him.

Makayla scans the rows, her eyes fixing again on the small pillow left in the bassinet in place of Liam. *Who would do this?* She steps through an empty middle row to the aisleway on the other side, searching the rows for Liam. A young couple, no older than twenty-five, glance at Makayla as she marches toward their seats. Their faces glow from the flashing lights on their screens.

Liam. Where are you? Please, please, be here. Makayla stops, seeing the blond head of hair poking out above a blanket on the woman's chest.

"Liam!"

The woman gapes at her as Makayla reaches over the man to grab her son.

"What are you doing? Stop!" she shrieks as Makayla starts to pry him away.

"That's my *son*." Makayla tightens her hold on the child's chest as the man clenches his hand around her forearm.

An unfamiliar wail erupts from Liam as Makayla draws him toward her. She strains to lift him out of the woman's grip. Makayla tugs harder and the blanket falls away, exposing the toddler's shoulder-length curls.

The man stands from his seat and pushes Makayla back. She lets go, staring at the screaming girl in a pink onesie. *It's not Liam.*

"Get your hands off my child!" The man takes a step toward Makayla, blocking her path to their row as the woman tries to console their toddler. Even in the dim light, his eyes are fierce.

"What's going on?"

Makayla turns, recognizing the auburn-haired flight attendant who greeted her upon boarding.

The man swings his finger toward Makayla's face. "She tried to take our kid!"

"Ma'am." The flight attendant's voice takes on a firm tone. "I need you to return to your seat right now and to remain in the main cabin."

A platinum-blond attendant emerges from the first-class galley, appearing startled by the commotion. She marches toward them.

"I'm sorry. I wasn't trying to take your child." Makayla closes her eyes, trying to think through the near-debilitating pain between her temples. When she opens them, light floods the cabin. "My baby. He's—" The aisle sways beneath her feet, and she forces herself to inhale. "I can't find him. Have you seen a baby brought through here?"

The man shakes his head. He shoots Makayla a cautionary glance before taking his seat, then rubs his palm up and down his crying daughter's back.

"Ladies and gentlemen." A female voice comes over the intercom. "We have a passenger who is looking for her infant son, and we would appreciate your assistance in locating him. We've turned on the cabin lights and ask that you please look around your seats and notify one of the crew if you locate the infant. Thank you."

"I haven't seen your baby; I'm sorry," the auburn-haired attendant says.

"What about the lavatories up in the front?" Makayla asks, turning to the blond attendant standing behind them.

"They're empty." The first-class flight attendant purses her lips; then something in her face shifts, and Makayla imagines she must see her desperation. "But I'll check them."

"Thank you." Makayla watches her proceed to the front of the plane, scanning the rest of the first-class seats on the way.

In business class, Makayla spots the gray-haired woman setting down her knitting supplies and standing. Makayla continues to the now brightly lit main cabin. Several passengers are up from their seats, looking around for Liam, along with three flight attendants sweeping the aisleway. Every overhead bin has been opened, but it does nothing to ease the constriction in her heart.

She crosses the middle row to her seat, where Liam's bassinet remains empty. Even the young woman seated across from her has gotten up to look for Makayla's baby, leaving her pink headphones draped over her armrest.

It feels like a rock has been dropped into the pit of her stomach. *This cannot be happening.*

Makayla drops to her hands and knees to peer beneath her seat. "Liam."

She runs her hand atop the thin carpet, knowing he couldn't have gotten out of his bassinet on his own. And even if he did, it didn't explain the pillow being in his place. Makayla grips her armrest and stands.

She follows the young woman down the aisle, scanning every row and overhead compartment in horrified disbelief.

None of this even feels real.

CHAPTER FIVE

MAKAYLA

As she nears the lavatories in the middle of the aircraft, Makayla feels like she's moving outside of her own body. *How could Liam be gone?*

She slows, spotting the *Friends* episode playing in front of an empty seat. It's where the old woman was struggling with the flight attendants earlier. She looks around. Rose is nowhere in sight. From what Makayla witnessed, the woman was in no shape to be helping with the search for Liam.

From the rear of the plane, Derek moves up the aisle toward Makayla, glancing side to side at each row. Makayla passes the lavatories and sees that one is occupied. She pushes open the door to the lavatory she used earlier, and the empty space fills her with an overwhelming sense of helplessness.

She crosses the exit row behind the lavatories, but the elderly woman isn't in the rear cabin either. Makayla flags down the flight attendant.

"Yes?" Derek asks, closing the gap between them.

Makayla forces a breath from her lungs, straining to form words through the increasing pressure between her temples. "Have you seen the elderly woman? The one you were helping earlier. She was in row twenty-four. Rose . . . I think that's her name. One of the lavatories is occupied. And I'm wondering if she could've—" She brings a hand to her forehead. "Could've taken my son in her confusion."

But Rose was in her seat when Makayla came out of the lavatory. And she didn't have Liam. It doesn't seem possible that she could've taken him and hidden him somewhere before Makayla came out of the bathroom. But it also doesn't seem possible that Liam could be gone.

And why isn't Liam making any noise from wherever he is? As terrifying possibilities swirl through her mind, her whole body trembles.

"Oh, yes. I saw her being helped into the lavatory a few minutes ago." His expression hardens, wariness evident in his eyes. "But she didn't have your baby."

Makayla's gaze skirts the back of the plane. "Have you checked the other lavatories?"

"We're looking everywhere."

"Then where's my *son*?"

Heads turn toward her.

"We're doing everything we can to help you find him."

The calm inflection in his voice makes Makayla want to scream. She turns and knocks on the door to the occupied lavatory.

"Hello? Rose?"

No response.

Makayla knocks harder. "I'm looking for my baby. Could you—"

Derek presses his hand on the lavatory door. "Your baby isn't in there, ma'am. She's already quite confused, so let's wait until she comes out."

Makayla gapes at him. "But what if he is?"

The attendant purses his lips. "Just give her a minute. If she doesn't come out soon, I'll get one of my female coworkers to open the door."

Makayla leans her face toward the door. "Rose!"

Why isn't she answering? What is she doing in there?

Makayla lifts her hand to bang on the door when she hears the toilet flush from inside. Seconds later, the door unlocks and wobbles back and forth as Rose attempts to open it. Makayla pushes on the door, her heart sticking in her throat as she braces herself for the best- and worst-case scenarios at the same time.

As the door flings open, Rose's startled eyes meet Makayla's. Her white hair sticks up in varying directions from the back of her head.

"Have you seen my baby?" Makayla asks as Rose pushes past her in the direction of her seat.

Rose turns. "No, dear. Have you seen Roger? Maybe he knows?"

"Let me help you back to your seat," Makayla hears Derek say as she steps inside the lavatory, her lungs deflating as her eyes adjust to the dark, empty space.

The floor shakes before the plane lifts into the air, and Makayla puts a hand on the wall to steady herself.

"Ladies and gentlemen, we're expecting a bit of rough air up ahead, and I'm turning that fasten seat belt sign back on. Please take your seats if you're up, and make sure your seat belts are securely fastened."

She retreats into the aisleway, aware of the flight attendant approaching as he looks around at the passengers beginning to take their seats. She's hit with a wave of nausea as her panic intensifies.

Makayla covers her mouth with her hand and grabs Derek by the arm. "We haven't found him yet. We can't stop looking!"

"Right now, I need you to return to your seat. We'll keep looking, but the plane's already been searched."

"Wait." Makayla's eyes lock on the door opposite the now empty lavatory as she realizes it isn't another restroom. She brushes past Derek toward the door marked CREW ONLY. "What's in here?"

"It's the crew rest area."

She twists the handle and pulls.

"Hey! You can't go down there."

Makayla starts down the narrow metal staircase. Derek's heavy footsteps follow.

When she gets to the bottom, Makayla peers around at the three sets of empty bunk beds that line the walls before lifting each of their half-opened curtains. "Liam!"

Derek grabs her by the forearm. "Ma'am, I need you to return to the main cabin."

"Let go of me!" She yanks her arm free. "Has this been searched?"

"Yes. Britt came down here a few minutes ago. This area is off limits to passengers. You can't be down here." He points to the stairs. "Let's go."

Makayla spins around, opening the storage compartments beneath one of the bunks, which contain two roller bags. She reaches to unzip the first bag, but Derek places his hand on top.

"This is the crew's luggage. And that's my bag. Your baby isn't down here."

She lifts her eyes to his, catching a whiff of expensive cologne. "Just let me check."

His lips form a hard line as he shakes his head. "No. You're not going through the crew's bags. Britt already checked down here."

"This is ridiculous!" she yells. "My son's missing and you're worried about *what*? Me seeing your underwear? Or finding my son in your bag?"

Derek slowly lifts his hand off the bag while Makayla's chest heaves with rage. Makayla unzips it in one swift motion to find it half full of neatly folded men's clothes. She moves to the next bag, which is filled with women's clothes and toiletries. She stands and opens two more compartments. The first is empty, and the second contains three more bags. This time, Derek helps her open them.

The floor dips as Makayla hopelessly assesses the bags' contents, causing her to fall to the side. Derek grabs her by the arm, steadying her.

"Like I said, he's not here. And now, you need to go back to your seat."

She swallows the golf ball–size lump in her throat.

The door at the top of the stairs swings open. "Derek?" The blond flight attendant appears at the top of the staircase.

Derek turns to mount the stairs. "Yeah. We're down here."

Makayla follows.

The flight attendant frowns when she sees Makayla, then brushes her bangs away from her eye with the back of her hand. "I already checked down there."

"I know," Derek says when he gets to the top. "She insisted on having another look."

Makayla steps into the aisle behind him, seeing the petite woman who recovered Liam's pacifier earlier standing beside the attendant.

The attendant turns to Makayla with a somber expression. "No one has seen your baby. And we've run out of places to look. Can I have your full name so I can alert the pilots? That way, they can notify the appropriate ground authorities."

Ground authorities. What on earth could they do? "So, you think he's been kidnapped?" A cascade of horrific scenarios rips through her mind.

"We don't know, ma'am. This is an unusual situation, and we need to be informed of the next steps."

As the walls of the plane seem to move inward, Makayla puts a hand to her temple. "Is there an air marshal on board? Someone who could help us?"

The attendant shakes her head. "Sorry, no. Air marshals are mostly on flights in and out of DC."

Makayla exhales, and her gaze falls to the woman's name pin, *Britt*, which she recalls reading earlier. She squares her shoulders, hoping to add strength to her voice. She heard once that using someone's name helps them take notice. *Take you seriously.* "Britt, I don't understand. Where could he be?"

The floor shakes, and Makayla grabs on to a seat back to steady herself.

"We're doing our best to help you. Can I have your name?" Britt repeats. "And then I need you to return to your seat until the seat belt sign turns off."

Makayla inhales as much as her lungs allow. "It's Makayla. Makayla Rossi. And my son is Liam. He's only three months old."

Her heart feels like it's beating into her throat. She lifts a hand to her neck. The attendant's grave expression only intensifies her fears. Her lip quivers.

"And how long has he been missing?"

"Um. I'm not sure." She strains to make an estimation but can't think about anything other than where Liam could be. And who took him. An image of his sweet little form stuffed inside someone's suitcase leaps again into her mind.

An overhead bin shuts behind her, making her jump.

The petite dark-haired woman puts a hand on Makayla's back. "I think it's been about thirty minutes since you were first asking if any of us had seen your baby."

Makayla nods, unable to form more of a response.

"Okay. Thank you." The two flight attendants exchange a glance before making for the front of the plane.

"It's okay; just take a deep breath."

Makayla swallows as the woman holds her palm between Makayla's shoulder blades.

"I'm Jemma, by the way."

A tear slides down Makayla's cheek.

"Your son can't have gone far," Jemma says. "He's still on the plane. And he'll be found."

Makayla scours the faces of the seated passengers scattered around her. Many of them have returned their attention to their books and seat-back screens without the dread of their own child being missing.

A surge of anger flows through her like an electric current. Someone on this flight, possibly one of these very people, took Liam. She knows it now, as certain as she's ever been. They know exactly where he is.

CHAPTER SIX

Anna

"You said you've flown for Pacific for seven years?" Miguel asks.

"That's right." Anna sits tall to take in the snowcapped mountain range below, which is visible through a gap in the clouds.

"Funny we've never flown together before, since we're both based out of LaGuardia."

"Yeah, it is. I'm scheduled to start captain upgrade training the day after tomorrow, so if all goes well, this will be our only time flying together." She tilts her head toward the empty, fold-down seat behind Miguel's. "Unless one of us is in the jump seat."

"That's great. I'm sure this will be the last time we fly together, then." Miguel reaches into his flight bag on the other side of his seat and withdraws a worn, leather-bound book.

He opens it to a bookmarked yellow page.

"*Too Busy to Die*?" she asks after reading the faded title on the spine.

His mouth forms a smile. "That's right. It's by H. W. Roden. Ever heard of him?"

She shakes her head. "Nope."

"I'm a sucker for a 1940s detective novel. Read this one several times already, but I'm struck by something new each time I read it." He lifts his gaze. "You a reader?"

"Not really."

"Oh, man. You're missing out."

Anna offers Miguel a slight smile before stifling a yawn and leaning against her seat. Aside from talking, there won't be much to do to keep herself awake for the five-plus hours remaining, but Miguel is already immersed in his novel. She thinks about her plans for after they land. Feeling the weight of her phone in her blazer pocket, she wonders if she's gotten a reply to her text.

The flight attendant call buzzer sounds, jarring her from her thoughts.

Miguel pushes the flight attendant button on his interphone panel. "This is Miguel."

As Miguel listens to the other end of the call, Anna thinks of the night earlier this summer when she found herself capable of something she never thought possible.

"For how long?" Miguel asks into his headset, his expression elsewhere.

Since that night, she's hardly seen Carter, aside from each climbing into bed on occasion when the other was already asleep. Their schedules never seem to align. They were supposed to go out to dinner last week, on her birthday, but Carter never showed. She ate dinner alone, calling the hospital on her way home from the restaurant to be told by one of the nurses that Carter was in the middle of surgery. By the time he got home, she was asleep. The next morning, she left for the airport before he woke and had a single text message from him: Sorry.

He couldn't help it, she knows. But she still wanted more.

Anna wrestles with the guilt of going through with her plan as her gaze travels across the controls. While she knows it's wrong, to back out now would come at the cost of her own happiness.

"Are you sure you've checked everywhere?" Miguel says. "Lavatories? Crew compartment?"

Anna turns to Miguel, registering the look of concern on his face. She turns up the volume control under the flight attendant call light on her interphone panel.

"Yes." A female voice comes through her headphones. "Everywhere."

Miguel frowns, staring out the windshield. "I'll let them know. In the meantime, keep looking. And call me back if you find him."

"What is it?" Anna asks after he hangs up.

He presses his lips together before meeting her eyes. "A three-month-old infant has gone missing in the back."

Anna feels her brows knit together. "Missing?"

"The mother left him in the bulkhead bassinet while she got up and used the lavatory. When she got back to her seat, he was gone. He's been missing for half an hour." He seems to key on something in her expression. "The crew says they've looked everywhere," he adds before Anna can ask.

"So, they think someone's taken him?"

"They don't know what to think."

Anna stares back at Miguel. "If someone *has* taken him, there's only so many places to hide a baby on board. We're bound to find him."

Miguel doesn't respond.

"Right?" She's not even sure what the protocol is for an in-flight child abduction.

"We need to call dispatch." Miguel manipulates the radio panel and tries several times to contact dispatch without success.

"We must be outside of radio contact range," Anna says, looking at their nav screen.

"Yeah, you're right." Miguel starts typing on his keypad. "I'll have to send them a message."

Anna stares out the windscreen at the waning daylight, thinking of the poor mother who's lost her baby. It would be a sickening feeling. She could hardly imagine anything worse.

CHAPTER SEVEN

TINA

The dull vibration atop Tina's nightstand pulls her from her restless sleep. She reaches through the darkness for her phone, sitting up when she sees the incoming call from her squad supervisor.

She clears her throat. "This is Tina."

"Tina, it's Special Agent Castillo." There's a slight echo to his voice, like he's talking through his Bluetooth in the car. "An infant has gone missing on board a Pacific Air flight currently en route to LaGuardia from Anchorage, and we need you to come in. The kid is only three months old, and we don't yet know what we're dealing with."

"Okay." Tina draws back her sheet and swings her legs off the side of her bed. *How does an infant go missing on a plane?* "They've searched the aircraft?"

"Yes, and there's no sign of the child. We've advised the flight to check everyone's luggage. The mother left her baby in the bassinet while she went to the lavatory, and when she came back, he was gone."

Her earlier phone call with Jason comes flooding back to her, and she remembers Isabel is asleep down the hall—not with her father. "I actually have my daughter this weekend. She was supposed to be with her father but—"

"I need you at our headquarters within the hour. Is that a problem? I hope not, because you're the only analyst assigned to this task force who's not on vacation."

In the last six months, three of their intelligence analysts have retired. With their positions still unfilled, Tina is stretched thin, fulfilling roles on three separate task forces.

She lowers her phone to check the time. It's 1:25 a.m. If she leaves in the next twelve minutes, she can catch the last train of the night into the city. As long as she can get Felicity to watch Isabel. "It's not a problem. I'll get there as fast as I can."

Tina opens her work laptop as the train pulls out of Newark Penn Station, using the virtual private network provided to her by the FBI to get online. Aside from one other passenger, she's alone in the train car, her heart still racing from having to run from the parking lot to catch the train before the doors closed. Fortunately, her neighbor Felicity came to the door at Tina's middle-of-the-night knocking and, although startled, agreed to come over and stay with Isabel until Tina returned from work.

She opens the email from Special Agent Castillo and reads through the demographics of the missing child's parents. Liam Rossi, the couple's only child, was born in May. *Liam.* Tina stares at his name, thinking of the baby being taken on the flight and the reason he hasn't yet been found.

She swallows, pushing the thoughts from her mind to focus on her task. She runs a criminal record check on both parents, which turns up nothing. Makayla Rossi has had no employment record since 2010, but Jack Rossi works as a senior account manager at Rothman Securities. Tina flags his employment and makes a note to include it in her report. Special Agent Castillo said this could be a targeted kidnapping. *How much money does Jack Rossi have access to?*

She searches the purchase history for the Rossis' current address and sees the couple purchased the condo for over $4 million the previous year. She flags this too. It's more than most investment bankers could afford on a single salary, but most investment bankers aren't senior account managers at Rothman Securities.

The same month they purchased the condo, the couple's previous address sold for $1.1 million. She pulls up the Rossis' joint tax return from last year and sees his gross income was $500,000. After taxes, they were left with roughly $300,000. Even with a hefty down payment, the mortgage—along with the building's HOA fees—seems like a stretch.

She finds several social media accounts for various Jack Rossis. Pressed for time, she puts that aside to focus on Makayla. On Facebook and Instagram, there's only one Makayla Rossi with an address in Tribeca. Tina starts with her Instagram and sees Makayla has over one hundred thousand followers. She scrolls through the professional-looking photos of mountainscapes, rivers, and wildlife. In one image, a moose drinks from the edge of a stream.

In another photo, Makayla beams at the start of a trailhead, with Liam in a carrier on her chest. The next photo shows Makayla on the shore of a lake, standing behind a stroller. She's flanked on one side by an older man, presumably her father. Seeing Liam's little face in the stroller, Tina's stomach turns.

She scrolls through older posts, recognizing photos taken along the Hudson River Park. She comes to a video of Makayla and stops. She retrieves a pair of earbuds from her purse and connects them to her laptop's Bluetooth before pressing play.

Makayla appears to be sitting on a couch, and Tina notes she's even prettier up close. She turns up the volume as Makayla speaks, her large green eyes staring into the camera.

"Hey, guys. As some of you know, today is the ten-year anniversary of the passing of my mom, Lydia Banks. You might know her from starring in *Prom Queen* or from the amnesiac episode she suffered on live TV before she died."

Tina brings a hand to her chin. *She's the daughter of Lydia Banks?* Tina read the actress's memoir several years after her death. It was right after Jason left, and she found comfort in relating to Lydia's account of how her first marriage ended. After filming *Prom Queen*, Lydia Banks married her supporting actor, Tommy Brecks, at the age of eighteen. Their divorce was highly publicized a year later, after Tommy's headlined affair with his supermodel costar was plastered all over the tabloids.

In her memoir, Lydia described learning about Tommy's affair on the cover of a magazine in an LA grocery store while he was away filming in New York. Tina's marriage ended differently: she came home from work to a half-empty closet and Jason's wedding ring on the kitchen counter. Later that night, she got an email from him explaining he needed a change and was starting a new life in Florida with someone else. But she remembers understanding the devastation Lydia described after being abandoned by the person she set out to build a life with. Different circumstances, but both felt shitty.

Tina also related to Lydia's account of early motherhood, how the actress worried when she was pregnant that she might not be cut out for that kind of life, but then it came so naturally, taking her by surprise.

She remembers the actress's famous TV interview in which—right in the middle of a talk show appearance—she forgot where she was. After she died in a car accident later that same day, the clip of her suddenly appearing dazed and confused was all over the news. There was even a Netflix documentary made about it a couple of years after it happened.

"To me, she was the best mom I could ever ask for," Makayla says in her Instagram video, smiling to reveal vividly white teeth. "And I wanted to take this opportunity to help raise awareness about transient global amnesia. It's been a while since I've shared this, and you can click the link in my bio to learn more. I hope that by raising awareness about the disorder, you can help keep someone safe if they ever experience this."

Makayla blows a kiss into the camera as the video ends.

Tina clicks the link in Makayla's profile, which takes her to a video from a major news station. When the video starts to play, Tina recognizes the blond reporter who stands in front of a green-screen image of the Manhattan skyline.

"Tonight on *True Investigations*, we will hear from the daughter of actress Lydia Banks, whose *rare* disorder led to her fatal car accident, and explain how you can be aware of the signs of someone experiencing transient global amnesia—and how to help keep them safe. But first, a look at what a woman in Texas caught on her video doorbell, and why you should have one."

Tina fast-forwards until she spots Makayla sitting in an overstuffed chair across from the same reporter. A fireplace flickers between them. Tina hits play, but the video remains frozen.

Tina looks out the window and sees the reason she's lost service. They've gone under the Hudson. When they emerge under Manhattan, the video resumes playing. Tina moves her finger to the bottom of the video to rewind to the beginning of the interview.

The blond newscaster crosses her legs. "Had your mother experienced an amnesiac episode before?"

Tina stops, her fingertip hovering an inch away from her laptop screen.

Makayla shakes her head. Her hair is longer, blond with no trace of red, and she wears less makeup than in the more recent video on her social media page. "No. We believe that talk show interview was the first time it happened. She'd been having migraines for a few years, which increases your risk of developing transient global amnesia. She'd also just gotten the news that her sister had cancer. Emotional stress can be a trigger for the memory disorder."

The TV host's eyes widen. "Wow. Okay."

Tina pauses the video and types *Lydia Banks amnesia interview* into her internet search bar. She clicks on the video at the top of the results, recognizing the auburn-haired actress as the video plays.

Across from Lydia Banks, a brunette talk show host leans forward on a blue couch. "So, what kept you from saying anything after you learned of your father's affair?"

Lydia's brows knit together in horrified confusion. "How did you know that?"

The TV host glances to the side before plastering a smile on her face. "Your memoir, remember?"

Lydia stares blankly at the woman.

The brunette shoots the camera a look before letting out an uncomfortable laugh. "Okay, let's move on to another question. When you said that working with Hayden Graham was one of the best *and* worst experiences of your life, what did you mean?"

Keeping her eyes on the screen, Tina reaches into her purse and finds a pack of gum. Hayden Graham went on to become an A-list actor after costarring with Lydia Banks in *Prom Queen*. They were like the John Travolta and Olivia Newton-John of the eighties.

Tina folds her gum into her mouth as she watches Lydia furrow her brows without responding.

The TV host offers a forced smile. "Okay, let's move on to my next question. On screen, the two of you were very believably in love. But you say that off camera, the chemistry between you and Hayden Graham was very different. Tell us about that."

Lydia stands up. "I never told you that. How do you know this?" She looks around the room, her petrified stare settling on the camera. "Where am I?"

The train brakes to a stop. Tina looks up to see they've arrived at Moynihan Train Hall. She stops the video, staring at the still image of Lydia Banks looking dazed. Tucking her laptop into her bag, Tina opens her recent-call log on her phone. She puts her phone to her ear as she steps onto the platform, and the call connects after the second ring.

"Special Agent Castillo."

"It's Tina. I'm almost to the office. And I think I've found something."

CHAPTER EIGHT

MAKAYLA

As the captain's voice comes over the loudspeaker, Makayla stares at Liam's empty bassinet.

"Ladies and gentlemen, as you are already aware, an infant has gone missing aboard our flight. We have notified the authorities on the ground, and they've requested our crew inspect everyone's luggage. Flight attendants will be coming through the cabin in just a moment to conduct this search. Your cooperation is appreciated."

She leans forward, cradling her head in her hands. If Liam is inside someone's luggage and not making a sound, then he's . . .

"If you have any information regarding this infant's whereabouts, we ask that you come forward immediately. Thank you."

A flight attendant passes her seat, and Makayla reaches for her arm.

"Britt?"

She turns.

"I can help search the luggage so it goes faster." If Liam's inside someone's suitcase, he will be running out of air. If he hasn't already. The thought makes her lightheaded.

Britt outstretches her palm. "No, I need you to remain seated."

"What about the cargo hold? Down below? Has that been searched?"

Britt shakes her head. "He can't be down there. The only access to that part of the plane is through the cockpit."

Makayla unbuckles her seat belt. Learning there's somewhere they haven't yet checked causes a flicker of hope to pulse through her. "We can't know for sure unless we check. I want to see it." She starts to get up.

"No, you can't." Britt steps forward, blocking Makayla's access to the aisle. "We don't allow passengers into the cockpit during the flight. It's against our security policy. There's no way your baby could be down there. Like I said, the only access is through the cockpit, which has been secured since takeoff."

Makayla's chin quivers as she lowers herself to her seat. "Can you at least ask the pilots to check?"

"We're already doing everything we can." Britt's expression softens. "But I'll see what I can do."

Makayla nods as a sob escapes her lips. Britt continues toward business class, and Makayla reaches for Liam's blanket inside the bassinet. She lifts it to her cheek. As the familiar lavender scent hits her, tears escape her eyes.

She leans into the aisle, craning her neck. In the back, Derek and another flight attendant open overhead bins. Derek withdraws a backpack from the compartment and rests it on an armrest to unzip it. He reaches inside before replacing it in the overhead storage space.

Makayla scans the faces around her for a hint of guilt, or a shifty gaze, someone who meets her eyes and looks away too quickly. She searches for anyone who appears too intent on their phone. Anything that could indicate they took Liam. But none of the surrounding passengers return Makayla's stare.

She faces forward and rests her head against her seat. It feels as if the plane is spinning. Hearing voices in the cabin in front of her, Makayla leans again into the aisle, peering through the opened curtain to business class. Britt removes a duffel bag from above the older woman's seat, rifles through it, and returns it to the overhead bin.

When Britt gets to her row, Makayla is dizzy. After peering beneath her seat, Britt opens the compartment above Makayla's head. The flight attendant's eyes fall to the diaper bag next to Makayla.

She points to it. "Can I see inside that, please?"

Makayla's jaw falls open. "That's my bag."

"I know. We're searching everyone's luggage."

The young woman across the aisle watches Makayla intently from between her pink headphones as Makayla slides the diaper bag across her lap, opening it so Britt can look inside. Britt leans forward, pulling the bag open wider before she digs around inside.

She offers Makayla a sympathetic smile before searching the overhead compartment across the aisle. "Thank you."

Makayla feels numb as she replaces the diaper bag on the seat next to her. Did the flight attendant really think she'd hidden her own child inside her bag? Seeing his burp cloths beside his rattle in the shape of a moose hits her like a thousand knives slicing into her heart.

Her chest heaves from the sob she's unable to contain. The crew says they're doing everything, but then, why can't they find him? And what are the authorities on the ground going to do? Help them when they land in a few hours? They need to find Liam *now*.

"Do you want me to take her out of the carrier?" she hears Jemma say from behind her. "I'm more than happy to. Just can't guarantee I'll be able to coax her back in there. She might howl, but she's completely harmless."

Makayla reaches for her phone, realizing Jack has no idea what has happened. In the background, Jemma's husband continues to talk about the dog, and she wishes he would just open the carrier and stop talking.

"She hates this carrier," Jemma's husband says. "Howled for an hour after we put her in there. Our vet prescribed her an antianxiety pill. What's the name of it again, Jemma?"

Makayla calls Jack through her internet messaging app, but it rings four times before going to voicemail. She hangs up and tries again, willing him to answer. Jemma's talking again, so loudly Makayla can hardly think.

". . . Anyway, she fell asleep by the time we got to the airport. Surely, it's worn off by now, and I mistakenly put the rest of the pills in my checked bag. We tried traveling without it on the way to Anchorage, and she howled for half the flight. Even bit me when I put her in the kennel. But I understand. You need to check everywhere. I just hope she doesn't cause too much of a disturbance."

"No need to open it," Britt says. "I can see her inside the kennel."

Makayla's head is pounding by the time it goes to voicemail again.

"Jack, call me as soon as you get this. Liam is—" Her voice breaks. She puts a hand over her mouth. After a long breath, she lowers her hand. "He's *gone*, Jack. And we can't find him anywhere. Oh, God." She sniffs. "I don't know how this could've happened. Please call me."

She hangs up and closes her eyes, tears spilling onto the sides of her face. When she opens them, she checks the time on her phone. It's the middle of the night in New York. Jack must be asleep. He leaves his phone on silent at night so that he's not disturbed at all hours by his clients.

Or is there another reason he isn't picking up? Makayla forces the image of Sabrina—her fitted dress clinging to her size-two waist with her hand on Jack's shoulder as they laugh together, their faces inches apart—from her mind.

A new message from Cori appears on her screen. I'm up feeding Aurora and remembered what I meant to tell you yesterday! I just found out my friend Zoe who owns that yoga studio by your condo is getting divorced. I'll tell you about it tomorrow—you won't believe what her husband did! It's so crazy. A row of wide-eyed emojis. How's your flight?

Makayla sits up straight and looks around the cabin. Britt is now in the last row of this section, and there is still no sign of Liam. She isn't sure if she feels better or worse. Where could he be?

Makayla swallows and types a reply to Cori. Liam has gone missing on the plane. A tear escapes her cheek and falls onto the screen. I'm really scared.

Three dots appear below her text as Cori types a reply. Seconds later, her message appears. What?!! How is that possible?

Makayla's thumbs tremble as she taps a reply. I don't know. But he's gone, Cori. I feel like I'm going to throw up.

Another text. Don't worry, I'm sure you'll find him. Could one of the crew have picked him up, trying to console him or something? Or a passenger seated around you?

No. The crew knows he's missing, and we've searched everywhere. They just made an announcement and are searching everyone's luggage. I can't believe this is happening.

OMG! I'm so sorry! I wish I was there with you. I'm sure it's hard, but try to stay positive. I know you will find him. Let me know if there is anything I can do. I'll stay awake until I hear you've found him. Hang in there—hugs!

Makayla lowers her phone, wishing she could share in Cori's optimism. *But how can I when Liam is nowhere to be found?* She surveys the young woman who she asked to keep an eye on Liam while she went to the bathroom. She's reclined in her seat and refocused on the screen in front of her.

Makayla studies her. After what happened, how could she be so carefree? He isn't her child, but still. The young woman's gaze darts toward Makayla as though she can feel Makayla assessing her. She looks back at her screen, but Makayla doesn't look away. How could she not have seen someone take Liam from his bassinet? *And had she really not known that I was asking her to watch Liam?*

She had the perfect opportunity to take him if she wanted to. But if she did, then where is he?

CHAPTER NINE

TINA

At her cubicle, Tina replays the clip of Lydia Banks's decade-old interview while Castillo stands behind her, watching with interest. Beside him stand two field agents assigned to the resident agency that serves JFK and LaGuardia airports. Aside from a couple of bowed heads wearing AirPods at screen-lit desks, the four of them are the only ones on the twenty-third floor at this time of night. The normally bustling cubicles surrounded by glass-walled offices and conference rooms are dead quiet.

Although Tina has worked late into the night before, she's never seen the place so still. Besides hers, the cubicles and offices are vacant. It feels weird, like being in a classroom in the middle of summer break.

The clip finishes with Lydia Banks ripping off her microphone and storming off stage. Tina turns to Castillo.

"You might remember that after she died, Lydia Banks was diagnosed with transient global amnesia. After I found this, I called and spoke with the neurologist on call at Manhattan General. She said that people with this disorder experience short-term memory loss but still remember who they are."

Special Agent Castillo crosses his arms in the reflection of Tina's laptop screen. "You confirmed that Makayla Rossi actually *has* a three-month-old infant, right?"

"Yes. A birth certificate came up when I searched our database. I also saw photos of Liam on her social media account." Tina turns to look up at her squad supervisor. "When I asked the neurologist if this disorder runs in families, she said it's debatable. The cause of the memory disorder isn't completely understood, but some researchers believe there is a genetic component. It rarely affects people younger than forty, but it does happen. Makayla Rossi is thirty-six. This may not be what's happening, but if the crew can't find the baby after a second thorough search of the aircraft, I think we need to consider the possibility that Makayla is having an amnesiac episode—even if it seems like a stretch."

"Do we know for sure that the kid got on that plane?"

Tina swivels in her chair at the older field agent's question. By "the kid," Agent Pratt must mean three-month-old Liam. She hasn't worked with him much, and although he's known for being extremely good at his job, he also has a reputation for barking orders and being difficult to work with. *Pratt the Prick* she heard him called more than once behind his back. Their few interactions so far have proved this to be true.

Agent Pratt turns to Castillo. "Or are we taking the mother's word for it?"

"I assume other people on the flight saw the baby, but I'll contact the flight and see if any of the crew can confirm that the infant was on board." Castillo withdraws his phone from his pocket and steps out of Tina's cubicle.

Pratt refocuses his attention on Tina's laptop screen and the frozen image of Makayla's mother.

"I requested the airport security footage from around the time Makayla Rossi went through TSA," Tina says. "But I'm still waiting on it."

Agent Pratt's eyes flicker with surprise. "Okay, good."

"Do we know what she was doing in Alaska?" the younger, more pleasant field agent asks Tina. Tina hasn't met her before tonight. Castillo introduced her as Agent Ruiz.

"From her social media, she was visiting her dad in Anchorage."

Ruiz leans against the edge of the cubicle, studying the screen before turning to Pratt. "Can you get me his name and address? I'll request one of our Anchorage field agents go to his home. Find out if he dropped off Makayla—and the baby—at the airport." She lifts her gaze to meet Agent Pratt's. "And ask what kind of mental state Makayla was in before she left."

Tina opens Makayla's social media page and clicks on a post in which Makayla tagged her father's account. It's a selfie of the two of them wearing matching smiles at a forested trailhead, and she hovers her cursor over Makayla's father. She takes a sip from the mug at her desk and feels a burn in her throat. But it's not from the reheated break room coffee. Bolded words appear below her cursor: *With Jason Kowalski.*

She clicks on the name to go to his profile, ignoring the pit in her stomach as she realizes Makayla's father shares a first name with her ex-husband. The image of Makayla and her father about to embark on a hike sears itself in her mind, and a rush of heat rises to her cheeks. *Will Jason ever be a better father to Isabel?*

"What about the baby's father? Do we know where he is?"

"His name's Jack Rossi. And he's at home in Tribeca."

Tina copies the name of Makayla's father into their Accurint database, which allows her to run a comprehensive public-records search. She clicks on the name that tops the results of all the Jason Kowalskis living in Anchorage and recognizes the sixty-three-year-old man's driver's license photo from Makayla's social media. Tina spins around toward Agent Ruiz. "Here you go."

Agent Ruiz leans forward and uses her phone to snap a photo of Tina's screen. "Thanks."

The agent steps out of the cubicle, leaving Tina alone with a frowning Agent Pratt.

"What do we know about Jack Rossi?" he asks.

"He's a senior account manager at Rothman Securities." Tina clicks an opened tab on her web browser where Jack Rossi's confident, smiling headshot appears on the Rothman Securities website. "To open an account, the firm requires a minimum investment of fifteen million dollars—more than Goldman Sachs. Last year, the firm reported having over five billion in assets under management." Tina opens another tab displaying a straight-faced Jack Rossi on the cover of *Forbes* beside a bold headline, *The Money Man*. "Rossi was on the cover of *Forbes* last March. The six-page spread detailed Rossi climbing the ladder to become the firm's top account manager, aside from Lionel Rothman." Tina scrolls through the article, pausing on a photo of Rossi in his Financial District office. He stands, arms crossed, in front of a floor-to-ceiling window with views of the East River, flanked by Lionel Rothman and Rothman's daughter, the firm's managing director. *It's all in the family* is printed across the photo. "According to the article, Rossi has built a client list of extremely wealthy, high-profile investors, including Malcolm Zeller, the pop star turned business mogul, making Rossi one of the most in demand wealth managers on Wall Street. His client accounts total nearly a billion dollars. However, I took a look at the Rossis' personal finances and—"

Agent Ruiz reappears at the edge of Tina's cubicle, her phone in hand. "One of our Anchorage field agents is en route to the home of Makayla Rossi's father. I should hear back from him soon."

Pratt turns to face Ruiz. "Makayla Rossi's husband is an account manager at Rothman Securities. If this *is* a kidnapping, he may get contacted for a ransom."

If he hasn't already, Tina thinks.

"We're going to need a warrant to live monitor every account Jack Rossi has access to," Pratt adds.

"I'm on it," Ruiz says, nearly colliding with Castillo when she retreats to make the call.

"Hold on, I want you to hear this," Castillo tells her. "None of the crew on Flight 7038 can confirm actually seeing the infant on board." He looks beyond Ruiz to Tina and Pratt. "During boarding and takeoff, the mother had the baby inside a wrap against her chest, but the crew never saw the infant, only a bulge beneath the wrap that they *presumed* to be the baby. They're going to check if any passengers saw Liam and get back to me. They also said the mother doesn't appear to be having any memory loss—aside from not being able to find her son." He lowers his eyes to meet Tina's. "What about the airport security footage? Have you checked that?"

Ruiz stands still, waiting for Tina's answer.

"I requested it." Tina turns to her screen and opens her inbox. "Looks like it just came through." She clicks the link to the security video sent by the Ted Stevens Airport TSA.

Castillo and the field agents hover over her as the video loads.

When the feed begins to play, Tina checks the time stamp in the corner. "TSA logged Makayla going through security at 4:32 p.m., so she should appear in the next minute or so."

Tina rests her elbow on her desk as a family of four moves through the security line. "There." She straightens and points to the redhead who steps to the front of the line, holding out her ID for the security officer. "That's her."

A gray fabric baby carrier is wrapped around Makayla's back and shoulders. Tina leans forward as Makayla sets her diaper bag on the conveyor belt of the x-ray machine. With a palm against the bulge beneath the wrap, Makayla strides toward the metal detector next to the luggage scanner.

Tina enlarges the image as she strains to see beneath the wrap, but the bulge is tucked completely inside the fabric. Not even the hair on Liam's head is visible. Makayla turns her back to the camera, blocking any view of the bulge beneath her wrap, as the TSA agent waves her through the metal detector.

Agent Ruiz's phone rings inches from Tina's ear, making her jump. "Agent Ruiz."

As Ruiz leaves the cubicle to take the call, Tina keeps her eyes on the security footage.

Makayla retrieves her diaper bag and disappears from the video frame before Tina can get another glimpse at the front of her wrap.

"Well, that was no help," Agent Pratt says.

Tina presses her lips together before pausing the footage.

"Is this all we have?" Out of the corner of her eye, Tina sees Special Agent Castillo's finger pointing at her screen. "What about at the gate?"

Tina shakes her head. "The security camera was down at Makayla's gate. Various other locations and all the entrances and exits have cameras, and I've requested those feeds as well, but I told them to send me the footage from the security line first. Since we don't know which doors Makayla entered through and the exact time, it could take me all night to go through the rest."

Ruiz returns to Tina's cubicle after making the call. "Anchorage FBI just spoke with Makayla Rossi's father."

Tina turns as Ruiz slips her phone into her trouser pocket.

"He dropped Makayla and Liam off at about four and was shocked to hear of his grandson's disappearance. The officer said he was adamant Makayla was fine. Her father *did* say that Makayla fell and hit her head on their hike yesterday, but that she seemed okay."

An uneasiness settles over Tina. "According to the doctor I spoke with at Manhattan General, mild head injury is one of the triggers for transient global amnesia."

After watching Makayla's mother's TV interview, Tina dreads the thought of Liam never boarding the flight. "If he's not on that plane, then where is he?"

Castillo sighs. "I'm going to call to have the Anchorage airport searched."

If Makayla left him in some public area of the airport, he should've been found already.

Tina turns to Ruiz and Pratt, who are still standing behind her desk. "What about the gate agent? Maybe they could confirm seeing the baby with Makayla when she boarded."

"Good idea. I'll contact the airline." Ruiz pulls out her phone. She turns to Pratt on her way out of Tina's cubicle. "You still want that warrant for the accounts at Rothman Securities?"

Pratt nods. "Yeah. Right now, we have no idea what's happened to the child. We can't rule out anything yet."

Tina turns back to her laptop to check if she's been sent the rest of the footage from Anchorage Airport.

"We need to go speak with the baby's father."

Assuming he's speaking to Ruiz, Tina opens the new email from Anchorage TSA.

"You coming?"

She clicks the link to the footage captured by the entrance camera closest to the Pacific Air check in.

"Let's go," Pratt barks.

Tina twists in her chair and realizes she and Agent Pratt are the only ones in her cubicle. Ruiz and Castillo have already disappeared down the hall.

"You want me to come with you?" Unlike the agents, Tina is a civilian employee. She hasn't been trained to work in the field.

"That's what I just said."

"But I don't—"

"It's a friendly interview. I'll do the talking. I need you to brief me on everything you know about the Rossis on our way. Earlier, you were going to tell me about their personal finances. And I want to know more about what the neurologist said about that amnesia disorder."

"What about the rest of the airport security footage?"

"Bring your laptop. You can start looking at the footage on the way back." He's already at the edge of her L-shaped cubicle, heading for the elevators. As Tina stands from her desk, he calls over his shoulder, "But not now. Like you said, it could take all night. And the kid may not have that long."

CHAPTER TEN

ANNA

A buzz from the interphone fills the cockpit.

Anna presses the "ATT" button on her intercom panel and keys the microphone. "Anna here."

"It's Aubrey."

Anna recognizes the cabin supervisor's voice.

"I have an update on the search. Can I come in? Popcorn," she adds, using the code word they designated at the start of the flight that signals she's not under duress.

Miguel lifts the toggle switch to unlock the cockpit door, ignoring the standard visual check protocol as he nods in approval.

"Okay, door's unlocked."

Aubrey opens the cockpit door and enters the flight deck. Miguel and Anna both turn, slipping their headphones off one ear.

After closing the door behind her, Aubrey steps closer to the two pilots. "We've searched everywhere. Again. There's no sign of the baby."

The mother must be freaking out. *I would be.* "How is that possible?" Anna asks.

"Your guess is as good as mine," Aubrey says, tucking her blond hair behind her ear. Her gaze falls to the hatch on the floor, leading to cargo hold. "The mother asked Britt if she could see inside the cargo hold below, even though Britt told her there's no access to it except through the cockpit."

Anna glances at Miguel, knowing how he'll respond. All the crew are trained to be wary of passengers creating a ruse, like a child abduction, to gain access to the cockpit. She's surprised Aubrey would even ask.

"Well, she can't. It would be a security risk to let her into the cockpit," Miguel says.

"Britt told her that too. I just thought I'd let you know."

"Thanks, Aubrey," Miguel says, sliding his headphone over his ear. "I'll let dispatch know so they can relay it to the FBI."

"Flight 7038, dispatch, how do you read?"

Miguel presses his transmit switch. "We read you loud and clear, now, finally."

"Roger. I've got FBI Special Agent Castillo on the line, and he's requesting to speak with you. Are you available for me to patch him through to you?"

"Roger that. You can patch him through now."

Anna pulls on her other headphone to listen to the call and turns up the volume knob on the overhead speaker so Aubrey can hear the conversation.

"This is Special Agent Castillo with the FBI. Can you hear me?"

"Yes, we read you loud and clear. Our crew has just finished the thorough search of the aircraft, but the baby hasn't been found."

It's only been a half hour since dispatch relayed an electronic ACARS message from the FBI requesting the crew search the aircraft a second time, along with everyone's luggage. So why is the agent calling so soon? It was her understanding that the captain would contact dispatch with the results of their second search, not the other way around.

"Okay. We need to know if any of the crew or passengers actually *saw* the baby on board before he went missing. Anyone besides his mother."

Anna turns to Miguel. *They're doubting the baby's on board?*

"Stand by," Miguel says over the radio. "One of the flight attendants is in the cockpit right now." He lowers his headphones and twists in his seat to face her. "The FBI needs confirmation that someone besides the mother saw the infant on the flight before he went missing. Did you see him?"

Aubrey shakes her head. "I didn't. But I can ask the others."

"Ask the passengers too," Miguel adds.

He dons his headphones as Aubrey leaves the cockpit. "That flight attendant didn't see him, but she's going to ask if anyone else did. I'll contact dispatch and let them know as soon as we find out."

"Thank you. We appreciate your help."

Anna turns to Miguel after he signs off with the FBI agent. "It *is* strange that we haven't found the infant yet, but doesn't it seem awfully quick to be doubting the mother's account of her baby being on board?"

"It does. But until we find him, I'm not sure what to think. There's only so many places on this plane where he could be. It could be their protocol. They likely can't rule anything out until he's found."

"Yeah, probably," Anna says as Miguel opens his novel to his book-marked page. How can he be so calm? Especially with a baby of his own on the way? Maybe he's been flying long enough to hear almost everything. But she doubts he's ever had an infant go missing in flight. She stares out the windshield at the full moon illuminating the night sky. "Unless they know something we don't."

CHAPTER ELEVEN

JACK

Jack shoots up in bed, jolted from sleep by the sharp pounding outside his bedroom. In the darkness, his eyes dart to Makayla's side of the mattress, and he remembers she's on her way home from Alaska with Liam. Despite the air-conditioning, his hairline is damp from sweat. Lionel's betrayal—and threat—comes flooding back to him.

He's wondering if he dreamed the noise, when three more sharp raps beat against the door to his condo. His pulse quickens, and he swings his legs onto the floor. He unplugs his phone, checking the screen as he rushes out of his bedroom in his boxer briefs.

He has a missed Wi-Fi call, along with a voice message from Makayla. Seeing the time, he guesses she still has a few hours to go on the flight. The pounding against his door persists as Jack passes through the kitchen. Groggy from the scotch he polished off before his few hours of sleep, he flicks on the lights, squinting when he reaches the door.

The building has a twenty-four-hour doorman, so it must be one of his neighbors. He thinks of the young tech entrepreneur down the hall who once rapped on their door by mistake after coming home drunk. Jack peers through the peephole. A gray-haired man in a suit stands beside a woman around Makayla's age wearing a white blouse.

"This is the FBI, Mr. Rossi." The man lifts up a gold badge below his chin. "We need to speak with you. It's urgent."

That was fast. Jack presses his palm against the door before turning the lock and swinging the door wide.

"Mr. Rossi?"

"Yes?"

"I'm FBI Agent Mike Pratt." The man extends his badge toward Jack before motioning to the woman at his side. "And this is my colleague, Intelligence Analyst Tina Farrar."

The woman nods. A ripple of apprehension runs down Jack's spine.

Agent Pratt folds his badge into an inner pocket of his suit jacket. "I'm afraid we have an urgent matter to discuss with you. May we come inside?"

Jack makes no effort to move, mentally replaying his boss's threat. *If you breathe a word of this to anyone, you'll be the one to take the fall.*

Should he call a lawyer? Or would that make him look guilty? He looks between the agent and analyst, feeling completely unprepared for their questions. Then, it strikes him that he shouldn't appear like he knows why they're here.

"What's this about?"

A flicker of pity appears in the agent's brown eyes. "It's about your son, Liam."

CHAPTER TWELVE

TINA

Tina watches Jack Rossi's expression falter before he casts a wary glance at the phone in his hand. Wearing only his boxers, he didn't seem startled by their presence on his doorstep in the middle of the night. Only now, at the mention of his son.

Rossi lifts his gaze. "What's happened?"

"May we come in?"

Tina glances at Pratt. The agent's expression is stoic, unreadable beyond the fact that this is not good news.

Rossi steps back, allowing them inside. "Is Liam all right?"

Tina shuts the door behind them. "Could we have a seat?"

Rossi motions to his living room. They pass a white baby grand as they follow him through the condo. "Please tell me what's going on."

Tina and Pratt sit side by side on Rossi's white leather couch. Tina glances out the window, which would offer sweeping views of the Hudson during the day. Rossi sinks into a velvet armchair across from them, seemingly unbothered to be wearing only his boxers.

Agent Pratt's mouth is set in a hard line. Tina remains quiet, allowing him to lead the interview.

"Have you spoken to your wife this evening?" Pratt asks.

"She texted me before boarding her flight to LaGuardia. I just saw a missed call from her less than an hour ago, but I was asleep, and my phone was on silent. I haven't checked the message yet."

Pratt leans forward, resting his forearms onto his thighs. "Your son, Liam, appears to have gone missing in flight from Anchorage to LaGuardia."

"Missing?" Rossi shoots Tina a confused look before returning his attention to Agent Pratt. "How is that possible? I don't understand."

"It seems your wife, Makayla, got up to use the lavatory while Liam was asleep in his bulkhead bassinet. When she returned to her seat, he was gone."

Rossi's expression turns to shock. The shift in his demeanor from when he first opened the door gives her the feeling Rossi was expecting different news from them.

"But haven't they searched the plane?" he asks.

Pratt nods. "They have. And there's no sign of him."

Rossi brings a hand to his temple.

"I understand you're a senior account manager at Rothman Securities?"

"Yes." Rossi's voice comes out a hoarse whisper.

"How much money would you estimate that you manage?"

"Um." Rossi runs his hand up the back of his hair, appearing to be either doing a mental calculation or debating telling them the truth. "Around eight hundred million. Why?"

"Given the amount of money you have access to, we wanted to see if you've been contacted for a ransom."

Rossi straightens. "Ransom? No, no I haven't. You think someone *took* him? For money?"

"We're considering all angles at this point."

Rossi sits forward, narrowing his eyes. "Meaning you have no clue what's happened to my son."

The truth in his statement causes Tina to glance at Pratt.

Pratt ignores Rossi's comment. "So, you haven't been contacted by anyone?"

Rossi checks his phone in disbelief as Tina and Pratt look on in silence.

"No," he says after a moment, shaking his head before playing Makayla's voice message.

"Jack, call me." Tina recognizes Makayla Rossi's voice from her video on social media. But there's a wobble to it now. "Liam is—" She breathes into the phone. "He's *gone*, Jack. And we can't find him anywhere. Oh, God—" Her voice breaks. "I don't know how this could've happened. Please call me."

Rossi lowers his phone, staring at the screen until it goes black.

Pratt gestures toward her. "Analyst Farrar found that you were featured in a *Forbes* article last spring. It's possible that it made you a target." The agent's eyes bore into Rossi's. "Has anything suspicious happened at your work recently?"

Rossi shifts uncomfortably in his seat, as if trying to read the agent's expression. "What do you mean?"

He's worried about something, Tina thinks. *But what?*

"Since that article ran, have you had any suspicious encounters with anyone? Or has your wife?"

Tina watches Rossi's whole body go rigid. *What's he hiding?*

"It could be anything at all," she says. "Even if it seems small, it might still help us."

Thirteen stories below on the street, a police siren wails.

"No. Nothing comes to mind."

He's lying, Tina thinks.

Pratt clears his throat. "We understand your wife's mother had a memory disorder." He casts a sideways glance at Tina.

"Transient global amnesia," she adds.

Rossi narrows his eyes at the agent. "What does that have to do with Liam being missing?"

"Has your wife ever had any short-term memory loss? Any amnesiac episodes that you're aware of?"

Rossi shakes his head in bewilderment. "No. Never. What her mother had was a rare disorder." He looks between the pair sitting on his couch. "Why?"

"Has your wife been under any emotional stress lately?" Tina asks.

"She just had a baby a few months ago, but aside from that, no."

"Any migraines?"

"She gets headaches sometimes, yeah. But what does that have to do with my son going missing?" He raises both hands in the air, his agitation evident on his face.

Pratt and Tina exchange a look before Pratt laces his long fingers together atop his lap.

"Anchorage FBI has confirmed with your wife's father that he dropped Makayla and Liam off at the airport earlier this evening. However, when we checked the airport security footage, we were unable to verify whether Liam went through security with your wife."

"Of course she took Liam through security! She texted me from the gate." Rossi scoffs. "What are you trying to say? You should be looking for *my son*, not making wild accusations against my wife!"

"We are," Pratt says, his voice remaining calm despite Rossi's outburst. "Anchorage authorities are searching the Ted Stevens Airport as we speak."

Rossi gapes at the agent. "This is crazy! Makayla's fine."

"We aren't saying that she *didn't* take Liam through security," Tina says. "Only that from the footage, we cannot be sure. And no one on the flight can confirm seeing Liam aside from a slight bulge beneath your wife's wrap. We—"

Rossi jumps to his feet. "How on God's green earth did no one on a flight see a *baby*? Everyone notices babies. They're terrified to sit next to them because they cry." Jack's voice breaks on the last word. As he sinks back onto the couch, it's as if all the anger has bled out of him. He puts his face in his hands.

Agent Pratt shoots Tina a sharp look. In the hall, Pratt told her to keep her "trap shut," and she shrugged it off. She'd met enough guys like him to know they liked to be in charge of anything, even if it's just ordering at the drive-through at McDonald's. But from everything Pratt was going on about in the car, Rossi needs to know there's a possibility his son didn't get on that plane.

Tina keeps her voice low. "We have to consider every possibility until we know what's happened to your son."

Instead, Rossi slides his hands to his temples. "How could this happen?" He lifts his eyes to Pratt's. "You need to find him! He has to be on that plane." He points toward the sky out the window.

Pratt raises his palms in the air. "We understand this is incredibly upsetting, but I can assure you the entire aircraft has been thoroughly searched. We're—"

"Upsetting?" Rossi stands from his seat at the agent's effort to placate him. He glances down as if realizing for the first time that he's only wearing his underwear. "I don't care. Have them search it again!"

"We're doing everything we can. We promise you that," Tina says.

Jack looks unconvinced. "I need to call my wife."

Pratt shoots Tina another look as they stand from Jack's couch.

"Of course," Tina says before making for the door.

Pratt lingers in the room and pulls out his card. "If you think of anything, and I mean *anything* that could help us, call me."

Jack takes the card before leading the agent out of his condo. Tina waits beside the piano for her colleague.

Pratt pauses, turning his head toward the adjacent hallway when they move past the kitchen. "Is there anyone else in the condo with you?"

Jack shakes his head. "No."

"I thought I heard something."

"There's major renovations going on down the hall. They've practically gutted the apartment after a water pipe burst."

"It's the middle of the night," Tina says.

"Oh, right." Jack brings a hand to his forehead. "I can't think straight with Liam missing."

Pratt takes a last look down the hall before following Tina out of the condo. She assesses Jack Rossi for a final time before he shuts the door.

He's hiding something, she thinks. *But what?*

CHAPTER THIRTEEN

MAKAYLA

Makayla gets up from her seat, unable to stay there any longer. Liam is on this plane—somewhere—and she has to find him. As she slips into the aisle, she's startled by a sudden laugh from the girl who sits across from her. The girl's eyes are glued to the small screen on her tray table. Makayla looks away and makes her way toward the rear of the plane, focusing her attention on the flight attendant moving through the rear cabin.

Britt strides up the aisle toward Derek, who's been checking overhead compartments one by one, and taps his shoulder. After closing the bin, he turns toward her.

Makayla nears the lavatories, scanning the cabin as she continues toward the attendants. Still no sign of Liam. A man close to her father's age on the far aisle watches the video on the small seat-back screen in front of him while taking a sip from his soda can. She sees it's the Netflix special on her mother, and a current of irritation runs through her. *How can anyone be watching TV right now?*

Rose catches Makayla's eyes when she gets to the elderly woman's middle row.

"Is it time to get off, dear?" She reaches for her seat belt buckle with tremoring hands.

"No." Makayla shakes her head. "Not yet."

"Oh." The woman's hands fall away from her seat belt. "Have you found your baby?"

Makayla swallows. "No."

"That's terrible. I wish I had paid closer attention when you were in the bathroom, but I'm afraid I was too engrossed in that TV program those stewardesses turned on for me. It was called . . . um . . ." She snaps her fingers. "*Friends*."

Makayla stands still, surprised at the woman's clear recollection surrounding the time when Liam went missing.

Rose extends her arm, patting Makayla's hand with her ice-cold fingers. "I know he'll turn up, dear. At least you know he couldn't have gotten off the plane."

Makayla studies the woman. She doesn't appear confused at all now, like she was earlier. *Is it normal for people with dementia to have moments of lucidity?*

Makayla pulls her hand away. *Could the woman have been faking it?* She scans Rose's row, unsettled by her clear recall of events.

Makayla remembers the flight attendants coaxing Rose back into her seat when she went to the lavatory, and Rose eating from a bag of pretzels, contentedly watching *Friends*, when Makayla emerged from the bathroom. *There couldn't have been time for her to take Liam and stash him somewhere. Could there?*

No, she thinks. *Plus, where would she have put him? Everyone's bags have been searched.*

Rose yawns and leans her head against her seat. Makayla continues down the aisle, trying to shake her uneasiness at the elderly woman's sudden moment of clarity.

A swarm of guilt washes over her when she moves past the lavatories. *If only I'd taken Liam with me.* A twentysomething flight attendant who Makayla can't recall seeing before rifles through a backpack on the adjacent aisle at the rear of the plane. Makayla swallows. The luggage search is almost done.

Their backs to her, Derek and Britt speak in hushed tones when Makayla approaches.

"I never saw him. Did you?" Britt asks.

Derek shakes his head, unaware of Makayla's presence behind them. "No. I mean, there was something beneath her wrap, but I never saw the baby."

Makayla stops. *Are they questioning whether Liam was on the flight? Is that why they don't seem worried about finding him?*

"Are you talking about my son?"

Britt whips around, a flush of color rising to her cheeks. She purses her lips. "We're trying to do our best to help you find him."

"By doubting that he was even here?"

From the surrounding seats, a few heads tilt in Makayla's direction.

"We're here to help you find him," Derek says. "And that's what we're doing."

On the adjacent aisle, a bin snaps closed. "That's the last bag on this side," the twentysomething attendant says to them before striding toward the front of the plane. Makayla stares at Britt and Derek, trying to read their expressions.

"My son was *here*," Makayla says, a wobble to her voice as she says the last word. "And he still is—somewhere!" She waves her hand through the air. "Did you check under everyone's seats?" Someone must be hiding him.

"We've checked every bag on board."

The pity in Britt's eyes makes Makayla's throat tighten.

"Is there anything I can do?"

Makayla recognizes Jemma's voice before she whips around.

"You saw him! You saw my son."

Confusion flickers in Jemma's brown eyes.

"When you boarded," Makayla adds. "You saw Liam inside my wrap." She points behind her. "They're questioning whether he was ever on board."

Jemma looks to the attendants. "I did."

Makayla exhales. "Thank you."

"To be fair," Jemma adds, "I didn't actually *see* your baby, but I saw a bulge beneath your wrap. And his pacifier that fell out. I have no doubt that he was there."

Makayla's heart sinks. A wary look crosses between Britt and Derek when Makayla turns toward them.

"He was here!"

Britt lays a hand on Makayla's shoulder. "We're not arguing with you."

But Britt's placating tone does nothing to convince her.

The floor lurches beneath them. Makayla falls to the side, catching herself on the armrest of an empty seat. Derek stumbles backward while Britt presses her palm on top of a seat back.

"Folks, this is your captain speaking. We're experiencing some unexpected turbulence. For your safety, we need everyone to return to their seats and remain there until the fasten seat belt sign is turned off."

The armrest vibrates under Makayla's grip before the plane lifts roughly into the air. She pushes herself upright, grabbing the sides of the empty seats on either side of the aisle. In front of her, Jemma leans against a row.

"We need you both to return to your seats," Derek says while Britt moves to the back of the plane.

"Not until I find my baby."

"I promise we're doing everything we can to find him."

The floor rattles. Makayla searches his face. The concern in his eyes looks genuine.

"But right now, we have to keep you safe," Derek says. "You can get back up as soon as it's safe to do so."

"No." Makayla digs her heels into the unsteady floor. "I'm not sitting down until I find Liam."

The plane dips, causing Makayla to fall into the seat behind her. Derek's eyes widen with concern. He leans toward her.

"This is not safe. I'm ordering you back to your seat. Right *now*," he says, irritation in his voice.

"It's okay." Jemma extends her hand and helps Makayla out of the seat. "It doesn't mean we'll stop looking."

Derek blocks the aisleway behind him with folded arms. Makayla reluctantly follows Jemma atop the swaying floor.

"I'll help you as soon as we're allowed to get up," Jemma says. "Why don't I sit by you until then?" Jemma moves past her empty seat in the exit row, where her husband watches them both with a guarded expression.

Makayla feels herself nod, as if she is existing outside of her own body. There's something surreal about Liam's disappearance, like it's too horrific to be true.

At the front of the cabin, the attendant with hair the same color as her mother's is bent over the young woman sitting across from Makayla's seat. The girl's pink headphones are pulled down around her neck. As Makayla continues toward them, the flight attendant gestures to Liam's empty bassinet against the bulkhead wall. A sinking feeling forms in Makayla's gut as the young woman shakes her head.

Makayla hurries down the aisle, practically stepping on Jemma's heels, wanting to know what's being said. When the flight attendant notices her, a guarded expression washes over her face.

"Thank you," Makayla hears her say to the young woman before she retreats into business class.

Makayla takes her seat next to Jemma after peering into Liam's empty bassinet. She drags her gaze across the aisle toward the girl pulling her headphones over her ears. The floor shakes, and Makayla buckles her seat belt.

This is crazy. Liam didn't just get lost. Someone took him. Makayla assesses the girl as she leans back her head and closes her eyes, despite the rough turbulence and brightly lit cabin.

Makayla has a good idea of what the flight attendant was asking her. And the shake of the girl's head confirmed her answer. *The crew doesn't believe Liam was ever on board.*

CHAPTER FOURTEEN

JACK

Jack lowers himself onto his couch in the spot where the FBI agents had sat moments earlier. When they first arrived, Jack was certain Lionel had sent them to arrest him for fraud. He couldn't have been more wrong. The leather is warm against his bare legs as he drops his phone to his side. Makayla didn't answer, even though he let it ring for a full two minutes.

His phone rings in his hand. His heart races, but when he checks the screen, it's not Makayla. It's her father. He takes a deep breath, remembering the FBI saying that Anchorage authorities had already spoken with his father-in-law.

"Hey, Jason."

He has few things in common with Makayla's father, a retired architect and avid outdoorsmen who detests life in the city. With Jack's long hours and living on the other side of the country, he hasn't spent much time with Jason, despite Jack and Makayla being married for more than a decade. But Jason has always been warm to him.

It's been over two years since Jack's seen him, aside from the occasional video chat on Makayla's phone when Jack happened to be home. It strikes him how much he's missed in his family's lives—not just his relationship with Makayla's dad—being an investment banker, working around the clock. And for what? Imprisonment for fraud? The time he's already lost with Liam . . . he'll never get back. And now, he might never see his son again.

"Jack! Have you heard what's happened?" His father-in-law's normally cheerful voice is plagued with panic, a sickening reminder that this is really happening. Liam is gone.

"Yes, the FBI was just here."

Jason breathes into the phone. "So, have they found him?"

"Not yet."

"I don't understand how the hell Liam could be lost on that plane."

Jack leans forward, resting his forehead against his palm. "Neither do I."

"The FBI agent who came to my house asked about Makayla having memory loss—I'm assuming because of her mother." Jason scoffs. "I told them that was ridiculous. But I don't understand how he could go missing on the *plane*."

Jack thinks about the FBI asking him if he received a ransom demand. "I agree. Have you spoken to her? I just tried calling, but she didn't answer."

"No, I called you first. I assumed Makayla's phone wouldn't have service on the flight."

"Everything was fine when you dropped her off, right?" He feels bad for entertaining that something could be wrong with Makayla, but after the FBI's allegations about her mother, he has to be sure.

"Yeah." A pause. "She hit her head on our hike yesterday, but she assured me it was nothing. And—"

Jack straightens, pulling his forehead away from his hand. "Wait. She hit her head? They didn't tell me that." His gaze lands on the grand piano Makayla inherited after her mother's death.

"It was more of a bump. I mean, it scared me when she fell, but she was adamant she was fine. And she seemed to be. Even insisted we finish the hike when I offered to turn back. You don't think . . ." His voice breaks.

The silence that follows fills Jack with an incredible sense of dread. He spoke to Makayla just before she left for the airport, and she seemed a little spacey, but that's because she was tired. *She was fine. Wasn't she? Of course she was fine. The nonsense the FBI is talking about is just that, nonsense.* Jack takes a deep breath and holds it a second, then lets it out. He hasn't always told Makayla everything. *Could she be hiding something from me as well? A condition?*

"No, I don't," Jack says, his words firm, as if trying to convince himself. Jack forces the doubt from his mind. The FBI questioning Makayla's coherency only tells Jack one thing: they have no idea what's happened to Liam. "I'm going to try calling Makayla again."

"Won't her phone be on airplane mode?"

"I can call her through an internet messaging app. She used it to call me after Liam went missing. I had a voice message from her when I woke up."

"Okay. Please call me as soon as they find him."

The possibility that they might not surfaces in Jack's mind. He swallows the thought. "I will."

As soon as he hangs up, Jack tries Makayla. He closes his eyes while her phone rings. And rings.

He places the call on speaker and gets up from the couch, heading straight for his work laptop on the kitchen island. He sets the phone on the marble counter and logs into Rothman Securities, letting the continued ringing drown out the terrifying scenarios that have him paralyzed with horror.

"Jack?"

He swipes his phone off the counter at the sound of Makayla's voice.

"It's Liam. He's gone. He—" Her voice breaks into a sob.

"I know. The FBI were just here."

From the sound she makes next, he knows she's broken down into tears.

He thinks of Lionel and how much is at stake—for both of them— if the fraud is exposed.

"We'll find him. It's going to be okay," he says, as much to reassure himself as his wife. Makayla goes quiet. They both know he can't promise that.

CHAPTER FIFTEEN

MAKAYLA

Makayla wipes a tear from her cheek as she hangs up with Jack, feeling no better after their brief conversation despite Jack's reassurance that they would find their son. She leans her head against her seat. At least the FBI is investigating, but from what Jack said, they have no leads whatsoever. It was useless to think they could figure out what's happened to Liam from the ground in New York.

Next to her, Jemma sits, quietly keeping her company. Makayla cocks her head toward the girl across the aisle. *Did she really think I was asking where the bathroom was when I asked her to watch Liam?* It was obvious Makayla hadn't taken Liam with her. The girl knew she had her baby with her—she even saw them at the gate when she handed Makayla her water bottle.

"When I was a kid, I had this greyhound. Her name was Roxy," Jemma says.

Makayla turns, wondering why Jemma thinks this is the time to tell her about her childhood pet.

"I loved that dog so much." Jemma smiles. "I still joke with Chad that she was the love of my life."

Makayla manages to return a half smile, wishing Jemma would stop talking so she could concentrate on where Liam could be.

"I grew up with a single mom who worked two jobs, so Roxy and I spent a ton of time together when my mom was at work." Jemma tucks a short, dark strand of hair behind her ear, revealing a small diamond stud earring. "Anyway, this one time, my mom and I took her to a dog park, one of those with a gated fence so you could take their leashes off."

Makayla twists to look around the cabin as Jemma continues to share her long-winded story. All the flight attendants must have returned to their seats.

Jemma places a warm hand on Makayla's knee. "You know?"

When Makayla meets the woman's eyes, she's waiting eagerly for her response. "Mmm," Makayla says, having no idea what Jemma just said. She imagines that Jemma's the type to give a Starbucks barista her life story if they would lend an ear.

"But someone left the gate open," Jemma continues. "And we couldn't find Roxy anywhere."

Makayla exhales, wanting to tell her this isn't the time for a heartwarming dog story. But she knows this woman's just being nice. *Probably trying to take my mind off my baby and not understanding that there's nothing that will take my mind off it until he's found.*

"We put signs up all over town. I was worried sick; afraid I'd never see her again. I didn't sleep for the next three days until this old man called saying he found her." Jemma's gaze travels to Liam's empty bassinet. "My mom always kept the leash on Roxy after that," she finishes.

Makayla follows Jemma's stare. Was Jemma relating her mother losing their dog to Liam going missing? *That I should've kept a better "leash" on my son?* Or was she just trying to distract Makayla with an anecdote from her childhood, oblivious to the story's implications?

She looks across the aisle. Pink Headphones' eyes remain closed, and Makayla thinks of her shaking her head moments earlier when the flight attendant pointed to Liam's bassinet. She *had* to have seen Liam inside it. Why would she pretend otherwise?

There could only be one reason why she was lying.

Makayla remembers seeing two bags in the girl's overhead bin when Britt came through to search their luggage: a backpack and a small suitcase. She watched Britt pull down the backpack, but had she searched the other bag? Makayla was so horrified by Britt asking to look inside her diaper bag that she hadn't paid close enough attention.

She casts a cursory glance at the fasten seat belt sign that glows above her head as she unbuckles. The floor dips when she stands. She steadies herself against the bulkhead wall, her eyes falling to the empty bassinet before she steps in the aisle.

She throws open the overhead compartment. The backpack falls out, hitting the young woman's leg before landing beside Makayla's foot.

Makayla grabs the suitcase with both hands.

"What are you doing?" The girl gapes at her, flinging off her headphones.

"I need to check your bag."

Makayla tugs it out of the compartment as the plane tilts to one side. She stumbles backward and nearly falls into an empty row as the suitcase crashes to the floor. Bile rises to the back of her throat at the thought of Liam inside it.

"It's already been searched!"

The girl reaches for her suitcase, but Makayla beats her to it, jerking the bag out of her reach.

The business class curtain is swiped open. The flight attendant with hair the color of her mother's marches toward her with wide eyes.

"What's going on?"

The young woman jabs a finger at Makayla's head. "She's trying to go through my bags even though they've already been searched! She probably broke my laptop inside my backpack, which almost hit me in the head before it fell to the floor."

Makayla ignores her and unzips the side of the suitcase.

"Hey!" The girl grabs Makayla's forearm and gives it a shove. "You need to stop."

The girl grips the bag's handle and lifts it away from Makayla. On her knees, Makayla pulls it back down, terror ripping through her.

"What are you so afraid I'll find? Did you take my son?"

"No!" She puts her other hand on the handle and tears the suitcase out of Makayla's grip.

The girl falls to the aisle floor, nearly bringing the attendant down with her.

"You both need to return to your seats before someone gets hurt!" The flight attendant glares at Makayla. "Every bag on this aircraft has already been searched."

Makayla stands. "I'm not sitting down until I see what's inside that bag."

The girl wraps both arms around her suitcase while glowering at Makayla.

"That's enough."

When Makayla turns, Derek is standing behind her.

"I'm ordering you to take your seats. All luggage needs to be returned to the overhead bins before someone gets injured."

"What about my *son*? What if he's hurt? I just—"

Derek holds up his palm. "Sit. Down."

Jemma gets up from her seat. "Excuse me."

Derek pivots.

"She's lost her baby," Jemma says. "Can you just let her look inside the bag? For her peace of mind?" She lifts a hand toward Makayla. "I'm sure she'll take her seat if she can see that her son isn't in there."

Derek's chest lifts beneath his sweater-vest with his deep inhale. He looks at the girl being helped to her feet by the other flight attendant. "Could you please allow this woman to see that her son isn't inside your bag?"

She presses her lips together, casting Makayla a dirty look before thrusting her bag toward her. "Fine."

With shaking hands, Makayla takes the suitcase and lays it on the empty row of seats behind her. Her heart throbs as she unzips the top. A mess of unfolded clothes covers the top of the bag. Makayla uses both hands to toss the clothing items onto the seat, moving her open palms through the fabrics before removing nearly everything inside.

Her breath sticks in her throat as she stares at the lining of the suitcase, empty aside from a hairbrush and pair of socks. A firm hand settles on her shoulder.

"Please return to your seat."

She lifts her gaze to meet Derek's. There's pity in his eyes now too. There's also concern, but she gets the feeling his concern is for her—not her missing baby. Jemma peers over the row of seats, her hand covering her mouth as she stares at the empty suitcase.

"I'm sorry," he adds.

"I told you!" the girl says when Makayla moves into the aisle. "Can you at least put my clothes back?"

"I'll take care of it," Derek says. "We need everyone to take their seats."

Makayla feels several pairs of eyes on her as she returns to her row. When she sits down, the young woman flashes her a look of annoyance before pulling her headphones over her blond hair.

"Excuse me." Makayla reaches her hand toward the auburn-haired female attendant's arm as she starts toward the front of the plane. She's the one whose hair reminded Makayla of her mother's when she boarded the flight.

She turns. Makayla sees her name pin reads *Aubrey*.

"Are we going to land?"

Aubrey looks to Derek as he lifts the suitcase into the overhead bin before shaking her head. "We haven't been informed that we're diverting."

Makayla's jaw goes slack. "But we can't keep flying for hours without knowing where my son is!"

The overhead compartment snaps closed. Makayla watches Derek retreat toward the rear of the plane.

"Right now," Aubrey says, "we're flying over northern Manitoba. It's very remote. It's going to be another hour or so before we're even in range of a major airport, but even then, it would be up to the captain. I promise we're doing everything we can to help find your son. This is a very unusual situa—"

"*Unusual?* Like I lost my purse? Someone's taken my son! It's more than unusual—he's been *kidnapped.*"

"I know this is hard. But right now, I need you to stay calm."

Makayla crosses her arms, her panic morphing into anger. "I want to speak to the captain. Now."

"I'm afraid he can't come back here. It's a safety issue."

Makayla blinks back the tears that blur her vision. "I don't care. My son is missing, and I need to know when we're going to land. He should be crying, wherever he is!" Tears come despite her trying to hold them back. The bright cabin lights and intercom announcements should've woken Liam up. *Why isn't he making any noise?* She thinks again that it could already be too late to save him.

Aubrey's eyes dart to the front of the plane. "Look, I'll ask him if he'll speak to you through the interphone. I can't promise that he will, but I'll ask. And I need you to stay here until it's safe for you to get up."

Makayla wipes away a tear that escapes down the side of her face. She can only nod, being too overwhelmed to speak.

Aubrey disappears into business class. Makayla peers around the main cabin. The girl across from her has closed her eyes again. Jemma has taken her seat beside her husband, and Derek is nowhere in sight.

Makayla faces forward and pulls the screen out from inside her armrest. The home screen lights up, and she taps the image of a plane above the words *Flight Tracker.*

She brings a hand to her mouth. Aubrey was right. They're over northern Manitoba. She uses her fingers to zoom out and finds Winnipeg on the map, which looks to be about five hundred miles south. In the corner of the screen, their cruising speed is displayed at 550 mph.

Makayla reclines against the seat back, adjusting her head to the side to keep pressure off the tender spot at the back of her head. There's no way they'll continue all the way to New York with Liam missing on board.

Makayla reaches for her phone. There's a new message from Cori.

Have you found him yet?

Makayla heaves a sigh before responding. No. No one is taking me seriously that he's been abducted. I'm freaking out.

Oh, my sweet friend. I'm so sorry. You must be panicking! Do you want me to wake up Fletcher? He plays golf with the CEO of Pacific Air. Maybe he can make some calls.

That's okay. Thank you though. She appreciates Cori's offer, but no matter how well connected Fletcher is, his phone calls won't help find Liam any sooner.

She stares at the plane following the curved line southeast on the small screen. If they divert to Winnipeg, they should be on the ground within an hour. She closes her eyes, praying they find Liam before then.

CHAPTER SIXTEEN

TINA

Tina drums her fingers on her thigh as they pull away from Jack Rossi's building and head east. Agent Pratt hasn't said a word to her since they left the Rossis' condo.

"I said I would lead the interview," he says a minute later, finally breaking the awkward silence. "Which meant you don't chime in unless I ask you to."

"Sorry. I guess I spoke without thinking. I thought the interview went pretty well." She replays their conversation with Jack Rossi in her mind, too focused to take offense at Pratt's comment.

"The neurologist you spoke with said that headaches are a risk factor to developing that amnesia disorder, right?"

"Migraines, but yes. She was familiar with what happened to Lydia Banks and said the actress had a history of migraines too."

Pratt sighs. "If Makayla Rossi *did* have an amnesiac episode and left the baby somewhere in the airport, it explains why they can't find him on the flight. But if that's the case, what I don't like is why the baby hasn't been found. That was several hours ago. Unless someone took the opportunity to snatch him from the airport, which could kill our odds of finding him."

"When Makayla went through security and boarded the flight, she was wearing her baby wrap. If she forgot she had a baby, why would she keep the wrap on?"

"Maybe she thought he was still with her, because she didn't remember leaving him."

Tina looks out the window, considering it. She pictures Isabel when she was a baby, so innocent and vulnerable, and how unthinkable it would've been to leave her behind. "Maybe." She turns to the agent as he slows for a red light. "Did you see the fear in Jack Rossi's eyes when you asked him about having any suspicious encounters recently? He looked terrified."

"I agree." Pratt keeps his eyes on the road. "He's hiding something."

"Do you think he's lying about the ransom? I know he checked his phone, but I wonder if he was stalling. Debating whether to tell us."

The light turns green, and they accelerate through the intersection, passing scaffolding that clings to the apartment building to their right and a man jogging along the sidewalk. The last few years as a single mom have made her understand why people work out at ridiculous hours. Otherwise, you would never get it done.

"There's something he's not telling us," Pratt says. "He broke eye contact with me when I first mentioned his work. We need to take a look at the accounts he manages." Pratt's phone chirps as he takes a right on Broadway, in the direction of their field office. "It's Castillo," he says before answering through the SUV's Bluetooth.

"I've got you on speaker. We're on our way back from interviewing Jack Rossi."

"What'd you learn?" Castillo's voice echoes through the car.

Pratt merges into the left-hand lane. "Rossi denied having been contacted for a ransom, but he appeared pretty jumpy when asked about having any suspicious encounters with anyone since being featured in *Forbes*."

"Interesting," Castillo says.

"He also conceded that he manages nearly a billion dollars at Rothman Securities," Pratt continues. "He told us his wife has a history of headaches, which is one of the risk factors for transient global amnesia according to the neurologist Tina spoke with."

"Along with the mild head injury she could have from falling on her hike yesterday," Tina reminds them. "Have you heard anything more from the flight? Or the Anchorage Airport search?" She pulls out her phone.

"They're still searching the airport, but they haven't found anything so far. I've requested the flight divert to the nearest major US airport. But they're currently flying over a remote area of Canada, and their assigned dispatch has lost radio contact. They sent the flight a message through their aircraft communication system, so we should hear back soon."

"What about the gate agent for Makayla's flight? Was Ruiz able to track them down?"

"Not yet," Castillo says. "She got the name and number of the agent from the airline, but she's off work now and isn't answering. Ruiz is requesting an Anchorage officer go to the gate agent's address as we speak. So, hopefully we'll know soon."

"In the meantime, we need to start monitoring Rossi's accounts. See if he's pulled a large sum from any of the accounts he manages," Pratt says.

On her phone, Tina pulls up driver's license records to access the full name and date of birth of the CEO of Rothman Securities, then plugs the name into their database.

Pratt glances at Tina as he slows for another red light. "We'll serve our warrant to the head of Rothman Securities once we verify the address on his license. He should have a way to access everything. Or at least give us someone in the company who can."

"Already got it." Tina extends her phone in front of the middle console. "Lionel Rothman has an address on the Upper East Side."

"Good work. But this time, I'll do the talking."

CHAPTER SEVENTEEN

ANNA

On the display panel to Anna's left, **COMPANY MSG** flashes green.

"We have a new ACARS message from dispatch." She presses a button on the panel.

The message appears on the screen. If all means of locating infant exhausted, FBI requests land nearest suitable US airport.

Anna's heart sinks. If they divert, it will ruin her plans for after they land. A ping of guilt rips through her for her selfish motivations, thinking of the distraught mother in the back.

Outside the flight deck windows, the wing strobes suddenly emit white flashes as they enter a cloud layer. At the same time, the airplane bounces in turbulence. Anna is thrown upward and caught by her harness.

"There wasn't any weather forecast on our route." Miguel switches on the seat belt sign and fumbles with the weather radar controls.

The radio announces, "Pacific Air 7038, contact Minneapolis center on frequency one three four decimal five five."

Miguel acknowledges the new frequency and dials it in on the radio control panel. He waits to check in while another aircraft replies to a call from air traffic control.

A woman's voice cuts in. "Attention all aircraft, SIGMET Alpha three valid until ten hundred Zulu. A line of severe weather extending across Minnesota, Wisconsin, and Northern Michigan, tops to flight level four zero zero. Strong upper-level wind shear and hail to one inch possible."

The flight attendant call buzzer sounds.

Miguel presses the "Attendant" button on his intercom panel. "This is Miguel."

Anna checks in with Minneapolis Center on the radio while Miguel listens to the attendant on the other end of the call.

"Okay, thanks," Miguel says.

He resets his intercom panel back to VHF 1 and turns to Anna. "They've checked everywhere, including everyone's luggage, and haven't found the baby. And none of the crew or passengers can confirm actually seeing the child aside from a bulge beneath her baby carrier when she boarded." He sighs into his microphone.

"Even after she laid him in the bassinet?"

Miguel shrugs. "Apparently not."

It seems strange that no one saw him, but then Anna remembers it's not a very full flight. The FBI was so quick to want confirmation of the baby being on board. She wonders if that is their protocol or if they know something they aren't telling them.

Miguel punches the VHF 2 button on his intercom panel. "I'm going to call dispatch." He presses his transmit button. "Dispatch, Flight 7038."

A male voice comes over the radio. "Flight 7038, dispatch, go ahead."

"You can tell the FBI that none of our crew or passengers can confirm ever seeing the infant on board. And per the FBI's request, the crew has conducted a thorough search of the aircraft, including everyone's luggage. But there is still no sign of the child."

"Roger that. Did you see our ACARS message about the FBI's request for you to divert to the nearest US airport? Due to the deteriorating weather across the Great Lakes, a diversion doesn't seem feasible."

"Yes, I agree," Miguel says. "And with that weather, I don't see a suitable airport much closer than LaGuardia."

Especially, Anna thinks, without proof the child is even on board. She stares out the windshield into the darkness.

"You can tell the FBI that landing won't give us any more places to look. Every part of the aircraft where the infant could be is accessible whether we're on the ground or not," Miguel adds.

"Okay, I'll pass that on," the dispatcher replies.

The flight attendant buzzer sounds. Anna takes the call.

"This is Anna."

"Hi, it's Aubrey. The mother of the missing infant is asking to speak to Miguel about whether we're going to divert. I didn't promise anything but told her I would ask. She's obviously distressed, and I think it would help to calm her down."

"Okay, hang on."

Anna turns to the captain after Miguel signs off with dispatch. "Aubrey says the mother of the missing baby is asking to speak with you about when we're going to land."

"That's fine," Miguel says, meeting her eyes. "If Aubrey can put the mother on the phone, I can talk to her briefly."

Anna catches the wary look in Miguel's eyes after she finishes the call and hangs up. As much as she's been wanting to become captain, she doesn't envy him tonight. Maybe she's not as ready for the added responsibility as she thought. She can see the weight of his decision written all over his face.

Anna is blanketed by uneasiness as she imagines the mother in the back. *Would she harm another passenger—or the crew—if she's convinced someone on board abducted her baby?*

She hopes that Miguel can calm the mother down. They still have hours to go until they reach LaGuardia.

CHAPTER EIGHTEEN

MAKAYLA

Makayla opens her eyes. The few minutes since Aubrey agreed to talk to the captain feel more like hours. She presses the flight attendant call button above her head. The fasten seat belt sign is still on, even though the turbulence is less noticeable.

She leans into the aisle to look behind her. No one is coming. She sits forward, stretching her neck to try and see through the crack in the curtain separating her from business class.

This is ridiculous. Liam's life is in danger, and I'm being told to sit here and keep calm.

She unbuckles herself, gets up, and yanks the curtain aside before slamming into Aubrey.

"Oh!" the attendant shrieks, placing a hand over her heart. "I told you to stay seated." She raises a palm in the air, seemingly registering the spark of anger on Makayla's face. "But I talked to the captain, and he agreed to speak with you. I'll take you to the phone up front."

Makayla silently follows her through the well-lit business and first-class cabins, scanning the floor of each row and every seated passenger. They move past the first-class galley and lavatories, and Aubrey stops outside the cockpit door. With her back to Makayla, she lifts the phone hanging from the wall.

"I have the mother of the missing child here to speak with you." She glances over her shoulder at Makayla. "I'll put her on." She pivots, extending the phone to Makayla.

Makayla snatches it from her hand. "My name's Makayla. And I'd like to know when we're going to land."

"Hi, Makayla. I'm Miguel."

His calm tone does nothing to soothe her.

"The FBI has requested we divert to the closest major US airport," the captain says.

Makayla leans against the cockpit door. *Thank God.*

"However, there's a severe thunderstorm warning and tornado watch right now from Minneapolis to Chicago. I can't risk the lives of everyone on board to divert."

What about Liam's life? "But we have to find my son!"

"I understand that, ma'am. But every part of this aircraft where your son could be is accessible while we're still in the air. Landing isn't going to change that. We don't need to be on the ground to search the entire plane, and I can't risk everyone's life to do so."

Makayla gapes at the cockpit door. "But the flight attendants aren't police! They aren't trained in performing searches for missing children." She feels the flight attendant's eyes on her from the side. "They obviously haven't been able to find out who's taken him. Every person on this plane needs to be searched, along with their bags, *again*. We need help—my son could be dead before we get to LaGuardia." Saying it out loud makes her feel like she might throw up.

The captain breathes into the phone. "I understand your need to find him. We are in contact with the FBI, and they are working with us to find your son."

"I saw on the map we are north of Winnipeg. Can't you land there?"

"Winnipeg is also within the area affected by the thunderstorm, so I can't risk landing there either. But if the situation changes, we can reevaluate."

Makayla suddenly feels cold. "What do you mean?"

"Well, like if he's found on board and in need of emergency medical attention, then we'll reevaluate the best course of action."

"One of the crew told me there's a luggage compartment accessible through the cockpit. Have you checked down there? Just in case . . ."

"No one's been in the cockpit besides me, the copilot, and one of the flight attendants since takeoff. So it's not possible for your baby to be down there."

Makayla leans forward, pressing her forehead against the wall. "Could you check it anyway, just to make sure? I know I can't come into the cockpit, but can you send me a photo of that compartment when you check?"

"There's no way your child could be down there. I'm needed on the radio," the captain says, "but I can assure you we are doing everything possible to help find your son. We're still expecting some rough turbulence. For your safety, please return to your seat."

Makayla numbly hangs up the receiver. Aubrey steps aside for her to move past the narrow passageway. Makayla meets the wary gazes of several passengers as she slowly returns to her bulkhead row.

The girl seated across from her has taken off her headphones and is intently scrolling through her phone. Rose looks to be asleep a few rows back. Jemma, leaning close to her husband, is saying something in a low voice but stops when she spots Makayla, offering a look of sympathy before Makayla sinks to her seat.

She stares at Liam's empty bassinet. *This is insane.* How can the crew act as though nothing has happened?

She removes the screen again from her armrest and pulls up the flight tracker. If they continue all the way to New York, there's nearly three hours left in their flight. The aircraft suddenly drops. Makayla feels weightless as she's lifted away from her seat before slamming down hard when the plane corrects for the drop in altitude. Begrudgingly, she reaches for her seat belt and secures it across her lap.

Liam is on this plane—somewhere. She's not waiting three hours to find him. If the crew won't help her, she'll have to find him herself.

She digs inside the side pouch of her diaper bag for her phone. She'll call Jack again. Maybe he can somehow convince the FBI to get the flight to land sooner. And get the crew to do more to help her find him.

"Where am I?"

Makayla cocks her head toward the familiar voice bleeding from the girl's phone across the aisle. Its speakers emit a short laugh. Pink Headphones lifts her head, her eyes widening when they meet Makayla's.

"You're on *Mornings with Sally*."

Makayla gapes at the girl's device. It's been a long time since she's heard her mother speak, but she would know her voice anywhere.

"I don't understand. How did I get here?"

Those were some of the last words she spoke before she died.

CHAPTER NINETEEN

TINA

Light floods the penthouse condominium when Tina and Agent Pratt step off the elevator onto the black marble floors of Lionel Rothman's grand entryway. The white-streaked marble continues up a spiral staircase to their left. Lionel appears on the far side of the immaculate living room, cinching a robe around his waist as he strides toward them. He also wears slippers, Tina notes, and pajama pants despite it being August, although you wouldn't know it's the hottest day of the year from the condo's temperature. It's a few degrees cooler than the building's lobby, a welcome reprieve from the sticky night air outside.

As they wait for him to cross the large space, Tina's eyes drift to the black-and-white painting hanging to the right of the entryway. She's always been interested in art, despite having no talent of her own, and recognizes the piece immediately as Picasso's "Le Taureau noir." A small light hangs directly above the canvas, and Tina guesses the painting is illuminated even when the rest of the lights are off.

"I'm Agent Mike Pratt, and this is my colleague, Analyst Tina Farrar."

Tina turns from the art piece, realizing it is an original, when Rothman reaches them.

Pratt extends his hand. "Thank you for your cooperation in allow-ing us up. We're sorry to wake you."

Tina detects a slight tremor in Pratt's voice. *Is he nervous being in the presence of Lionel Rothman?* She watches the two shake hands, wondering if Pratt would've apologized if Rothman weren't the most well-known financier in the country.

"That's all right. But you're lucky my wife is in the Hamptons escaping the summer heat. There's nothing she hates more than having her sleep interrupted." After dropping his hand to his side, Rothman looks between Tina and Agent Pratt. "What's this about?"

If he's alarmed by the FBI's presence in his home in the middle of the night, he doesn't show it.

Pratt withdraws the warrant from his suit jacket pocket and unfolds it for Rothman to read. "We have a warrant for every account managed by Jack Rossi at your firm. And any other accounts he may have access to."

The color drains from the Rothman Securities founder's face as his eyes fall to the warrant. "So, it's true?"

Tina recalls Lionel's quote from the *Forbes* article. *Jack is like a son to me.* Maybe Jack called him. Or it's possible Liam's disappearance got leaked to the media. Once the story gets out, it will likely be everywhere.

"You've already heard?" Pratt asks.

Rothman looks between Tina and Pratt. "Heard what? Has Jack been arrested?"

Pratt glances at Tina in confusion. "For what?"

Rothman frowns. "Well, I assume my suspicions are correct that Jack's been committing fraud." He attempts to smooth the back of his thinning gray hair. "Why else would you be serving this warrant?"

Tina works to hide her surprise as she mentally replays Rossi's reac-tion when Pratt asked if anything suspicious had happened at his work.

"Jack Rossi's infant son has gone missing aboard his flight home to New York with his mother."

Rothman's eyes widen briefly before he narrows them at Pratt. *"What?"*

"We're investigating the possibility that Jack's son was kidnapped due to the amount of money Jack has access to at your firm. His being on a recent cover of *Forbes* may have made him a target. We need to see if any large sums have gone out for a ransom."

"My God." Rothman sways slightly on his feet.

For a moment, Tina worries he might faint.

"I think I need to sit down."

"Of course," Tina says as they follow Rothman past the ten-foot French doors leading to an expansive lit-up terrace.

When they reach the living area, Lionel moves around a glass coffee table and slowly lowers himself onto a Chesterfield sofa. Beside it, two bronze sculptures sit atop rectangular white marble plinths. Tina sinks into an art deco armchair beside Pratt. The penthouse has to be worth upward of $20 million. Being the only unit on the forty-third floor, the condo is dead quiet.

The investment manager blows a breath out of his mouth before locking his eyes with Pratt's. "So, Liam's been kidnapped?"

"We don't know for sure. We're considering all possibilities. Are you aware of Jack Rossi receiving any threats since being on the cover of *Forbes*?"

Rothman shakes his head. "No. Jack's been flooded with new clients and interviews from other media outlets. But no threats. At least not that I know of."

"What makes you suspect Jack was committing fraud?" Tina asks. She feels Pratt's head snap in her direction but keeps her gaze trained on Lionel's.

The financier grips both knees with his hands. "Last month, I noticed a discrepancy between Jack's client's statement and the account balance. When I questioned Jack, he blamed it on a printing error. At the time, I believed him." Rothman peers at the night beyond the large window on the far wall, flanked by forest-green silk curtains. "I've known Jack since he was a boy. He's like a son to me, and I wanted to give him the benefit of the doubt." The older man clears his throat, running his thumb and index finger down the sides of his chin. "But recently, Jack reported major client losses to me after a venture capital investment of his went under."

He averts his eyes from the window to meet Tina's. "We're talking about one hundred *million* dollars in losses. So, I looked into it. Jack *did* lose money in that investment, but not *that* much." Rothman swallows, as if struggling with what he's about to say. "I'm afraid Jack siphoned half of this investment to himself and is still hiding it—somewhere. Maybe an offshore account or in one disguised as an investment. And I believe he's been doing this for a while."

Tina's phone vibrates inside her purse on the floor beside her feet. Both men turn to the sound of the noise. Pratt frowns.

"Sorry." She reaches inside her bag, thinking it must be Special Agent Castillo. Seeing her neighbor's name on the caller ID, her heart stills.

"Did you report it?" Pratt asks, refocusing his attention on Lionel.

Biting her lip, Tina debates whether to get up from their interview to answer it. With a flush of guilt, she ignores the call and slips her phone back into her purse, mentally conjuring the reasons why Felicity would be calling in the middle of the night. None of them are good. Occasionally, Isabel wakes and has trouble falling back asleep. Hopefully, that's why Felicity is calling. She'll call Felicity back as soon as they're done.

Tina forces herself to focus on Rothman as the investment manager shakes his head.

"Not yet. I confronted him about it only this week. He denied it. Said he could prove where the deficit funds were. I wanted to believe him . . . even though I knew in my gut he was lying. Anyway, I agreed to let him produce this supposed proof before I went to the authorities. But I guess my gut was right."

Tina studies him. In his bathrobe, with tufts of hair sticking out at odd angles, the city's most successful financier looks much more fallible than the powerful man pictured in the recent *Forbes* article with Jack Rossi.

Pratt shifts in his chair. "Do you have access to the accounts Jack manages? Or is there someone in your firm who can? We need access tonight—as soon as possible—to see if there's any pending transactions for a ransom."

Rothman smooths the front of his robe. "I should run your warrant through my legal team first." His gaze travels out the window.

Tina glances at Pratt. Banks are notorious for roadblocking the FBI when being served warrants, dragging them through their legal team and not getting back to them for thirty to forty-five days. They don't have time for that.

She studies the financier, wondering what his motivation would be to stall the investigation. Given the endangerment of his employee's child and his suspicions of fraud, it seems Rothman should be more than willing to help.

Is he protecting Jack Rossi? Or something else? She thinks of Rothman's beautiful daughter pictured in the *Forbes* article with Rossi and remembers Pratt asking if Rossi was alone in his apartment. The article stated they were childhood best friends. She wonders what they are now. From the looks of it, they are still very close.

Rothman lets out a sigh. "But I have access to everything. I still directly manage a percentage of Jack's client accounts. It's how I've been able to set him up with some top clients. When Jack started working for me, mine was the name everyone knew—the man the rich wanted managing their money. But I could only manage so much. Jack's clients got the promise of me investing a portion of their assets, but now he's made a name for *himself*, which was exactly what I hoped he would do." Rothman pushes himself to his feet with the help of the armrest. "I'll get my laptop."

Tina and Pratt wait in silence as Lionel disappears down a dimly lit hallway. Tina casts a look at Agent Pratt, who avoids her eye contact.

She guesses that, like her, Pratt is relieved Rothman is cooperating, given the time-sensitive nature of the situation.

She thinks about the Rossis' financial records, his salary of a few hundred thousand after taxes, and their water-view Tribeca condo. *Was he supplementing his income through fraud, like Lionel suspected?*

Tina reaches inside her purse to see if Felicity left her a voicemail and sees that she did. Rothman reappears from the hallway, now wearing a pair of reading glasses and carrying a silver laptop in one hand. Tina drops her phone back into her bag. She'll have to wait to call her back. Rothman perches on the edge of the sofa, opens the computer atop the coffee table, and begins to type.

After a moment, Rothman flips the laptop around. "Here are all of Jack's accounts. You can see the end balances as of yesterday, but you'll have to go through each fund to look for any pending transactions."

Pratt leans forward.

"It'll take a while," Rothman continues. "And it's possible any transactions made after the close of yesterday's business day won't show up until the start of business hours."

Tina stares at the list of eight-figure balances on the laptop screen. If Rothman confronted Jack yesterday, staging his son's kidnapping and ransom might've seemed the perfect way to cover his fraud. Which would also mean that Makayla is in on it. They could claim they *had* to take that money out to cover the ransom demand. They had no choice. Still, it wasn't a foolproof plan. Faking a kidnapping and ransom wouldn't do anything to fix Rossi's account balances in a federal investigation, but, she surmises, it would provide Rossi an explanation to give to his clients for their missing money. She's seen enough as an analyst to know that desperate people take desperate measures. And they don't always think things through. It would also explain why they can't find Liam on the flight.

Jack would have had to hire someone to stage this, or Makayla did it. But who would do such a thing? To their own child?

"You don't think Jack embezzled from the wrong client, do you?" she asks.

"If my suspicions are correct, Jack's in way over his head. We have a lot of very powerful clients who would undoubtedly go a long way to protect their assets. Most of our investors don't get to where they are by being passive individuals. And I can't speak to all of their moral codes." A gasp escapes Rothman's throat. "What if one of them enlisted some criminals to hit Jack where it hurts the most?"

"Anything is possible at this point," Pratt says. "Can you give us administrative access to all these accounts? We need to live monitor everything. Analyst Farrar can give you our emails." Pratt stands with his phone in hand, and Tina thinks Rothman's fears surrounding a vengeful client make more sense than Rossi staging his son's kidnapping. And apparently, Pratt has been thinking the same thing. He turns to Tina. "I'm going to get a warrant for the Anchorage office to go back and search Makayla's father's house."

CHAPTER TWENTY

MAKAYLA

Makayla tears her eyes from the young woman's phone to meet the girl's gaze. Her enlarged blue eyes are trained on Makayla's as a different female voice plays through the girl's phone speaker.

"These were some of the actress's final moments before the tragic car accident that claimed her life when she ran a red light after fleeing the recording studio."

Makayla resists the urge to swipe the girl's phone out of her hand. *My mother's interview.* She probably saw the Netflix special, then pulled up the full interview on YouTube.

Why couldn't the girl have kept watching her Reese Witherspoon rom-com?

The girl taps her phone screen and gapes at Makayla. "Your mom was Lydia Banks." She extends her phone into the aisle. "That actress that lost her mind before she died."

A spark of rage surges inside Makayla's chest. Her mother didn't lose her *mind*; she lost her *memory*. Makayla stares back at the girl, her anger morphing into confusion. *But how does she know this?*

"I remember my mom crying when it was on the news," Pink Headphones says, waving her phone in the air. "This says she had an amnesia disorder." Her eyes widen. "That must be why the flight

attendant asked me if I *actually saw* your baby. You could have that too."
She unbuckles herself with one hand and steps into the aisle. "Do you
even remember him being with you?"

Makayla scoffs at the absurdity of the girl's question. "Of course
I do."

"No one saw him. Not even me, and I was sitting right here." She
gestures to her seat over her shoulder. "And you obviously forgot that
my bags were already searched. You were here when the flight attendant
came through and watched her go through my stuff."

"You need to sit down." Makayla fights to keep her voice calm.
"What is wrong with you?" Makayla presses her flight attendant call
button.

"You accused me of taking him!"

Makayla shrinks back from the girl's pointer finger, which stops
within an inch of her cheek. "Get your hand out of my face."

The girl slowly lowers her arm. "I don't think you even brought
him on board."

Makayla tugs at the buckle of her seat belt and stands to her feet.
"How dare you! Of course he was on this plane! He still is. He was lying
right there when I asked you to watch him. I know you saw him. And
there's only one reason why you'd be lying about it." The thought sends
chills down Makayla's spine.

The girl shakes her head. "I'm not lying. You're not thinking
straight."

"What's going on?"

They turn to find Britt standing in the aisle a few rows back, hands
on her hips.

"Both of you need to sit down. Now."

The girl jabs her finger toward Makayla's chest. "Her mom was
Lydia Banks—that child-star actress who lost her memory before she
drove like a maniac and died in that car crash. I bet her daughter has the
same thing. Her baby isn't missing. He was never on board!"

Makayla's nostrils flare as she fights the urge to shove the girl away from her. *Stay calm so you can find Liam,* she tells herself.

Makayla suddenly remembers her hair being blond on the nearly decade-old Netflix documentary. Did the girl actually recognize Makayla from watching it, or did she already know who Makayla was?

Makayla lowers her face toward the girl's, staring into her big blue eyes. "How could you even find out who my mother was without knowing my name? My *full* name."

Makayla racks her brain trying to remember if she's ever seen this girl before. She's sure she hasn't. Could the girl have targeted her somehow? Stalked her online? She thinks about her photography blog, which only has a small following; her public social media pages; and the awareness campaign she created about transient global amnesia after her mother died.

The girl takes a step back, but Makayla doesn't break eye contact. Did she see her mother's illness as an opportunity to abduct Liam?

But why?

The girl swipes her hand through the air. "You said it."

Makayla furrows her brows. *When?*

"Then I realized you were on that Netflix special. Your hair was lighter, but it was definitely you."

Britt moves in between them. "I need you both to take your seats."

"Fine." The girl crosses her arms and plops down.

Britt turns to Makayla. "You gave me your full name so the pilots could give your information to the ground authorities, remember? We weren't standing that far from here when you told me. She probably overheard you."

Makayla does remember. Now.

Britt's eyes search her own, and she can guess what the flight attendant's thinking. But Makayla forces away the thought that there could be more she's not remembering. Any mother would have trouble thinking straight with her baby missing. Makayla steps forward, scanning the faces of those seated around her.

"Someone on this flight has Liam."

"Ma'am, I need you to return to your seat." Britt's voice is sharp.

"Not until I find my son." Makayla strains to see beyond Britt. She catches Jemma's eye, who regards her with pity. Rose looks to have fallen asleep across the aisle, while the retirement-aged couple seated in front of Rose look on with wide eyes. Makayla's gaze darts to the man seated on the far side of the plane who's reading on his tablet, looking maddeningly calm.

Derek comes to stand behind Britt.

"We've already checked everywhere." Exasperation seeps from Britt's sharp tone.

"You can't have checked *everywhere*—otherwise Liam would've already been found. We need to look again. I have to find my son!" Her voice breaks, and the last word comes out a croak.

Derek steps past Britt and closes his grip around Makayla's elbow, his mouth set into a hard, thin line. His eyes are void of the compassion they held when Liam first went missing.

"We agree that his disappearance doesn't make sense. But I'm ordering you to take your seat."

Makayla's lower lip quivers as she draws in a steadying breath. But she makes no attempt to move.

Derek loosens his hold on her ever so slightly. "We're doing everything we can to help you, but you must calm down and comply with our safety instructions."

"I haven't lost my memory. I've lost my *baby*. And I need you to help me. And believe me!" She motions toward Jemma watching them from the exit row. "You saw him! And you must've heard the whimper he let out when he dropped his pacifier. *Please* tell them."

"I—" Jemma glances at her husband. "I'm sorry." She grimaces, meeting Makayla's eyes with a look of apology. "I didn't actually see your baby, like I said before. Or hear him. I wish I had. I only saw his pacifier."

"Sit down." Derek steps forward, motioning to her seat.

Makayla shakes her elbow from his grip. "My baby is *missing!*"

"We know, ma'am."

He's not even addressing her by name, she notices. She wonders if the crew has somehow already learned about her mother. Is that why they're questioning whether Liam ever came on board? Could that be why they aren't landing? Was the captain lying about the thunderstorm and tornado watch?

"It's a federal regulation that you remain in your seat with your seat belt fastened until the captain turns off the seat belt sign." Derek's once kind voice now sounds robotic.

"I'm not sitting down until I find my son."

"You have no choice. It's the law. You're endangering yourself and those around you by moving about the cabin. If you refuse to comply, then we'll have to restrain you."

Makayla sets her jaw, locking her eyes with Derek's, before lowering herself to her seat.

Derek leans over her, his face softening. "Thank you. We're doing our best to help you find your son."

No, you're not, Makayla thinks as he retreats toward the rear of the plane. *How could they be helping when they don't even believe Liam was on board?*

Makayla peers down at Liam's diaper bag on the floor and her baby wrap, now in a messy heap on the empty seat beside her. She reaches for the fabric, cool from the air vent above, before checking her phone to find a new message from Cori. Any updates?

She drums out a reply, her thumbs fueled by anger at the crew's lack of concern. The crew says they're doing everything, but they've stopped looking, saying they've already checked everywhere. We're not even going to divert. They found out about my mom and don't think I brought Liam on the flight. They think I've lost my memory like her.

Makayla presses her lips together after hitting send. She knows Cori will believe her. She only wishes she had someone to defend her sanity on the flight. Cori's mom is a bestselling romance author, and

Cori knows what it's like having a famous parent. She understands better than anyone—even Jack—Makayla's pain over the public scrutiny surrounding her mother's infamous TV interview.

What?! How can they not believe you?

Makayla glances at Pink Headphones, who rips open a snack pack of almonds before popping a few into her mouth. Makayla hadn't remembered giving her full name to Britt when she accused the girl of knowing it. And she has no recollection of Britt searching both the girl's bags—only one—even though she was sitting right here when Britt came through the cabin to search their luggage.

She envisions the look on her mother's face in the interview the girl just replayed. She's seen the interview countless times, and the image of her mother's final moments will be forever seared in her mind.

Makayla covers her mouth with her hand as she allows her gaze to settle on the empty bassinet. Her mother clearly had no idea what was happening to her when her amnesia set in. Lydia was so certain of her own cognition and perception of events that she refused to entertain the possibility she was confused. It's why she left the recording studio before anyone could stop her.

Makayla's fingers tremble against her lips. A few moments ago, she didn't think it possible to feel any more fear than she was already experiencing. But she was wrong.

She collapses against her seat and considers—for the first time—the possibility that the crew's suspicions could be right. *What if Liam was never on board?*

Her heart sticks in her throat just considering the possibility. Because if she boarded without Liam, then . . .

It would mean that she left him somewhere in the Anchorage airport, somewhere between where her dad dropped her off and the gate. But if that was the case, then why hasn't Liam been found?

CHAPTER TWENTY-ONE

TINA

After the elevator doors to Lionel Rothman's penthouse close, Tina turns to Agent Pratt. "You think Jack and Makayla Rossi staged their son's kidnapping to cover up his fraud?"

"It would explain the look on Rossi's face when we asked about anything unusual happening at work. Also, why they can't find the kid on that plane." Pratt folds a stick of gum into his mouth without offering one to Tina. "I got the warrant for Makayla's father's home in Anchorage while you were getting the account access from Rothman. We'll find out soon if they're hiding the kid there."

"Although," Tina thinks aloud when the doors open to the opulent lobby, "wouldn't Jack realize that staging a kidnapping and a fake ransom would draw the FBI's attention to his accounts?"

Pratt motions for her to go first. "People do irrational things when they fear they're about to get caught. Maybe Rossi got scared after his boss confronted him about the fraud and hatched up a plan."

"A ransom *would* give Rossi an excuse if his clients raised an alarm over their account deficits," Pratt adds as they move side by side through the quiet Upper East Side lobby.

"I still don't see how Rossi could've planned to get away with it. We can trace the transfer."

Pratt shrugs. "Maybe he didn't think it through. Or he could be planning to transfer funds into his personal account and then withdraw a large sum of cash. If we hadn't got wind of Rossi's alleged fraud, we wouldn't be looking that deeply into his accounts aside from the 'ransom.'"

She thinks about the Rossis' water-view Tribeca condo. If he gets caught, Jack has a lot to lose, not to mention facing a potentially lifelong prison sentence.

"I'm going to need help from one of our forensic accountants to go through everything," Tina says. "I'll call Special Agent Castillo on our way back to the office."

After Rothman's accusations, they'll have to launch a separate investigation into the firm's accounts to determine whether Jack Rossi has been committing fraud, but tonight, they need to focus on finding Liam.

Tina's phone vibrates in her purse. She digs it out, thinking of Isabel and the call she still hasn't returned. It's a text from Felicity. **Everything's fine but if you can, call me when you get this.**

Tina calls her back without listening to the voicemail as the doorman wearing a bespoke suit opens the door for them. The muggy outside air is a stark contrast to the overly air-conditioned lobby.

Felicity answers after the first ring. "Sorry to call you. I know you're at work. And everything's okay, but Isabel had a nightmare. She woke up crying, and she's having trouble falling back asleep. She seems pretty upset, and I was wondering what you normally do to help her?"

Tina's heart drops into her stomach. She should be there with Isabel, not her neighbor. Isabel has gotten these night terrors since she was little. They started right after Jason left.

"I normally let her come sleep in my bed. And I tell her a story while rubbing her back."

"I'll try that."

"Thanks." Except the only stories that seem to soothe her are memories of fun times she and Isabel have had together, Tina thinks.

Pratt casts her a look before moving around to the driver's side of the SUV, apparently realizing she's on a personal call.

Tina opens the passenger-side door and climbs inside. "Can I talk to her?"

"Yes, hang on."

Tina hears the creak of a door opening. There's a pause before Felicity speaks in a whisper.

"It looks like she finally fell back asleep."

"Okay, good." But her relief is muddled by the thought of Isabel crying herself back to sleep without her. For the second time that night.

"All good," Felicity adds. "Sorry to bother you. We'll see you when you get home."

"Thanks, Felicity."

Tina puts on her seat belt after ending the call.

"Everything all right?" Pratt asks, making a turn for the financial district.

His question comes out as a mixture of annoyance and concern.

"Yeah. Fine."

He shoots her an inquisitive look. "You sure?"

"It's my daughter. I had to leave her with my neighbor tonight." Tina swallows the large lump that's formed in her throat. "She was supposed to be with her dad this weekend, but he . . ." *He bailed, breaking her heart and ignoring his responsibility as her father.* "Canceled last minute."

"That's tough."

Tina turns to him, surprised by the warmth in his tone.

"My wife passed away when my kids were eight and ten."

"I'm so sorry."

"Thank you." He keeps his eyes on the road. "It was a long time ago. My kids are grown now. But I remember those days of juggling the demands of work as a single parent. Somehow, they turned out to be a couple of pretty well-rounded adults."

"Right now, I think my daughter's growing up to be someone who's getting used to disappointment." The last word sticks in her throat, and the welling up of emotion takes her by surprise.

"I know it's hard, but you'll get through it too." Pratt meets Tina's gaze after stopping at a red light. "I'm sure your little girl will grow up to be a strong woman like her mother."

Tina nods, blinking back the tears that spring to her eyes. The light turns green, and Pratt accelerates through the intersection. She studies him for a moment before looking out her side window at the buildings speeding past.

CHAPTER TWENTY-TWO

JACK

Jack rubs his eyes after refreshing the client account dashboard. The balances are still the same. When he spoke with Makayla, he couldn't bring himself to tell her about the FBI's suspicions—that she'd lost her memory like her mother. He didn't bring up the possible connection with his work, either, telling Makayla only that they were gathering information. She was already so beside herself, obviously crying.

He pictures her alone on the plane, with Liam missing. *I should've gone with her.* Instead, he stayed back to appease Lionel. The man to whom, until earlier this week, Jack thought he owed everything.

He eyes the empty whiskey glass in the sink that he'd downed before going to sleep, when there hadn't seemed anything worse than to be facing a lifelong prison sentence if he went down for Lionel's fraud.

All these years he believed Lionel was looking out for him. *Mentoring* him. A second father. In actuality, he'd been covering himself if the firm were ever investigated, setting Jack up to look guilty of the biggest Ponzi scheme of the decade.

Jack recalls Lionel teaching him how to change a tire when he was fifteen, and showing up at Jack's high school graduation when his own father didn't make it. He stares at the account balances. All this time, he hadn't really known Lionel at all.

How could I never have known? Not even suspected.

He wonders if Sabrina knows. A memory of her hair blowing in the wind as they rode the ferry to Governors Island on a summer Saturday while they were in high school flashes in his mind. When they were still best friends. Before everything changed.

Jack wishes they hadn't dated in college. Their friendship was never the same after that.

Jack tilts his head toward the living room window and stares at the lit-up skyline of Jersey City across the river. This very condo was purchased with the help of stolen money—money that Jack was stupid enough to believe he'd earned. Lionel's threat after Jack told Lionel he was turning him in rings in his ears. *No one's going to believe you. They were your accounts, Jack. Every single withdrawal was done using your log-in code. If you breathe a word of this to the authorities,* you'll *be the one they find guilty.*

If Lionel gets caught, he'll be facing life imprisonment. Jack contemplates the possibility that Lionel had Liam kidnapped so he could blame the account deficits on a ransom. He knew Makayla was flying home tonight with Liam. It seems unfathomable to consider it, but it's also unfathomable to think that all these years, Lionel has been committing the biggest Ponzi scheme since Bernie Madoff. Hell, Lionel could even be planning to make it look like Jack set up the kidnapping himself—just like Lionel did with the fraudulent account transfers. He could claim Jack had given into a kidnapper's threat that they'd kill Liam if anyone went to the police, then embezzled the funds to get his son back.

The more Jack considers this, it doesn't make sense. If the FBI investigates the firm's accounts, they'll see that no ransom has been made. More likely, the Feds would find the evidence of Lionel's years of embezzlement.

Jack sits tall. How could he not have thought of it before? Through the firm, he carried a kidnap-and-ransom insurance policy for himself and his family. Lionel helped Jack take out the policy after Jack's *Forbes* article came out, getting him a corporate rate on the insurance premiums. At the time, Jack didn't think it was necessary, but Lionel insisted on Jack getting the policy as a precaution. *You can never be too careful,* Lionel said.

Jack was the beneficiary, however, not Lionel. He should've told the FBI. He reaches for his phone, then stops. Telling the FBI about the insurance policy will only make him look guilty.

He studies his account balances on his laptop screen. *Could Lionel have taken out his own insurance policy on Liam?*

If Lionel was consumed enough by greed to steal hundreds of millions—possibly more—from those who trusted him, how far would he go to keep from losing everything?

But how would his boss orchestrate Liam's kidnapping from New York? Although, for enough money, it wouldn't be hard to find someone willing to kidnap an infant, especially if Lionel's plan was to allow Liam to be found once an insurance payout went through.

But if Liam is somewhere on that plane in the hands of a stranger, then why can't anyone find him? He refuses to entertain the most obvious reason why Liam wouldn't be making any noise.

Jack straightens, pressing his bare back against the kitchen barstool while he checks his phone screen. Makayla still hasn't called him back. The FBI's questions about Makayla's memory—and her mother—float in the front of his mind. *Maybe they were grasping at straws. They couldn't possibly have a legitimate reason to think Makayla wasn't in her right frame of mind.*

When Makayla's mom was diagnosed with amnesia after she died, Makayla told him all about the memory disorder. She said it was rare and mostly affected people over fifty. Makayla isn't even forty. Lydia suffered from migraines, which Makayla later learned had put her mom at a higher risk of developing this type of amnesia.

Now, Jack regrets telling the FBI about Makayla's headaches. It doesn't mean Makayla has amnesia. And if the FBI blames Liam's disappearance on Makayla's memory, thinking he was never on board, they could be searching for him on the ground rather than on that flight. Which was exactly what she said right before they hung up. *The crew even questioned whether I brought Liam on board.*

Terror grips him as if someone has reached inside and squeezed his heart. He can't just sit here and do nothing.

He slides off the stool in search of the business card the FBI agent gave him. He should've told the FBI about Lionel when they were here. Jack's silence has already caused them to lose precious time. A stab of guilt seizes his heart. He was so worried about Lionel's threat of framing Jack for fraud that he forgot that it doesn't matter what happens to him. All that matters is Liam.

Lionel's last words before Jack left his office haunt him as he spots the business card on the couch. *Take five million from some of your other clients' accounts to make up for the loss in Malcolm Zeller's. Aside from you and me, no one will ever be the wiser.* Lionel patted Jack on the back as he had countless times throughout Jack's life. *Everything's going to be fine, son.*

But Jack hadn't complied. *Is Liam's disappearance Lionel's way of taking matters into his own hands?* Jack's chest tightens at the possibility.

Taking the business card in his hand, he thinks about Sabrina. Lionel never answered Jack's question about whether his daughter knew about the fraud. Lionel made her the firm's managing director at its inception; she and her father have always been extremely close.

After what happened between him and Sabrina eight years ago, Sabrina is the one Jack would've thought capable of fraud. Now Jack wonders if her selfish ambition and lack of moral backbone were handed down and the apple didn't fall far from the tree.

Sabrina would likely rather die than go to prison. She's always detested Makayla. And Sabrina still holds a grudge for what happened between Jack and her all those years ago.

CHAPTER TWENTY-THREE

JACK

Eight Years Earlier

At the knock on his office door, Jack looked up from his spreadsheet, expecting to see Lionel. The firm's other account managers had already left for the night. Jack was used to being one of the last to leave, second, sometimes, to his boss.

But it wasn't Lionel. As a woman waltzed into his office from the unlit hallway, he recognized Sabrina's silhouette. She'd taken off her stilettos and sauntered toward his desk, her fitted dress straining against each long stride.

In one hand, she held a champagne bottle, her manicured fingers wrapped around its neck. In the other were two flute glasses.

"Heard you closed the Goldstein account." She smiled, lifting the champagne bottle in front of her chest.

Jack leaned back in his chair. "That I did."

She was no longer wearing the blazer she'd had on earlier in the day. Her cleavage spilled out of the dress's low neckline.

An uneasiness crept over him as she set the bottle and glasses on his desk. He worried this was going to be like the Christmas party all over again. When Sabrina cornered him in a below-deck hallway of the firm's rented yacht, she'd already had several drinks. Jack had left the group upstairs in search of a bathroom and got turned around, then found himself in an impossible situation. She confessed to still having feelings for him, admitting to never quite getting over their breakup in college.

At the time, he'd chalked it up to her being drunk—he'd had a few too many himself. Which was what he blamed for not resisting hard enough when she threw her arms around his neck and pressed her mouth—then her body—against his.

Now Sabrina stood by his desk, watching him with a playful expression. "Closing a big account always calls for a celebration." She flung her blond hair over her shoulder before untwisting the wire holding down the cork.

Jack glanced at the clock. Aaron Goldstein, the founder of the biggest online real estate marketplace, would be Jack's biggest client—by far. Landing the Goldstein account also meant he would be busier now than ever. It was after midnight, but he still had hours of paperwork if he was going to deliver the results he promised.

"Actually, Sabrina, I still have a lot of work to do."

An audible pop filled the office when Sabrina released the cork from the bottle. She poured a glass and extended it toward him. "Just one drink."

Jack hesitated.

"Come on. You deserve it," she added.

He accepted the glass. "All right." His eyes could use a break from the spreadsheet numbers. "Just one."

After pouring her own, Sabrina moved around the side of his desk, perching herself on the edge beside him. He got a whiff of her sweet perfume. The same scent he had inhaled when he kissed her neck on the yacht.

He pushed back his chair. "Sabrina—"

She laid her hand over his wrist. "Don't worry. We're just having a drink. Between friends."

Jack took a sip from his champagne and felt himself relax. They *were* friends. Had been since they were seven. And what happened on that yacht was a drunken mistake. They both knew it.

111

Sabrina crossed her legs. "You've been working for months to close this account. It must feel so good to have finally sealed the deal." She lifted her flute to her full lips.

"It does." He thought of all the meetings, phone calls, and late-night dinners he'd sat through these last few months. Then there were the hours he'd spent prepping for them, grinding out market analysis reports and sample investment portfolios. But it was a huge account, the biggest he would manage by far, and it had been worth it.

He thought of Makayla, home asleep, while he sat here sharing a glass of champagne with his childhood best friend. He hadn't been home enough lately, and he should have been celebrating with his wife.

Jack yawned. "Damn, I'm so tired. I can't believe I've still got so much to do."

"You've been working really hard."

Jack took another drink. Talking to Sabrina had always been easy. He missed talking like this with Makayla, who hadn't been the same since her mom passed. Even when he *was* home, she was preoccupied, putting all her energy into her awareness campaign for the amnesia disorder that contributed to her mother's fatal car accident.

"Maybe you should take a break for the night." Sabrina set down her glass and scooted closer to him. "Start fresh in the morning."

Jack finished what was left in his flute. He checked the time. Sabrina was right. He was exhausted. He turned off his computer, and Sabrina slid onto his lap.

"Whoa!" he said, abruptly standing.

Sabrina stumbled to her feet.

"We can't." He held out his hand. "I'm married. What happened before was a mistake—you know that."

Sabrina smoothed the skirt of her dress. "You need someone who understands you, Jack. Makayla's hardly spoken to you these last few months, while you've been under so much pressure to land this account."

Jack straightened. He'd told Lionel that in confidence. Heat rushed to his face.

"She lost her mother."

"Oh, come on. That was two years ago." She placed both palms on his chest. "It was always you and me."

She tilted her face toward his.

Jack peeled her hands off him. "Go home, Sabrina." He snatched his suit jacket off the back of his chair. "I'm leaving too."

She reached for his arm. "Jack! Wait."

He pulled away, striding for the door without looking back.

She was still in his office when he reached the elevator, and he was relieved to ride down alone.

The next morning, Jack threw open the door and burst into Sabrina's office. With her phone to her ear, she watched him storm toward her. The passive look on her face—as if she wasn't expecting this—only infuriated him more.

"*What have you done?*" he shouted.

She pursed her lips. "I'm going to have to call you back," she said before hanging up her desk phone. She batted her eyelashes. "What do you mean?"

Jack flexed his jaw. "You know what I mean. You gave my Goldstein account to Roger! After everything I did. That was *my* account. I spent the last three months trying to get them to invest with us. And not just us—with *me*." Jack pointed in the direction of Roger's office down the hall. "You can't do that. Roger's retiring later this year. Giving him that account makes no sense, and you know it."

She folded her hands atop her desk, not even bothering to hide how much she was enjoying this. "I can do whatever I think is in the best interest of the firm. I feel that account is a better fit for Roger. And I already spoke with Lindsey. When Roger retires, she's happy to take over the account."

Jack gritted his teeth. Lindsey was the firm's newest hire, and everyone knew she wouldn't last long. She rarely stayed past four o'clock, and she shopped online as much as she actually worked. Jack wondered how she even got hired in the first place.

"What the hell, Sabrina?"

She glanced at the glass office wall. "You might want to keep your voice down. We don't need any office rumors going around about us."

Jack took another step toward her desk. "So, what? Because I didn't let you come on to me last night, you think you can take the Goldstein account away from me?" He snorted. "Well, you can't. I'm going to see your father about this. Tell him what you've done. And why."

Sabrina's pink-lipsticked mouth curled into a sly smile. "No, you won't. Because if you do, I'll tell Makayla about the Christmas party."

Jack narrowed his eyes. "You want to tell her you threw yourself at me after I'd had a few drinks? That we kissed for a few minutes before I pushed you away and told you it could never happen again? Fine. You were the one who came on to me. I shouldn't have kissed you back, but it meant nothing."

Sabrina's smile faded. "We slept together, Jack. At least, that's how I remember it."

"I'm not even going to entertain this. You know that's not true." Jack turned for the door.

"And last night, when you stayed here so late, it was *you* who came on to me. I shouldn't have let it happen a second time, but you were so . . . forceful."

Jack whipped around when he reached her doorway. "How dare you."

Sabrina shook her head. "No, Jack. How dare *you*. If you go to my father about this, then I'll have no choice but to tell him my side of the story." She twirled a piece of her hair. "And you're a fool if you think he'd believe you over his own daughter."

CHAPTER TWENTY-FOUR

ANNA

Anna slides her phone out of her pocket while Miguel verifies that the correct LaGuardia arrival and instrument approach is loaded in the Multipurpose Control and Display Unit, which casts a green-and-magenta glow over the dimly lit cockpit. Seeing that she still hasn't gotten a reply to her last text, she checks the time. Feeling Miguel's eyes on her, she tucks her phone back into her blazer pocket.

She wonders how things got to this point. At first, she told herself she wasn't doing anything wrong. But now . . .

She hears Minneapolis Center calling an aircraft on the radio and realizes she hasn't been paying attention.

"Was that for us?" she asks Miguel.

Miguel looks up from pushing the buttons on his MCDU. "I didn't hear it. If it was, they'll call us again."

Through the cockpit windshield, a bright flash of lightning momentarily lights up the sky.

Anna glances at her map display on the instrument panel. "I thought our route was going to be too far northeast to be seeing that storm. But now it looks like it is just south of our track ahead." She points to the red and yellow patches on her map display.

"Me too." Miguel zooms in on the nav screen. "It must be moving north of where they predicted. Although that lightning seemed to be pretty far south."

He's right, she thinks, relaxing against her seat. *It wasn't that close.*

Her thoughts drift to the mother in the main cabin, still without her baby—and no trace of him anywhere on board.

"Did the mother say anything else when you spoke to her besides asking to divert?" she asks Miguel.

Miguel nods. "She wanted us to check the luggage compartment beneath the cockpit for her baby. And asked for us to send her a photo of it."

"A photo?"

"I'm assuming for proof that we actually checked it. But I told her there's no way her baby could be down there."

"Right," Anna agrees.

"Maybe you should go down there. I don't want the mother causing a big disturbance in the back, and it might appease her if we tell her we checked."

Anna cocks her head toward Miguel, surprised by his request. "We don't need to go down below to assure the mother her baby isn't there. The only access is through the cockpit. Plus, it's an FAA violation for either of us to leave our seats, except for physiological reasons, when there's only two of us. I'm not risking my pilot's license or the safety of the flight to go below when we already know the baby can't be there."

Miguel stares out the windscreen, appearing to consider what she said.

"And I don't think you should either," she adds.

"You're probably right," he finally says.

She presses her lips together, studying Miguel's expression. "You think the baby is really on this plane?"

His deep voice fills her headphones. "It seems hard to believe they wouldn't have found him already if he was. I suppose we won't know for sure until—"

A buzzer sounds. Anna sees the amber "ATT" light flashing on her intercom panel. She punches the "ATT" button and moves the transmit lever forward. "Yes, it's Anna."

"Hi, it's Aubrey; I'm outside the door with your drinks."

Miguel moves the door-locking lever to the unlock position. Behind them, the door unlocks with a click.

"Okay, door's unlocked," Anna replies.

"You guys want anything else?" Aubrey asks, holding two cups of black coffee in between the pilots' seats.

The pilots reach for their drinks as the nose lurches upward. Hot liquid spills over the side of Anna's cup and onto her pant leg.

"Oh, I'm so sorry," Aubrey says. "I only poured them two-thirds full, hoping that wouldn't happen."

Anna slides one of her headphones behind her ear and turns to the attendant. "Don't worry about it. Not your fault."

Miguel reaches up and turns on the seat belt sign as Anna wipes her leg with a napkin.

"You guys want anything else? Food?"

"No, thanks." Anna sets her now half-full coffee in her cup holder.

"Me neither," Miguel says. "Thanks, though. If I eat too much, I'll fall asleep."

He winks. But with a baby missing on board and the most turbulent flight any of them has had in a while, his joke falls short of a laugh.

The fuselage vibrates as they fly over a patch of rough air. Aubrey leans forward, placing a hand on Anna's seat back to steady herself. "One of the passengers discovered the missing infant's mother is the daughter of Lydia Banks."

Miguel turns toward her. "The actress?"

"Yep."

"Didn't she die in a car accident?" Anna asks, thinking it was about a decade ago when she saw the news story of her death.

Aubrey nods. "After losing her memory. She had a condition called transient global amnesia. It's some sort of memory disorder."

Anna twists in her seat to meet Aubrey's gaze. She glances at Miguel. "That must be why the FBI asked if the mother was acting confused."

"And is she?" Miguel asks Aubrey.

A bright flash of lightning, much closer than the last flash, fills the flight deck. Aubrey shifts her focus out the windshield. "She's definitely distraught. Which is understandable, but twice she's thought someone else's toddler was her own, so I'm not sure what to think."

Both pilots fix their attention to the red and yellow patches of weather depicted on their nav displays.

"Thanks for the update," Miguel says.

Anna hopes things don't escalate further in the back before they're able to land. Looking at the weather, they could have their hands full for the rest of the flight.

"Let me know if you change your mind on the food," Aubrey says before turning toward the door. After she leaves the cockpit, the door automatically locks with an audible click.

"We need to adjust our route to the north to avoid that weather." Miguel keys his microphone. "Minneapolis Center, Pacific Air Flight 7038, we need to deviate about twenty miles north for weather."

"Roger, Pacific Air Flight 7038, deviation to the north as necessary is approved. Advise when you can resume direct to Rockdale."

"Okay, we'll let you know, Flight 7038," Miguel replies as he types in the commands to turn the airplane to the left to parallel their course twenty miles to the north. When he presses the last button, the magenta course lines on their map displays jumps twenty miles to the north, and the airplane starts a gradual left turn.

"You should ask your husband about that memory disorder," Miguel says as Anna takes a drink from her coffee. "If it's hereditary."

Her coffee burns the back of her throat at the thought of Carter saving lives later today at Manhattan General while having no idea what his wife is about to do.

Seeing the look on her face, Miguel waves his hand dismissively through the air. "Never mind. I forgot what time it is. I'm sure he's asleep."

"Yeah, probably." She forges a smile, recalling what Miguel said at the start of their flight. *Hard to see what's right in front of you sometimes.*

Am I really going through with this? But she knows the answer. While she's struck by a tinge of guilt at what she's about to do, she also feels powerless to stop it.

CHAPTER TWENTY-FIVE

MAKAYLA

In her seat, Makayla stares at the bassinet where she laid Liam down after takeoff before falling asleep herself. She'd slept harder than usual.

Now that she thinks about it, she slept longer than normal last night at her dad's too. Her dad got up with Liam, and when she woke, she was surprised to discover the room brightly lit with midmorning sun. She runs her hand over the tender spot on the back of her scalp, wondering if her drowsiness could be due to her fall.

Did I hit my head harder than I thought? She pushes her doubts aside. *I laid him in that bassinet. I didn't imagine it. Liam was here, on this plane. And he still is. But where?*

She draws Liam's blanket to the side of her face, recalling her mother's infectious laugh so vividly she can almost hear it. It was distinctive. Erupting from deep within her.

Her mother was such an incredible person. It's why Makayla went on a campaign to raise awareness about TGA after her mom died. The disorder is rare, affecting less than 1 percent of people, even after age fifty. If someone at the recording studio had recognized what was happening to Lydia, they could've helped her. Called an ambulance instead of letting her mother get into her car that day. But no one knew what was wrong with her mom until it was too late.

Not only that, but what happened to her wasn't her fault, and Makayla couldn't have her remembered like that.

Even though her mother became an A-list actress before she turned eighteen, Lydia wanted nothing to do with fame. Her mother's teenage rise to fame took a toll, as it did on many child stars. Lydia's mother gave up on pursuing her own acting ambitions after having Lydia at the age of nineteen. Hoping to live out her own dreams through Lydia's acting success, she started taking Lydia to auditions as a toddler. Lydia's mother was over the moon when her daughter got her first role in a cereal commercial at the age of three and became known as the Wheat Crunchies Girl.

As an adult, Lydia spoke out about the negative effects stardom can have on mental health at a young, developing age. She became one of the first celebrities to advocate for the mental health of child stars. In Lydia's memoir, she shared her own battle with depression, revealing how her early fame and acting career also came with rejection and a pressure to perform. Being in the public eye as a child cultivated a need inside her to attain a level of perfection that was impossible to reach.

Makayla's mother also struggled with the lack of privacy she felt in her childhood, along with a sense of always being watched, especially after her infamous stalker incident. Lydia had been living alone when she woke to the sound of her bedroom window shattering in the middle of the night. She managed to dial 911 on the phone beside her bed before a disheveled man in his early twenties climbed inside the broken window and ripped the phone from the wall.

He sat on her bed, warning her if she tried to get up, he would kill her. Lydia remained stoically still, frozen in fear, as the young man launched into an angry rant about Lydia ignoring his fan mail and how they were meant to be together. Her intruder reached into his sweatshirt pocket, telling Lydia he would rather her be dead than apart from him.

At that moment, the police burst through her front door. After hand-cuffing him, the officers found a loaded 9mm in his sweatshirt pocket.

It was why her mother loved the seclusion of the Bainbridge Island property where Makayla grew up. Makayla recalls all the time she spent combing the beach for shells and sand dollars and playing make-believe on the forested, three-acre property, knowing it was likely the cause for her aversion to the city.

At the age of nineteen, the same year the stalker broke into her home, Lydia went through a highly publicized divorce. After being followed by paparazzi everywhere she went, Lydia quickly became overwhelmed by her worldwide fame and developed severe anxiety. During that time, Lydia's best friend and fellow actress died of a cocaine overdose.

Following a panic attack, Lydia was hospitalized, which triggered yet another media frenzy. Not long after, she decided her Hollywood lifestyle brought out the worst in her and chose to leave it all behind. She moved to Seattle, where she met Makayla's father, an architect whom she met through a mutual friend. A year later, she got pregnant with Makayla and never regretted retiring from acting to embrace motherhood and a normal life. When Makayla closes her eyes, a memory of her mother teaching her to ski in the Cascade mountains east of Seattle when she was five flashes in her mind.

Makayla clung to her mother's ski poles as her mom skied behind her on the groomed trail at Snoqualmie Pass, keeping her larger skis on the outsides of Makayla's. Thick patches of snow-covered evergreens lined the slope on either side. The first time her mom let go, Makayla's heart raced as she picked up speed on the slope. A snowboarder whizzed past her, and Makayla lost her concentration—and her balance.

Instead of slowing down with the snowplow position her mom had taught her, she turned off the groomed trail—heading straight for the tree line. Makayla panicked and wiped out, face-planting in the snow. By the time her mom reached her, she was crying.

"I can't do it!" she cried.

"Yes, you can."

Her mom tried to pull Makayla to her feet, but Makayla went rigid.

"No, I can't! Look what happened!" She reached to take off her skis. "I'm horrible at this."

"Failure isn't falling." Her mom put a gloved hand on hers. "It's not getting back up." She extended her hand to her daughter. "Let's go."

Her mother was the most radiant person Makayla had ever known. She had a magnetism that could light up a room. People were drawn to her mom in a way they weren't to Makayla. For as long as she could remember, Makayla had been introverted and struggled to make friends, preferring the solitary hours spent in nature and with her camera. Although Makayla wonders if her solitary tendencies stemmed from her mother.

While Lydia was naturally charismatic, she also had depressive periods during which she was distant and withdrawn. As a child, it was hard for Makayla to understand. She remembers there were times growing up when her mom was in bed for a week at a time.

Makayla thinks of her own withdrawal after her mom died. She'd gone to therapy, knowing her mother eventually had too, and it helped tremendously.

By the time Lydia wrote her memoir, she'd put years of effort into working through the scars left from her early rise to fame. Her mother was so much more than that final interview, which was why after Lydia died, Makayla went on an awareness campaign for transient global amnesia. She wanted her mother to be remembered for her achievements, not losing her memory. She wanted everyone to see her mother's love for life, for others, and for her family. The true woman that she was.

Makayla glances at the young woman across the aisle, back to scrolling on her phone. Why are people so quick to label others and draw conclusions based on a single moment in their lives? *How could she really think I've lost my memory? I've been coherent this whole time.* The girl has no reason not to believe Makayla. *Unless she's taken Liam,* Makayla thinks.

Makayla's gaze darts to the girl's phone. Could she be working with someone? Maybe she's texting them right now. But if she has taken Liam, then where is he? *And why is everyone doubting me?*

Guilt hits her like a log to the head. Her mom was such a good mother, while Makayla lost her baby on this flight.

She lifts her phone from the seat beside her to call Jack again. A new message from Cori appears on her home screen. Are you holding up okay? Have you found him?

Makayla sees that she never responded to Cori's last message. She starts to type a reply as Cori sends another text. I just had a thought. Maybe a confused older person took him by mistake? When my grandma had Alzheimer's, she used to try to pick up strangers' babies at the grocery store. Are there any elderly people on board?

Makayla thinks of Rose sitting a few rows behind her. If only that's what happened. If Rose took Liam out of confusion, they would've found him by now. She glances over her shoulder, but her view of the elderly woman is blocked by the seats in between them. With a ripple of uneasiness, she recalls the woman's clear memory of watching *Friends* when Makayla emerged from the lavatory.

Makayla faces forward and taps out a reply with her thumbs. At this point, I'm sure whoever took him did it on purpose.

Do you need me to call the police or something?

The FBI is involved. But there's only so much they can do on the ground. He's here—somewhere. But the crew doesn't believe me.

I am so sorry, my friend! I wish I could help in some way. I'm in total shock, but I know you'll find him!

Makayla wipes away the second tear that slides down her face. At least someone believes her. But what matters is finding Liam. And there's nothing Cori can do for her on the ground.

She calls Jack through her internet messaging app and puts the phone to her ear as it starts to ring. Jack will be outraged when he learns they've put the search for Liam on hold. Hopefully, he can relay the crew's incompetence to the FBI, and get them to help her find Liam before it's too late.

CHAPTER TWENTY-SIX

JACK

Jack runs his thumb along the edge of the FBI agent's business card, recalling the day he learned Sabrina's true nature. He never told Makayla what happened between them, afraid of what it might do to his wife during her fragile period following the death of her mother.

It took him years of landing new clients to finally manage the same amount of money he would've with the Goldstein account. Sabrina is still ice cold to him, even though it's been years. And she was the one who wronged *him*. But fortunately, she now keeps their interactions at the firm to a minimum.

Jack's phone rings on the kitchen counter. He drops the card and rushes toward his cell. Seeing it's Makayla's father again, his hope deflates. He prepares himself to tell Jason he still hasn't heard anything.

"Hey, Jason."

"Jack! The police are back with a warrant to search my home. They're looking for Liam. What the hell is happening?"

Jack hears a male voice in the background. He glances at the FBI agent's business card lying on the floor. "I—I don't know."

"Why on earth would they think he's here?"

The only plausible answer—and its implication that *they don't believe Liam's on that plane*—sends a ripple of terror through him.

A beep comes through his speaker. Jack extends his phone to see Makayla is calling him.

"Jason, I have to go. Makayla's calling."

"Thank God. Let's hope she's found him. Call me back when you find out."

Jack accepts Makayla's WhatsApp call without saying goodbye. "Makayla? Have you found him?"

"No."

Jack's insides curl up as Makayla continues.

"The crew says they've looked everywhere. I've looked again, too, but we can't find him."

How is that possible? "Are you sure they've looked everywhere?" *It doesn't make any sense. They can't have searched the entire aircraft—otherwise they would have found him. The crew must not believe Liam came on the flight. But why?*

Makayla's mother's infamous TV interview replays in his mind, but he shoves the thought aside, refusing to entertain the idea that Makayla got on the plane without Liam. He refrains from telling her about the FBI searching her father's home, afraid it might put her into a full-blown panic. "What about the luggage compartment? Have they looked there?"

"According to the crew, the only access to it is through the cockpit. I asked the captain, and he said no one's been up there tonight besides him and the copilot. He said there's no way Liam could be down there."

Jack paces the living room in front of the window. *But then where is he?*

"People are starting to act like I might be confused. The crew is acting like I didn't bring Liam on board with me. Like I lost my memory like my mom. It's *insane*, Jack. I don't know what's happening, but someone on this plane took Liam." A sob envelops her voice. "And they still have him—somewhere."

"Are they still searching the plane?"

"No! That's what's infuriating! They won't even land. The captain said he can't divert due to a thunderstorm. But I'm not sure that's true. They say they're doing everything, but I don't think they even believe me. You need to convince the FBI to have them search the plane again."

"When the FBI was here, they asked me if we've had any suspicious encounters with anyone lately. I told them no." Jack stops pacing, thinking about Lionel. He hesitates before telling her the next part. "They're considering that Liam may have been kidnapped for a ransom because of my job."

"*What!*"

"Don't worry—I haven't received a ransom demand." Jack realizes how stupid his words sound as soon as they leave his mouth. How could she not worry? Liam is gone. And nothing will make that better until he's found.

"I can't believe this," she mutters. "What else did they say?"

He debates whether to tell her. It would only upset her more. Looking down at his bare feet, he runs a hand down the back of his head. "They did ask me if you've had any amnesiac episodes, like your mom."

"They're wasting time! They need to help us find Liam. Not question whether he's even missing!"

"That's what I told them." He refrains from adding that he told them about her headaches. And that the FBI is searching her father's house for Liam. "The FBI is having trouble verifying that Liam went with you through TSA. They said your dad told an Anchorage officer that you fell and hit your head yesterday. Are you sure you're o—"

"That was nothing! I'm *fine*. I can't even believe this. Not from you. We need to find our son, Jack!"

From the wobble in her voice, Jack knows she's on the verge of tears, if she isn't crying already.

"I know. And I believe you."

"Really? Because it seems like you're doubting me too." She scoffs. "Of all people, Jack. I just texted Cori, and she offered to do whatever she could to help us. At least she isn't questioning my memory like everyone else, even my husband."

"Who's Cori?"

Makayla exhales with exasperation. "My best friend. We met at a mother's group a few months ago."

Best friend? How come he's never heard her name before?

"I know I've told you about her," Makayla adds as if reading his thoughts. "She and I talk all the time. You probably weren't listening."

Probably not. And most likely, this woman *is* Makayla's friend. Jack feels the hairs prick up on the back of his neck, thinking about what the FBI said. They seemed interested in any and all new encounters they've had.

He stares at his reflection in the large window. "How well do you know her?"

CHAPTER TWENTY-SEVEN

MAKAYLA

Makayla stares at the illuminated fasten seat belt sign above her head. "I know Cori very well. She lives in Tribeca, and we talk almost every day." Why is Jack asking? "This is ridiculous. We need to find Liam."

"The FBI wanted to know if either of us had any suspicious encounters with anyone since my feature in *Forbes* last spring. Even if it seems like nothing, it could be important."

"So, they are considering that Liam *has* been kidnapped." At least they're taking his disappearance seriously. She thinks of how much money Jack manages. It makes sense that someone could've taken Liam in hopes of a large ransom. But how would they have known she'd be on this flight? With a sinking feeling she remembers all the social media posts she's made to her public account, detailing her trip—and that she and Liam were heading home tonight. She feels sick to her stomach.

"How did you meet her? And when?"

"Cori's my *friend*. Not a suspicious encounter." Makayla glances around the cabin. The few passengers she can see have their eyes closed, attempting to sleep despite the overhead lights. And her missing baby. "I met her briefly at our mother's group park day last May. Then we connected through the group's Facebook page and realized we have a lot in common."

"Like what?"

"We need to find Liam."

"I know. What do you have in common?"

The air deflates from her chest. *This is so stupid.* "Her mother is Snow Browning. She wrote *First Kiss*," she adds, ignoring the pain in her head. She knows Jack would recognize her latest book since it was adapted into a movie.

"So, you met her after the *Forbes* article about me came out. Have you been to her home?"

"Jack, stop. No. She's been in the Hamptons all summer." Makayla winces from the familiar throb of pain right behind her forehead. *Not now.* The last time she got a migraine was right before she had Liam, and it left her bedbound for a whole day. "And she's been spending her summer vacation helping me get Liam onto the best preschool waitlists in our neighborhood."

"But you did meet her, right?"

Makayla unlatches her seat belt and stands from her seat. She's not going to sit here like nothing has happened when Liam could be stuffed inside someone's suitcase, suffocating. "Yes!"

Pain soars through the front of her head, so sharp she nearly loses her balance. *Oh, please not now.* She needs to stay focused. Liam needs her. Especially when she's the only one on this plane who's even looking for him. She grips the top of a seat back.

"Jack, you're wasting time. You need to convince the FBI to have them search the plane again—*everywhere!*"

Every head in the cabin turns in her direction. She hadn't meant to scream the last part.

Rose frowns in disapproval when Makayla approaches her seat. "Keep it down."

"Okay—I will. I promise," Jack says. "Just send me Cori's phone number and her Facebook profile so I can give it to the FBI."

Makayla surveys Rose, recalling the commotion the woman made that demanded the flight attendants' attention when Makayla got up to use the lavatory. *Had Rose done that on purpose to create a distraction?*

Cori's text runs through her mind. Are there any elderly people on board who might've taken him? Could the older woman be using her age and faking dementia to keep from being suspected?

Makayla's blood runs cold as the elderly woman returns her attention to the screen in front of her. *If she had,* Makayla thinks, *she couldn't have acted alone.* She would've needed help.

Makayla steps away from the woman's seat, considering the possibility. Her lungs deflate as she remembers Rose was already out of her seat before Makayla got up to use the lavatory. *Rose couldn't have known I would be getting up right then.*

I'm grasping at straws.

"Jack—"

"Makayla, you're right. It's probably nothing, but what if it's something?"

She reaches the lavatory where she should never have gone without Liam, glancing over her shoulder at Rose's white hair sticking up over the top of her seat. "It's *your* job and you being on the cover of *Forbes* that the FBI should be concerned about." She remembers Jack's excitement when he told her Lionel had pulled some strings to get him on the cover of *Forbes.* Despite having a baby, she's hardly seen Jack since the article came out. Since then, he's been busier than ever, getting flooded with new clients, along with a series of smaller media-outlet interviews. And now this. "You should be thinking about people *you've* encountered—not a friend I met at mother's group." She stops, staring at the ajar door. "Have you gotten any new clients lately? Or anything strange happen at work?"

Her vision blurs. She closes her eyes and opens them again. But her vision is still hazy. She presses her hand against the lavatory wall, resisting the urge to cry. Having a breakdown won't help find Liam. "What about Lionel?"

A pause. "What do you mean?"

"Have you called him? If the FBI thinks we've been targeted because of the firm, maybe he's had an encounter that could help us." Although, if Liam *has* been kidnapped for a ransom, why hasn't Jack gotten a ransom demand? "Lionel has access to more money than you do," Makayla says. "What if he's gotten the ransom demand?" Makayla checks her phone screen to make sure their call hasn't dropped. "Jack? You still there?"

"Yeah. Yeah, I'm here. I'll ask him. And send me Cori's info."

Makayla blinks in a futile attempt to clear her vision before sending him a screenshot of Cori's phone number and social media page. She's filled with immediate regret, knowing she is nothing but a genuine friend. It's also a waste of time, but maybe giving the information to the FBI will appease Jack.

"Fine. I sent it to you. You happy? Now *you* tell the FBI to have this plane searched again and get us on the ground as soon as possible." She refrains from stating the obvious before lowering her phone to her side: that if they don't, Liam may not still be alive when they land at LaGuardia.

CHAPTER TWENTY-EIGHT

MAKAYLA

Makayla steps into the rear cabin. She rubs the side of her temple, trying to remember if she packed her Advil in her checked bag or if she still has a bottle in the diaper bag. She squints from the bright cabin lights, which pierce her eyes like a knife.

Hit by a wave of nausea, she suddenly stops, bringing a hand to her forehead. The pressure inside her head is so intense it feels like it's going to push right out of her skull. She draws in a deep breath and forces one foot in front of the other, ignoring the concerned stare from a woman in a window seat. This is no time to be incapacitated from a migraine.

Was Jack really suspicious of her friend? Did he think it more likely they were targeted by a friend from her Tribeca mother's group than someone who wants the millions of dollars he has access to? It's ridiculous.

When she and Jack were dating, she felt certain he would always have her back. He was so enamored of her and her photography, always telling her that she was talented and encouraging her to never give it up. *Where is that man now?*

Hopefully, he can insist that they have the crew search the plane again. She tucks her phone into her back pocket. *At least Cori can tell the FBI I'm not losing my memory, since no one on this plane is taking me seriously.*

Her gaze settles on Derek's empty seat, and she thinks about the FBI's suspicions that Liam was targeted for ransom because of Jack's work. She doesn't know exactly how much money Jack manages, only that it's hundreds of millions. She's always been grateful for Jack's job and never considered it could put them in danger. She feels sick, thinking again about how she posted all about her trip—and when they'd be flying home—on social media and her photography blog.

Makayla scours the cabin for a sign of Derek, remembering Britt asking him about his mother at the beginning of the flight. And what he'd said about her medical bills, and the experimental drug she needed that wasn't covered by insurance.

Where is he?

Her head throbs. *What if Derek took Liam?* Had he seen Jack's *Forbes* article and kidnapped Liam for ransom to pay for his mother's treatment? Derek told Britt he'd picked up this trip for the overtime; he hadn't been regularly scheduled for it.

A stabbing pain rips through her temple as she unsteadily makes for the rear galley. *Where the hell did he go?*

Makayla thinks again of the disturbance Rose created before she went to the bathroom. She remembers putting her call light on *before* the older woman shouted at the flight attendant. Could Rose have seen? Is it possible she and Derek worked together to kidnap her son?

She slows when she approaches the door to the crew compartment that she and Derek searched earlier. The floor spins, and her stomach churns. She yearns to close her eyes to block out the painful light, but she has to stay awake. Keep looking for Liam.

Her pulse quickens when she reaches for the door handle. If Derek took Liam, he could've moved Liam to the compartment after she searched it, knowing she wouldn't look there again.

"Hey! What are you doing?"

Derek blurs as he rushes toward her from the front of the plane. Makayla reaches for something to keep her upright as her knees buckle.

Derek's hand encloses around her upper arm before she hits the aisle floor. He pulls her to her feet.

"I need some help here!" he calls out.

The cabin sways. Makayla leans against him to keep from falling over. She squints from the bright cabin lights, covering her eyes with her hand.

"Where were you?" she asks. "Where's my son?"

Derek shakes his head. "We don't know."

"What can I do?"

Makayla recognizes Britt's voice behind them.

"Help me get her to her seat," Derek says.

"No! I need to make sure Liam isn't down here." She pulls out of Derek's reach and staggers backward.

Derek grips her upper arm as she falls against the door. Britt grabs Makayla's other arm to keep Makayla on her feet.

"You need to sit down." Britt's voice is firm. "We already checked down there, remember?"

"I know, I just—" The plane spins. Makayla brings a hand to her mouth, fighting the urge to throw up.

"Are you okay to walk if we help you?" Derek asks.

Makayla meets his gaze. Genuine concern appears to be written all over his face. If he's faking it, he's a very good actor.

Makayla nods, wanting to confront him about taking her son but too weak to put up more of a fight. "I have a migraine. I need some ibuprofen. Or something stronger. I have a prescription, but I might've put mine in my checked bag."

"I can get you some out of our in-flight medical kit," Derek says. "But first let's get you back to your seat."

Makayla reluctantly lets Derek tuck his arm around her and lead her down the narrow aisle. She'll text Jack once she sits down and have him tell the FBI about the flight attendant's financial woes.

He looks over his shoulder when they reach the lavatories. "Thanks, Britt. I think we're good now."

"I'll get the ibuprofen," she says.

They pass row fifteen, where Jemma is leaning her head on her husband's shoulder. Makayla blinks to clear her vision as her eyes settle on the pet carrier slightly protruding from the seat in front of Chad, who appears to be asleep.

She can see the outline of the dog inside the carrier, but it looks different than it did when they boarded. Makayla stops. The animal hasn't made any noise the entire flight.

"I want to see inside that carrier."

"It's already been checked," Derek says, pulling her forward.

Makayla doesn't move. She stares at the travel kennel. It would be tight, but Liam could fit inside.

She turns to Derek. "Did you check it?"

He shakes his head. "Britt searched this cabin."

Jemma sits up, looking offended. "That's right, she did." She purses her lips. "And your baby wasn't in there. I've been doing everything I can to be helpful, and we were lucky to get Georgie back to sleep the first time. It was quite an ordeal." She frowns. "I thought you saw. Georgie's a nervous flier, and her sedative is wearing off. If we wake her up, she'll probably howl for the rest of the flight."

"Oh, brother! Don't do that!" Rose exclaims.

Jemma looks at Derek, ignoring the elderly woman across the aisle. "Do you need me to open it?"

"Yes!"

"No."

Makayla yanks free from Derek's hold, bringing a hand to her forehead at the stab of pain that shoots through the front of her skull.

"Yes!" she repeats. "I need to see inside. Open it! Or I will!"

Chad startles awake from Makayla's shout and looks at his wife. "What's going on?"

Jemma turns to him. "She wants to see inside Georgie's carrier."

"Again? We already showed that other flight attendant. And we're lucky we got Georgie to settle back down after we disturbed her. She's a horrible traveler."

Jemma puts a hand on her husband's leg. "That's what I told them."

Derek raises a palm in the air. "It's fine. Let your dog sleep." He encircles a strong arm around Makayla's back and pushes her toward her seat.

Makayla goes rigid, leaning against the force of his hand on her spine. "I'm not moving until I see inside that carrier." She reaches for the carrier, throwing herself so far into Jemma's row her stomach lands on Jemma's lap.

Jemma shrieks. Her husband clasps his meaty hand around Makayla's wrist before she can grasp the carrier under his feet. Makayla's head spins from the sudden movement of diving forward. Derek wraps both arms around her waist and tugs her back into the aisle. Jemma's muscled husband moves his hand to Makayla's shoulder, giving her an added shove.

"Oh, my!" Rose shouts before letting out a chuckle.

Makayla and Derek stumble backward. Sharp, synchronous gasps are emitted from the couple in the middle row, seated two rows back from Pink Headphones. Derek grunts as Makayla falls on top of him, landing on the floor a few rows up. Right beside Liam's empty bassinet. The girl with the pink headphones gapes at them with wide eyes. The curtain flings open behind their heads. Makayla makes out the blurry silhouette of the auburn-haired flight attendant standing over them.

Makayla rolls off Derek and uses Pink Headphones' armrest to get to her feet. Despite the pain radiating through her head, she takes a few unsteady steps toward Jemma's row when a hand grips her ankle. She trips but catches herself on an empty seat back before going all the way down.

She turns to see Derek sitting up on the aisle floor, holding onto her leg. She kicks out of his grasp.

"Whoa! Easy!" He blocks his face with his hand when her heel comes within inches of his jaw.

As soon as her foot is free, she hurries toward the pet carrier.

"Are you okay?" she hears Aubrey ask.

"She almost kicked me in the face!"

Makayla ignores them. She wasn't trying to hurt Derek. And she didn't. She only got away from him.

"She's going to hurt someone!" the man shouts from the middle aisle.

Jemma's eyes widen when Makayla reaches their row, out of breath. Chad sits forward as if ready to block Makayla from Georgie's carrier as Jemma's eyes travel behind Makayla. Makayla leans forward, about to reach over Jemma's lap, when her elbow is jerked backward.

She whirls to find Aubrey right behind her, tugging on the crook of Makayla's arm with an ice-cold grip.

"Get your hand off me!" Makayla tries to yank her elbow away, but Aubrey grits her teeth and digs her cold fingers into Makayla's flesh.

The floor drops as Makayla flails her arm back and forth. She feels Aubrey's grip slip away seconds before her elbow connects with bone. Makayla stumbles sideways and grabs the back of Jemma's seat to keep herself upright.

Jemma lets out a shriek as she gapes at the flight attendant standing behind Makayla. Makayla follows Jemma's gaze to see Aubrey covering her nose with both hands, bright red blood flowing beneath her fingers. Rose lifts a tremoring hand to her mouth while staring at Makayla in wide-eyed horror. Derek is on his feet at the front of the cabin, rushing toward them.

"Help!" Aubrey screams. "She attacked me!"

When Derek reaches Aubrey's side, he narrows his eyes at Makayla. Britt appears at the bulkhead holding a bottle of water, her jaw dropping at the scene.

Derek points to Makayla. "Don't move!"

Britt steps toward them. "You need me to call the captain, Derek?"

He spins. "Yes! Get permission to restrain her. She's out of control!"

CHAPTER
TWENTY-NINE

ANNA

"It's looking like we'll be tossed around quite a bit coming into Manhattan," Miguel says over the intercom. He casts Anna a wry smile. "This will be good experience for you just before your captain upgrade training."

"Pacific Air 7038, cross CYPER at flight level one eight zero and contact New York Center now on frequency one two five decimal three two five," Boston Center commands over the radio.

Miguel replies to Boston Center as Anna reaches up and sets eighteen thousand in the Flight Control Unit panel on the glareshield. The airplane starts a gentle descent as the autothrust system reduces the engine power to idle.

"That was close. I thought they were going to hold us up high, like they usually do," Anna says over the interphone.

"Yes, then they expect you to make the altitude restriction at CYPER. We should put those ATC guys in the simulator and let *them* see how they like it!" Miguel jokes, looking over the latest weather report for LaGuardia. "They're reporting heavy rain at LaGuardia, so I think we should select medium on the autobrakes," he adds. "As soon as the nose gear touches down, you may have to add more braking."

"Okay." Anna reaches up and pushes the "MED" button on the autobrake selector, causing a green "ON" light to illuminate.

Again, the airplane lurches from the turbulence, and Anna's shoulder harness digs into her collarbone. The flight attendant call buzzer sounds.

"I'll get that," she says, seeing Miguel is busy setting up for the approach to LaGuardia.

"This is Anna."

"Anna, it's Britt. We need permission from the captain ASAP to restrain Makayla Rossi, the mother of the missing infant."

Anna's brows knit together. "*Restrain* her?"

Miguel shoots her a look of surprise.

"You need to hear this," Anna tells him.

Miguel reaches down and turns up the volume knob on the flight attendant interphone.

"She isn't complying with our instructions to stay seated, posing a risk to herself and other passengers. She's been continuing to search the plane amid all this turbulence and throwing accusations at some of the other passengers. Just now, we were trying to get her back to her seat, and she elbowed Aubrey in the nose. There's blood everywhere. It might even be broken."

Anna winces. They still have a ways to go before landing—a long time to endure the pain of a broken nose without any medical treatment.

Miguel's eyes widen. "Okay, yes. Go ahead and restrain her if you're sure it's necessary. And can you ask if we have any medical professionals on board that could look at Aubrey's nose?"

Anna imagines the mother, hands zip-tied together in her seat while her baby is missing. Whether it's due to a memory lapse or not, she must be terrified.

"Yes, and believe me, it's necessary. She's become violent, and she won't stop. She's causing a *major* disturbance." Britt breathes a sigh into the line. "We've been dealing with a lot back here."

Miguel frowns, holding Anna's gaze.

"I understand," he says. "I just want to make sure you aren't taking undue measures. She has lost her baby."

"Well, we don't even know that for sure," Britt says, her tone sharp.

"Okay. Go ahead. If you're sure that it's necessary."

Anna stares at Miguel after Britt hangs up.

"I don't like that they're restraining her." Miguel frowns. "But we can't have anyone getting hurt either."

"No, we can't," Anna agrees, feeling oddly relieved. "I get that we have to protect our crew and passengers, but I can't say that I blame that woman for freaking out. I mean, her *baby's* missing." At least in *her* mind.

Although with Makayla Rossi restrained, they shouldn't have to worry about things getting out of control in the back, and they can focus on getting this plane on the ground.

CHAPTER THIRTY

MAKAYLA

Makayla ignores the condemning stares from the few passengers in the middle row as Aubrey lowers her hands a second time so that Derek can assess her nose.

"Are you okay?" he asks.

Blood runs down her chin. Jemma gasps at the blood smeared over the lower half of the attendant's face. Derek turns Aubrey by the shoulders to put himself in between her and Makayla.

"I've got this. Go use the medical kit," he says.

Aubrey sidesteps through the middle row before heading for the rear, obviously going out of her way to avoid getting close to Makayla.

Derek grips her by the arm again and drags her toward the front. "Wait!"

She turns to see his mouth set in a hard line.

He shakes his head. "No. That's enough!"

She digs her heels into the floor when she passes Chad, who blocks his row like a security guard.

"*Please.* Just let me see inside the carrier. Then I'll leave you alone. I can't sit down without knowing." She lifts her eyes to meet Chad's. There's a darkness in them, she thinks.

Derek wrenches her sideways and tows her toward the front of the plane, forcing her to sidestep a few feet toward her row. She tries to wrestle her arm free, but Derek has a death grip on her flesh. She leans all her weight in the opposite direction, keeping her eyes locked on Chad's.

"Why won't you let me look? What are you afraid of? If my baby isn't in that carrier, then show me!"

With gritted teeth, she jerks her arm to the right, twisting her body for added momentum. She manages to pull Derek back toward Chad's row, but somehow, the flight attendant maintains his hold.

"Makayla, I'm ordering you to take your seat. Now!"

She winces from Derek's tightened grip on her arm. She turns to him, her efforts to wiggle out of his hold only resulting in more pain in her arm.

"As soon as I see inside."

"No!" Derek shouts, bringing his head closer to hers.

Makayla turns to Chad, now right in front of her, his expression flat. *"Please . . ."* A sob erupts from her throat. "I won't disturb your dog. I just need to find my baby. Please let me look." Her voice wobbles as a tear runs down her face. "I—I need to know he's okay."

Makayla succumbs to a full-blown sob, her chest heaving with each breath while Chad displays no emotion.

"We already looked." Derek's voice is calm, softer now.

Despite his hold on her, Makayla pushes her shoulder against Chad's torso to get to the pet carrier, but it's like pushing against a linebacker. The man doesn't budge.

"I have the flex-cuffs!" Britt announces from the front of the cabin. "And a seat belt extension."

Derek grabs her from behind. Makayla screams in protest, flailing her arms and legs as he drags her backward to her seat. Chad comes toward them. He grabs Makayla's ankles, effortlessly overpowering her failed attempt to kick him away.

Jemma stands from her seat. "Don't hurt her!"

"She's the one hurting people, babe!" Chad calls over his shoulder.

Makayla grabs hold of a seat back. After losing her grip, she's flung into her seat by the two men.

Derek and Chad pin down her arms and legs. She fights against their hold as Britt buckles her seat belt, pulling it tight across Makayla's lap.

"Let go of me! I need to find my son!" Makayla breaks free of Derek's hold on her right arm long enough to pull her phone from her pocket. She tosses it on the seat next to her before the flight attendant secures a seat belt extension around her upper body, trapping her arms to her sides.

Makayla thrusts her body back and forth as much as the restraints allow. "Let me go!"

"You have the flex-cuffs?" Derek shouts at his coworker.

"They're right here."

Derek snatches something white from Britt's hand. Makayla starts to tuck her hands beneath her legs, but she's too late. Derek encases her wrists in a pair of adjoined zip ties.

"You're *cuffing* me? I'm not a criminal!" A painful pulsation rips through the side of her temple. She squeezes her eyes shut before opening them again.

"We have no choice." When Derek stands up, beads of sweat drip down the sides of his forehead. "You're a danger to yourself and the other passengers."

Britt heads for the rear, and Makayla writhes her wrists in opposite directions in a futile effort to free herself from the zip tie cuffs.

Seeing her phone still on the seat beside her, Makayla strains to twist enough to reach it. But with the seat belt extension pinning her elbows to her sides, she's not even close. She turns to the girl sitting across from her.

The girl is already staring at her, giving her a judgy look while chewing a large wad of gum. Ignoring the painful pulsation in her head, Makayla offers the girl what she hopes is a disarming look of desperation.

"Could you please help me reach my phone?" Makayla tilts her head to the side. "It's on the seat next to me."

The girl stares at Makayla blankly and moves her gum to the other side of her mouth. Hope drains from Makayla's chest. The girl lets out an exasperated sigh before she unbuckles herself and leans across Makayla's seat.

She reaches a long arm across Makayla and plucks her phone off the seat before dropping it into Makayla's lap. She plops back into her seat without a word as Makayla closes her fingers around her phone.

Fresh tears muddle Makayla's already blurry vision. "Thank you."

"Ladies and gentlemen," a female voice says over the loudspeaker. "One of our crew has sustained an injury to her nose, and we are requesting any medical professionals on board to please come forward to see if you can be of assistance. Thank you."

Makayla recalls the blood streaming down Aubrey's face and feels a pang of guilt. She hadn't meant to hurt anyone. *But I need to find my son. Why can't the crew understand that?* She blinks back her tears and sees a new message from Cori.

> Should I wake up Fletcher and have him make some calls? Maybe the Pacific Air CEO could get the crew to search the plane again.

Makayla wonders how much sway Fletcher could have with the airline. She knows he's in finance, but she's not sure on the specifics. But even if Fletcher *did* get the airline CEO to contact the flight, would the crew agree to search it again? When they don't believe she brought Liam on board the plane?

Yes, thank you, she replies, figuring she has nothing to lose by Fletcher making the call. At this point, she'll take all the help she can get.

More guilt stabs at Makayla's insides at not knowing more about Fletcher's job. Cori is always there for her when she needs her: staying up tonight and offering to help, listening to Makayla's suspicions about Jack and Sabrina's relationship, spending the summer getting Liam onto preschool waiting lists. *What have I ever done for Cori?*

She vows to be a better friend after tonight. She could call Jack again, but she's afraid the crew might take away her phone if they see her on it.

She taps the most recent conversation with Jack, where she last sent Cori's number for the FBI. Cori is such a good person. Would the FBI show up at her doorstep to question her?

She pushes the thought from her mind and types out a message to Jack as fast as her conjoined wrists will allow. They've restrained me! I'm in zip tie handcuffs and strapped into my seat! Fury builds inside her with each word. They're treating me like a criminal. Not letting me look for Liam! Tell the FBI to let me look for our son! No one else is!

CHAPTER THIRTY-ONE

JACK

Jack lowers his phone as he slides onto a kitchen barstool. Makayla screaming about this not being about her mother echoes through his mind. He's never heard her become unhinged like that before. He thinks back to the FBI questioning Makayla's mental state but dismisses the thought as quickly as it popped into his head. *She's lost Liam. We've lost Liam. She has a right to scream.*

He debates what to do with the message from Makayla with Cori's phone number and Facebook profile.

He knows this woman is probably a real friend to Makayla. It's much more likely that Lionel—or Sabrina—is behind this.

But it's strange to him how Makayla has gotten so close to this woman so fast. Makayla has stayed in touch with a few friends from college, but she doesn't form new friendships easily. She's slow to let new people into her life. Calling this woman her "best friend" when they only met a few months ago seems completely out of character for his wife.

It makes him wonder if she's been played. Did this Cori woman befriend Makayla to learn the details of her trip to Alaska?

Jack pinches the bridge of his nose. He doesn't know what to think. He needs to call the FBI.

Before dialing Agent Pratt, he logs onto his Rothman Securities account one more time. There're still no pending withdrawals.

He tries to clear his head as he starts to punch in the agent's number, preparing himself to tell Pratt about Lionel and his suspicions about Sabrina, and about this Cori woman. He's a few numbers in when a new message pops up from Makayla.

His jaw drops in disbelief as he reads her text. *They've restrained her? What the hell?*

His chest heaves with rage as he lifts his phone to his ear, calling Makayla instead of the agent. He lets her phone ring for a full minute before giving up and calling the FBI.

The agent answers immediately. "Agent Pratt."

"It's Jack Rossi. I want to know why my wife is being restrained on that flight!"

"Um, I wasn't aware of that."

"I just got a message from Makayla saying they've cuffed her and strapped her to her seat! Like a criminal. Or a crazy person." Jack forces himself to take a deep breath. *"Are they even looking for my son on that plane?"*

"I can assure you they are—"

"Then why are they cuffing my wife?"

"I don't know. Please try to stay calm. I can put a call in to the flight to find out."

Jack closes his eyes, trying to focus through the anger searing in his veins. "I know you've sent agents to search my father-in-law's home for Liam. This is outrageous! Liam is on that flight. They should be tearing that plane apart until they find him! Why don't you believe—"

"Mr. Rossi, I can assure you we are doing everything we can to find Liam. But until we do, we can't rule anything out."

"My boss, Lionel Rothman, has been committing fraud," he blurts out before he can stop himself. He swallows the trepidation that surfaces, knowing his confession could lead to life in prison. But none of that matters now. "I'm talking hundreds of millions of dollars. At least. I think he may have had Liam kidnapped so he could stage a ransom—or for leverage, to ensure I wouldn't turn him in."

There's a heavy moment of silence before Pratt responds. "How do you know this?"

"He admitted the fraud to me after I found a discrepancy in one of my client's statements."

"Why didn't you report it?"

Pratt sounds skeptical. Jack's stomach sinks. He should've told him when they were here.

"I just found out yesterday."

"Why didn't you say anything before?"

"I don't know. I was in shock." Jack exhales into the phone. "Lionel threatened to blame the fraud on me if I came forward. He admitted to making the withdrawals under my log-in."

The agent remains quiet, so Jack continues.

"Lionel's daughter, Sabrina, is the firm's managing director. She might be in on the fraud too. And she might have something to do with Liam's kidnapping."

"We'll look into it," Pratt says.

The lack of emotion in his voice doesn't give Jack any confidence. *The crew obviously isn't taking Makayla seriously. They're not even looking for Liam.* If Agent Pratt ordered the search of his father-in-law's home, he doesn't believe Liam is on that flight either. Jack wonders if he should tell Pratt about his suspicion that Lionel might've taken out a kidnapping policy on Liam after Jack's feature in *Forbes*. But then Jack would have to tell Pratt about his own. If Lionel *is* behind this, he would've made sure all fingers pointed to Jack.

"Is there anything else you want to tell me?" the agent asks.

Jack exhales. "Just that Makayla has a new friend, but they seem strangely close after only meeting a few months ago. It's unlike her to form a close friendship so fast, so I had Makayla send me her contact information."

"Okay, good. Forward that to me."

Jack agrees. After he ends the call, a gnawing sense of dread crawls over him. *Why didn't the agent seem more surprised about Lionel's fraud? Does he think I'm lying?*

Did Agent Pratt really not know Makayla had been restrained? Or had he ordered it?

He wonders what the FBI isn't telling him. *Why aren't they tearing that plane apart?*

He lifts his phone to call the agent back. He needs answers.

His phone lights up with an incoming call. Seeing the name, Jack hesitates. *Why the hell is Sabrina calling?*

He takes her call, fearing his earlier suspicions about her are true.

"Jack! Are you okay?" There's a warmth in her voice he hasn't heard in years. "I just learned about Liam."

Jack narrows his eyes. "How?"

"My dad called. The FBI came to his penthouse. Have they found him yet?"

He goes rigid. Agent Pratt didn't say anything about having been to Lionel's home when Jack told him about his boss's fraud. *Why the hell not?* "Why were they there?"

"I assumed you knew. They were asking about a ransom. Said they needed to monitor the firm's accounts. Sorry, maybe I wasn't supposed to say anything. I called as soon as I heard."

Jack doesn't respond. The FBI must've gone straight to Lionel's after coming here. Apparently, they didn't trust Jack to tell them the truth about getting a ransom demand, so they went to Lionel behind Jack's back.

He can only guess Lionel's reaction to the FBI showing up on his doorstep in the middle of the night, wanting access to the firm's accounts—especially if Lionel is behind Liam's kidnapping.

"I'm downstairs," Sabrina adds. "In your building."

"What?" He glances at the door to his condo. "Why?" Had Lionel sent her in the hope of throwing suspicion off him and Sabrina?

"I came without thinking. As soon as I heard. I just . . . I was so worried. Can I come up?"

Jack rubs his forehead. "Sabrina . . ."

"You're my friend, Jack. I'd like to be here for you—however I can."

Jack thinks back to how long he's known her. Sabrina had been his best friend for nearly as long as he could remember. Until he met Makayla. And when she took the Goldstein account away from him, the friendship ended completely.

"Please, Jack. Let me come up."

He heaves a sigh. "Fine. I'll call the doorman and tell him to let you up."

But he has to remember she's not his friend. He's letting her in for one reason: to find out if she had something to do with Liam's disappearance on that flight.

After calling the doorman, Jack waits by his door. The silence of his empty condo has never felt so loud.

CHAPTER THIRTY-TWO

MAKAYLA

The curtain flings open to business class. Makayla drops her phone on her lap and lays her forearm across it. Derek appears with the blond first-class flight attendant. He holds a bottle of water and two small packets in his hand.

He steps toward her. "How many ibuprofen do you want? There's two in each of these packets."

The first-class attendant lingers behind him, eyeing Makayla.

She hates to accept anything from the man who's keeping her from looking for Liam, but her head is screaming at her. And she needs to be as well as possible so she can find her son—even though there's nothing she can do from her seat.

"I'll take three."

Derek tears open both pill packets and drops three tablets in her palm. He opens the bottle of water but keeps it at his side.

"I can loosen the strap around your arms so you can drink this easier," he says. "But only if you agree to cooperate and not try to get up." He glances at the attendant standing behind him. "Otherwise, you won't be able to take these."

"I'll stay seated."

Derek leans forward and loosens the seat belt across her arms by only an inch before handing her the water bottle. She tosses back the three pills and chases them down with a large drink. The moment she swallows, Derek tightens the strap, cinching her arms against her ribs.

When he goes to take the bottle from her, she tries a different approach.

"Do you think you could take the restraints off?" She fights to keep her voice soft. "I'm sorry about earlier. I know you guys are doing everything. You don't need to restrain me. I'm not going to get up again until you say it's okay." She plasters a slight smile on her face.

"Sorry, you'll be restrained for the remainder of our flight. It's our policy for unruly passengers."

Her heart plummets to her feet. "Did you ask Britt about the pet carrier?"

"Yes," he says without missing a beat. "She checked it."

Makayla knows this is a lie. Britt hasn't come up from the rear of the plane since Derek went to the front. Unless he called her through the intercom, but she doubts it.

"Please, let me go!" Makayla reaches for Derek's arm with her zip-tied hands, but the seat belt around her arms keeps her from being able to move her hands beyond her armrest. "I'm not hurting anyone. The only person who's in danger on this plane is my son. My *baby*. Please." She chokes back a sob.

Derek purses his lips. "I'm sorry," he mutters before striding toward the rear of the plane.

Makayla screams in frustration. *"Nooooo!"* Her cry morphs into a wail and then a sob. *The crew already thinks I'm crazy.* And her outburst just proved they did the right thing by restraining her.

Makayla makes sure both flight attendants are gone before lifting her phone. She has a missed call from Jack, and she's glad to see her phone is on silent. Derek might've taken it away. That means Jack got her message. She can feel Derek's eyes on her from a few rows back.

154

Instead of calling, she sends Jack the text she was about to send before Derek appeared.

There's a couple seated a few rows behind me. She glances at her seat number. I think they're in row fifteen. They have a pet carrier and I have a horrible feeling Liam might be inside it. They won't let me look. Call the FBI and get them to demand the pet carrier gets checked, even if the crew says they already did. And let me know that you got this!

A new message pops up from Cori. Okay, Fletcher's awake. He's calling the CEO now.

Makayla inhales a deep breath as she sends a reply. They've restrained me and won't let me look for Liam! And no one else is looking for him either!

She holds her breath as three bubbles appear below her message. Cori's response comes seconds later. What!!?? They can't do that! Hang in there, I'll tell Fletcher.

Thank you.

Cori sends another message. I'm shocked and furious for you. Don't worry, this will all get sorted out. Liam can't be far, and he will be found!

Makayla rests her head against the seat back after reading Cori's texts. She doesn't doubt either of those two things. But she's terrified that Liam won't be alive when they do.

CHAPTER THIRTY-THREE

TINA

Tina sips coffee from her mug at her cubicle while Pratt steps away to take a phone call. The search of Makayla's father's home turned up no sign of Liam. So far, neither has the search of Ted Stevens Airport, which narrows the possibility of Liam being anywhere besides on that plane.

She catches movement in her periphery and looks up to see Ruiz striding past her cubicle.

"Did you ever get ahold of the gate agent?" Tina asks.

Ruiz slows, shaking her head. "No. I sent an officer to her address, but she wasn't home. And she hasn't returned my calls. I'll let you know if I hear from her."

"Thanks." Tina returns her focus to her laptop screen.

She double-checks the seat map of Makayla Rossi's flight before putting a check mark beside the name of the twenty-year-old female passenger in the aisle seat across from Makayla on the printed passenger manifest on her desk.

Tina thinks about her own daughter, wondering if she's still asleep. Often, when Isabel has a nightmare, a second one follows. She feels a pang of regret for not telling Felicity when she spoke to her. She won't have another chance for a while.

On her and Pratt's way back from Lionel Rothman's penthouse, Castillo had woken one of the bureau's forensic accountants, who works remotely, to go through all of Jack Rossi's accounts. A few minutes ago, the accountant called to say he couldn't find any pending or completed transactions in the accounts Rossi manages since Liam went missing. The same thing Lionel Rothman had said after logging into the accounts.

It is going to take a while for the accountant to complete a deeper audit to confirm Rothman's suspicions that Jack Rossi has been committing fraud. But for now, the accountant is monitoring the accounts for any withdrawals or new transactions.

Tina moves her pen down the manifest to the two passengers seated in the third row of the middle aisle in Makayla's cabin: Mark and Jordana Bauer. According to the information the airline sent over, they purchased their tickets together five weeks ago using a Visa, and they share an address in Wasilla, Alaska.

Tina types their names into her database and sees they're ages fifty-one and fifty-three, and neither has a criminal history. After placing a check mark beside both their names, she moves to the single passenger seated in the row behind them.

When she ran checks on the crew, she discovered that one of the flight attendants had recently been issued a notice of default on his home mortgage. She flagged his name before moving on to the passengers. She would have to wait until the start of business hours to dive deeper into the flight attendant's finances.

She'll run deeper background checks on all the passengers and crew later, but for time's sake, she's running preliminary checks on those seated closest to Makayla, looking for anyone with a criminal history or someone who bought their ticket with cash—or any other red flags.

She enters *Rose Bahnmiller* into her database, along with her upstate New York address. Her ticket was also purchased with a credit card.

After seeing the passenger in 15E is eighty-four and also has no criminal history, Tina makes a check beside her name when Pratt returns to her cubicle.

"That was Jack Rossi," he says, leaning against the desk to her right. "He accused Lionel Rothman of running a Ponzi scheme. Said he only found out yesterday, and that Rothman admitted it after Rossi discovered a discrepancy in his client's statement. So, pretty much the same story that Rothman told us, just in reverse."

"Someone's lying, or they're in it together." Tina finishes the last of the coffee in her mug. With each being so quick to accuse the other of the same thing, she's inclined to think the latter.

"Rossi thinks it's possible that Rothman is behind his son's kidnapping. That he might stage a ransom to cover up his fraud," Pratt adds. "Although, if Rossi were really worried about that, he should've told us when we were at his condo earlier tonight."

Tina replaces her empty mug on her desk, recalling the financier she met an hour ago. So rich. Is Rothman Securities all a fraud? If it is, it would be the biggest fraud of the decade. Like Bernie Madoff all over again. *Had Rothman done the unthinkable to cover it up?*

"Rossi also said his wife became very close to a new friend in the last few months, and he seems suspicious about their relationship. He's going to send me the friend's contact information. When I get it, I'll forward it to you. And he said his wife has been restrained on the flight."

Tina spins to face him. *"What?"*

"I don't know any more. But I'm guessing she must be freaking out and causing a disturbance."

"Of course she is! Her baby's missing."

Pratt shrugs. "Don't look at me. We'll have to find out more from the flight." He nods toward her computer screen. "Find anything?"

"One of the flight attendants, Derek Strous, has a loan default notice on his home mortgage. Also, I learned from the airline that he wasn't originally scheduled for this trip. He picked it up as an extra trip a couple of weeks ago."

Pratt crosses his arms. "Interesting."

"It *would* be easier to keep the infant hidden if you were the one conducting the search of the plane," Tina adds.

"I agree. Good work. Find anything on the passengers?"

Tina returns her attention to the flight's seat map, a sickening feeling settling in her gut after hearing the mother has been restrained. "Not yet. But I'm just getting started."

"Rossi's face told a different story earlier when he assured us nothing suspicious had happened at his work. Now he calls with this late confession accusing Lionel Rothman of fraud. It doesn't sit right with me that he would withhold that information until now." Behind her, Pratt exhales.

Tina whirls around. "What about kidnapping insurance?" She thought of it earlier when they were leaving Lionel's apartment, but then it slipped her mind after her phone call with Felicity. "The Rossis don't seem wealthy enough to be at risk over their income, but Jack has *access* to nearly a billion dollars, and the *Forbes* cover could put him at risk."

"It's worth looking into."

They won't be able to contact insurance agencies with a warrant until the start of business hours, so Tina types in the website that allows law enforcement to search for policies held by major insurance companies. She feels Pratt hovering over her as she types Jack's full name, address, and date of birth into the search field.

She leans back when the search yields a result. The type of insurance coverage is listed beside the policy number as *KR&E*.

Tina clicks on the policy for more details. "Rossi's got a kidnap, ransom, and extortion policy for himself and his immediate family members with coverage of twenty million dollars."

When Pratt leans toward the screen, Tina feels his breath on her shoulder. "No shit. That's a lot, even for that kind of policy."

Tina scrolls down. "It looks like Rossi is getting a corporate rate on the policy through the firm, but it's individual coverage. And it's in his name, not the firm's."

"How long has he had the policy?"

"Only since March of this year. It's possible he took out the policy after being featured in *Forbes*," she thinks aloud.

"It seems more likely that Jack and Makayla Rossi staged their son's kidnapping to cover up his fraud with insurance coverage. It seems crazy that they would do that, and I'm not exactly sure how they were planning to get away with it all. But if Rossi *is* committing fraud and Rothman found out, Jack Rossi would be facing life imprisonment. And if the mother's in on it, too, it would explain why the kid is nowhere to be found."

"Yeah, it would," Tina agrees as she hovers her cursor over the two passengers seated three rows directly behind Makayla.

"I'm going back to Jack Rossi's condo to talk to him again." Pratt straightens, and Tina can see the wheels in his head turning. "Do we have any proof that Liam went with Makayla Rossi to Alaska?" Pratt asks. "Aside from the Rossis' word for it? Or what Makayla Rossi's father told Anchorage FBI?"

"I went through her social media." Tina pulls up Makayla's Instagram page and scrolls through the photos for Pratt to see. "These were posted over the last week, one of them yesterday. Her baby was with her, clearly the same baby that she's been posting the last few months. And he looks to be about three months here." She clicks on an image of Makayla with Liam in a stroller in front of Lake Anchorage to enlarge it. "And they were definitely in Alaska."

Pratt leans forward, placing his palm on the desk beside her. "What if these were taken a few weeks ago? Makayla could've taken Liam to Alaska and then gone by herself this trip to fake his kidnapping. That would mean her father is in on it too, but parents do extreme things for their children."

"I'll need you to get me access to the TSA master list to see if Makayla Rossi traveled to Alaska recently."

"On it. Then I'm heading to Rossi's."

It takes Pratt a few minutes to give Tina a link and passcode to access the TSA list. Annoyingly, as an analyst and not an agent, she would have hit nothing but brick walls trying to access the list on her own. Now that she has it, Tina runs a search to see if Makayla Rossi went through TSA in the last few months, aside from her current trip.

"Let me know if you find anything else," Pratt calls over his shoulder on his way to the elevators.

After finding nothing, she stretches her arms above her head, glancing at her empty coffee mug. Before refilling it, she decides to finish screening the passengers in Makayla's cabin.

CHAPTER THIRTY-FOUR

JACK

Jack opens the door as soon as he hears the elevator arrive on his floor. Sabrina's gaze falls to his bare chest before she embraces him in a hug.

"I'm so sorry, Jack."

He steps back, wishing he'd thrown something on over his boxers. But it doesn't matter. What matters is finding Liam.

Sabrina closes the door behind her and follows him inside. When they reach the kitchen, Jack turns to the woman he's known since he was a kid. Her cutoff denim shorts and white tank top are a stark contrast to what she normally wears to the office. She looks younger, more like the girl he used to know.

She wore practically the same thing the night of their high school graduation, when she used the fire escape to sneak into Jack's bedroom after their parents had gone to bed. Jack's father had worked late, as usual, missing his graduation ceremony. Jack lay awake, trying to fill the void of his father's absence with the latest Pearl Jam CD, when Sabrina tapped on his third-story window.

After he pulled her inside, she withdrew a prerolled joint from her shorts pocket. They stayed up the rest of the night, making each other laugh, followed by shushing each other to keep from waking Jack's parents.

Jack wonders if Sabrina changed after working for her father. Or has she always been the ruthless woman he's come to know?

"So, what's happening on the plane? Have you talked to Makayla?"

Jack opens his bottle of scotch and, with a trembling hand, pours some into the crystal tumbler sitting on the counter. The amber liquid sloshes onto the white marble.

"Here." Sabrina steps closer. "Let me do that for you."

As he allows her to take the bottle from his hand, Jack gets a whiff of her freshly sprayed floral perfume. He studies her steady pour, wanting to believe she has nothing to do with Liam's disappearance.

"Remember the night, after our high school graduation, when I snuck into your room, and we stayed up all night listening to Pearl Jam?"

Her eyes meet his, and he wonders what it was that triggered her to recall the same memory he did moments earlier.

"Look, I know I can be heartless sometimes," she says. "When you rejected me all those years ago, it hurt. And I lashed out." She pushes the tumbler toward him after filling it halfway. "I'm sorry."

"Did you know about your father?"

"The fraud? Yes." She doesn't even blink.

Of course she did, he thinks. He nearly laughs at himself for being so naive. *She's a snake.* He was an idiot to ever doubt how much she and her father were capable of. To not see who they really were.

But he still doesn't understand their level of greed when they already have so much. "Is it really worth embezzling from clients and risking imprisonment to have a closet full of Prada?"

Her lipsticked lips lift into a wry smile. "It's a hell of a lot more than that, Jack, and you know it. Plus, I don't see you complaining about living in a place like this." She swipes her manicured hand through the air.

It's ironic to think how big his problems seemed before the FBI had shown up at his door. He'd lain in bed hoping Sabrina might be the key to making the whole thing go away, thinking she might be able to convince her father to turn himself in. But Jack should've known better.

She's never cared about anyone but herself. Not his marriage, not his job, not the people she and Lionel have been stealing from. He recalls standing in her office years ago when she threatened to lie to Makayla and her father about an affair that never happened. It strikes him that it was probably her idea to blame the fraud on him.

Now, it all pales in comparison to Liam's abduction.

Sabrina lays her hand on his forearm. "I wanted to tell you. Really, I did. We never meant for it to get so out of hand. But let's not talk about that now. It's only money. A bunch of numbers that keep daddy in brandy and cigars, summering in the Hamptons, and wintering in Palm Beach, and yes, my closet full of Prada. But none of that really matters, I know. Liam matters." She sighs. "You've done it right, Jack. Having a family. I should've spent more time with the people I care about, rather than sacrificing so much for the job."

Me too, he thinks.

"Now, I just want to be here for you until they find your son."

Jack wishes he could believe her. If there was a time he could use a friend, it was now. He leaves his glass untouched, knowing her being here now is likely part of her and her father's elaborate plan. He clenches both hands into fists. She and Lionel must've known Jack would suspect them—at least after he discovered the fraud yesterday. So she came here to convince him otherwise. Preying on him when he's at his weakest.

He thinks about the time it would've taken for the FBI to visit Lionel, and for him to call his daughter. Then for her to get here from her loft in Chelsea. Jack takes a step toward her, lowering his face toward hers. All those years ago, she tried to come between him and Makayla. But does she think she can mess with his *child*?

She tilts her face toward his, pressing her palms against his chest. Jack swipes the tumbler off the counter and hurls it across the room. Sabrina shrieks as the glass shatters against the wall.

Jack grabs her upper arms and squeezes. "Why are you really here? *What have you done?*"

"Jack, let go. You're hurting me!" Her eyes double in size as she squirms beneath his grip.

Jack leans closer. *"Where's Liam?"* His scream echoes through the apartment.

A drop of his spit lands on her cheek.

"I don't know!"

Jack grits his teeth, grappling with the urge to shake her. He glares at her, their noses almost touching. Terror seeps from Sabrina's hazel eyes when Jack's phone chimes on the marble countertop with a new message. He glances at the screen, keeping his grip tight around Sabrina's arms. It's from Makayla.

A floorboard creaks in the hallway leading to the bedrooms. Jack turns his attention toward the direction of the sound. Footsteps tread down the hall. Sabrina cocks her head to follow Jack's gaze.

A tall, dark figure emerges from the hallway with a gun pointed at Sabrina's head. Before Jack can move, a muffled gunshot fills the condo. Sabrina's head flops to the side.

She goes limp beneath his hold.

"Sabrina!"

The intruder stands still. A black balaclava covers his face. The masked man keeps his gun trained on Jack as he lowers himself to the floor with Sabrina's lifeless body.

"Sabrina!"

"Keep your voice down," the intruder barks.

Jack cradles his childhood friend's head in his blood-covered hands, gaping at the bullet hole in her temple and the vacancy in her eyes before looking up at her killer. The man steps toward him, aiming his pistol at Jack's chest with a gloved hand. Jack's heart hammers into his throat as his eyes settle on the silencer at the end of the barrel.

"Throw me your phone."

Jack carefully lowers Sabrina's head to the floor and stands.

The intruder steps closer, sharpening his aim at Jack's forehead. "Throw me the phone and put your hands in the air, or your son dies."

CHAPTER THIRTY-FIVE

MAKAYLA

Makayla twists her wrists and tugs as hard as she can to free herself from the zip ties. But they're too tight. All she's managed to do is rub the skin raw beneath the plastic.

"Something to drink?"

Makayla turns to the twentysomething attendant standing behind the drink cart, her back to Makayla. After pouring Pink Headphones a Coke, she glances at the water bottle on Makayla's lap. Without a word, she avoids Makayla's stare and pulls the drink cart backward.

A spark of outrage ignites in her veins. *They're seriously offering a beverage right now? Instead of looking for Liam?*

Makayla cranes her neck to look behind her at Jemma's row, but the restraint tied to her armrest keeps her from being able to lean far enough to see. She puts her phone on camera mode and angles it like a mirror between her knees, hoping to get a glimpse of the pet carrier. But the plastic covering containing the life vest hanging under her seat blocks her view.

Liam is in that pet carrier. He has to be.

Makayla sits up tall and strains to see over her seat. She can't see Jemma or her burly husband.

Makayla brings her hands to her face, but they're stopped short by the seat belt cinched tight above her elbows. She checks her phone. Jack still hasn't responded to her text about the pet carrier and the couple seated a few rows behind her.

She calls him with her arms pinned to their sides and puts the call on speaker, turning down the volume as not to alert everyone around her. She's not going to passively sit here for the rest of the flight. It rings. And rings. She needs to speak to the FBI herself. They need to know she's been restrained. And no one is looking for Liam.

Come on, Jack. Pick up the phone. Hopefully, he's on the phone with the FBI right now, giving them the information about the pet carrier. Makayla lets it ring for over a minute before hanging up. Keeping her voice down, she sends him a voice message, asking him to call her back.

She has a new message from Cori. The CEO is making calls right now to get them to take off your restraints. In the meantime, Fletcher said you should act as calm as possible so they don't have a reason to keep you restrained. Are you doing okay?

Makayla's lower lip quivers as she types a response. I can't think straight. I have a crushing headache. I don't understand what's happening. I'm going to lose my mind if I don't find Liam soon. It's starting to feel like I already am.

After a few seconds, Cori replies. You're not losing your mind. This will all get sorted out. Didn't you say you fell on a hike with your dad? Your headache could be from that. Fletcher said you can have memory loss with a concussion. You do remember bringing Liam on the plane, right? I mean, is it possible you could've left him at the gate? I know it seems like a stretch, but have they searched the airport?

Makayla feels a fresh flush of defensiveness at Cori's accusation but then is reminded of the blow to the side of her head, after she tripped over a branch on the trail. A fresh wave of terror rips through her. All the research she did on transient global amnesia after her mother died, and she can't even admit to herself that it's possible.

Mild head injury is a major risk factor for developing the memory disorder. This must be why the FBI brought up her fall to Jack. She recalls the pain that radiated through her skull when she came down on the rock. And how she downplayed the throb in her head to her father for the rest of their hike.

People under forty were rarely affected by transient global amnesia—and she had no other symptoms of developing the disease—so she hadn't let it worry her. But the pain in her head now is much more severe than what she experienced before.

Everyone who'd been around her mother the morning of her infamous TV interview, including her father, said the actress seemed completely fine. She showed no signs of memory loss until she went on live television and the amnesia struck in the blink of an eye.

She gets another text from Cori. Sorry, I didn't mean to question you. I'm sure you brought Liam on the flight. And there has to be some reasonable explanation for where he is. XO

Makayla pauses before typing out a reply, stung by her friend's accusations despite Cori's apology. I don't know what to think right now. I'm so scared, Cori.

"I just wanted to apologize."

She looks up to see Jemma standing over her.

"I'm sorry about Chad helping them to restrain you." Jemma gestures toward her seat. "He just didn't want anyone to get hurt."

I wasn't hurting anyone, Makayla thinks. *At least, not on purpose. And what about my baby? Isn't his safety important?* But she doesn't have the energy to argue.

"Just let me see inside your pet carrier," she says.

"Folks, this is your captain from up in the flight deck. We're passing by Buffalo, New York, and expecting some more turbulence as we make our descent into LaGuardia. We need all passengers to return to your seats and keep your seat belts fastened for the remainder of the flight. We're expecting to be on the ground in a little under an hour."

"I will—as soon as we land." Jemma retreats toward her seat.

Makayla reaches out her arms to block the aisle, but her zip-tied wrists are stopped short by her seatbelt restraint. Instead, she grabs the hem of Jemma's jacket. "Show me now."

Aubrey emerges through the business class curtain, nearly bumping into Jemma from behind. Her nose is red, but the blood has been cleaned from her face. Makayla's relieved to see she looks almost as she did at the beginning of the flight.

"Please return to your seat for our descent."

Jemma stares down at Makayla, who makes no effort to loosen her grip on Jemma's clothing.

"Excuse me, ma'am." Impatience permeates the flight attendant's voice. "I need you to take your seat."

"As soon as we land. I promise," Jemma says. "This will all get sorted out."

Sorted out? As if they are talking about some sort of clerical error—not a child abduction.

"Ma'am, you're blocking the aisleway," Aubrey adds, peering around Jemma to see what is holding her up.

Makayla lets go of Jemma's jacket. Aubrey eyes her with a wary expression and downturned lips as she follows Jemma toward the rear of the plane.

Makayla's gaze moves over her diaper bag before her attention settles on the empty bassinet attached to the bulkhead. Feeling the pinch from the zip tie, she looks down, twisting her arm to loosen the restraint, and spots the circular stain on the sleeve of her sweatshirt. She stares at Liam's dried spit-up, distinctly remembering the moment it happened.

It was when they were walking down the jetway to board the flight. She dropped her phone while trying to slip it into her pocket and bent down to pick it up. Liam spit up as she reached for her phone. Makayla could hear a roller bag coming behind her. Instead of stopping to dig a burp cloth out of her diaper bag, she wiped her sleeve dry with her hand.

I haven't lost my memory. Liam was here.

She twists in her seat, craning her neck to see behind her. If she's right, he's been only a few rows back this whole time.

CHAPTER THIRTY-SIX

JACK

Jack scans the room for something he could use as a weapon, seeing only the knife block on the other side of the kitchen. "*Tell me where he is!* I need to know Liam's okay."

"I said throw me your phone!" the man barks. *"Now!"*

Jack snatches his phone from the counter and tosses it toward his assailant before raising his trembling hands above his head.

The masked intruder flicks the nose of the gun toward the living room windows. "Close the blinds."

Keeping his hands in the air, Jack takes careful steps over Sabrina's body. Her eyes stare blankly at the ceiling. Horrified by the sight, Jack wrenches his eyes away. When he reaches the living room wall, he flips the switch to lower the shades.

"Please." Jack faces the man as the shades begin to close. "Whatever you want me to do, I'll do it," he pleads as the tall man dressed in black steps farther into the light. Jack's gaze drifts to the growing pool of blood around Sabrina's head, now seeping beneath the legs of the baby grand, then back to the intruder. "Just let my baby live." He chokes back a sob, unable to keep the fear from his voice. Fear not for himself, but from the sickening realization that Liam's disappearance was carefully orchestrated. The reality hits him—Liam was abducted and kept somewhere on that flight where the crew hasn't looked. And where he isn't making any noise. "Can you at least tell me where he is? I'm begging you."

"Shut up!" He points the pistol at Jack's laptop on the marble countertop. "Sit down. You've got work to do."

The man's thick Brooklyn accent is not far from Jack's own, making Jack wonder if Lionel hired him. Jack's gaze returns to Sabrina's lifeless form. But Lionel wouldn't have his daughter killed. At least not on purpose.

"Okay. Okay." He makes his way toward his laptop in silence, thinking that on the other hand, the fact that this guy is here—making demands—likely means that Liam will live.

Jack's entire body trembles as he sits on the barstool above Sabrina's lifeless form, bleeding out on the floor. *I'm sorry, Sabrina. So, so sorry.* The masked intruder creeps toward him, keeping his gun outstretched. Jack dares to look at him. He's close enough now for Jack to see that his eyes are brown.

Jack notes that Sabrina's killer is keeping his balaclava on despite the windows being covered so no one can see inside. Hopefully, it means he isn't planning to kill Jack as soon as he's done complying with his demands.

The intruder steps closer, stopping when the tip of the silencer is a few inches from Jack's temple. He lays a paper on the counter and points a gloved finger at the printed numbers on the top of the page.

"If you want your son to make it off that flight alive, you'll transfer ten million from each of your five largest client accounts into this account."

Jack can tell by the three-digit bank code and nine-digit account number that it's a foreign account, but he's not sure which country. He thinks maybe Singapore. Or possibly Japan.

He sits frozen, staring at the account numbers, aware of his childhood friend lying dead on the floor beside his chair. She and Lionel had nothing to do with Liam's kidnapping. Which means Liam is in the hands of—

The burly man grabs a fistful of Jack's hair, yanking his head back. He thrusts the silencer into Jack's throat, beneath his jaw. "You want me to blow your fuckin' head off or you want your kid to live?"

"I'll do it. I'll do it!"

Sabrina's killer shoves Jack's head forward and releases his hair. Jack coughs as the man withdraws the gun from his neck.

Jack's fingers fumble across his keyboard, and it takes him three attempts to get into his account. Once he's logged in, sweat drips down the side of his face, even though he's still in only his underwear in the air-conditioned condo.

"Calm down. We don't need you screwin' this up."

Jack breathes deep and accesses Malcolm Zeller's account first. He slides the paper toward him and types in the account number for the transfer. He pauses before putting in the bank code, overwhelmed by a surge of panic. How is Liam's abductor on the flight going to give Liam back without getting caught? What if Liam is only being kept alive until Jack transfers the funds?

"Let's go." The intruder pokes Jack's shoulder with the gun barrel.

Jack moves his hands away from the keyboard. "How do I know that my son is still alive?"

The large man tilts his ski-masked head to the side and cracks a sadistic smile. "You're gonna have to trust me."

He glances at Sabrina's blood seeping around the legs of his barstool. "No. I want proof of life before I move the money."

The killer lets out a raspy laugh. "You ain't the one in charge. Move the money. Or your kid dies."

Jack grits his teeth. "I want to see a photo of Liam alive on that plane."

The balaclava's mouth hole exposes the guy's smirk. "Don't got one."

"I can't transfer that much out of my clients' accounts without it getting flagged."

The man lowers his elbows onto the countertop, bringing his face toward Jack's. "Don't play games with me. I know you can move a lot more than that. But we're tryin' not to attract attention. How about this: I'll get you a photo of your *dead* baby if you don't transfer the money *right now*."

Jack gulps and replaces his hands on the keyboard. "All right. I'm doing it." What other choice does he have? With shaking hands, he schedules the transfer of $10 million from Malcolm's account.

The masked man straightens and moves directly behind Jack. "I need to see confirmation of each transfer."

"That's the first one."

The man's breath is warm on Jack's neck as Jack opens his next-biggest client account.

"You've only done one? What's takin' so long?"

"I'm going as fast as I can. Breathing down my neck isn't helping." Jack's pulse pounds in his ears as he wrestles with the reason why the man won't give him proof that Liam is alive. "Just let me think!"

Jack carefully types in the account number and schedules a second transfer of $10 million. The money won't reach this foreign bank account before the flight lands at LaGuardia. Are they really going to let Liam go before the money reaches their account?

Jack chews the inside of his lip as he initiates the transfer from his third-biggest client account, fearing they aren't planning to return Liam before the plane lands.

The FBI will be meeting the flight on the ground. There's no way Liam's abductor will escape with him in their luggage—dead or alive. The FBI won't let anyone go until they find Liam. Plus, the flight will land in plenty of time for Jack to cancel the transfers before business hours. It doesn't make sense.

The butt of the gun comes down hard on the back of Jack's skull. He cries out from the shock of the blow as pain radiates through his head.

"Hurry up!"

Jack winces. "I'm going as fast as I can. You're not helping!" He motions to the barstool beside him. "Sit down, why don't you? I can't think with you hovering over me." Or with his childhood friend lying dead at his feet. "And this will take a while. I still have a ways to go."

CHAPTER THIRTY-SEVEN

Tina

Tina reads over the ticket information provided by the airline for the female passenger seated a few rows behind Makayla: Jemma Neilson. She leans forward, reading that the name on the credit card used to purchase Jemma Neilson's ticket was "Gift Card," meaning it was likely a prepaid Visa. Tina brings a hand to her chin, seeing the ticket was purchased alone two months ago.

She pulls up the seat map and checks the name of the passenger seated beside Jemma. *Chad Wickham.* She drums her pen against her desk, looking at the sparsely filled plane. *Why would you choose to sit next to an occupied seat on a plane that is practically empty? And if Jemma Neilson and Chad Wickham are traveling together, why book their tickets separately?*

Tina glances over her shoulder to tell Pratt but remembers he left for Jack Rossi's condo. She quickly enters Jemma's full name into her database. Jemma's Long Island address matches what she gave the airline. A registered nurse license number for New York state appears below her name. She has no criminal history.

Tina retrieves the airline's ticket information on Chad Wickham. Her pulse quickens when she sees he purchased his ticket with cash—only one day after Jemma Neilson bought hers.

She copies his name into the bureau's public record database. When the results appear, Tina goes still. A red D pops up over his demographic information, meaning that Chad Wickham is deceased.

Tina jumps from her chair, knocking over her empty coffee mug, and looks around the mostly empty office. "Ruiz!"

Ruiz stands from her cubicle. "Yeah?" she says.

"I found something," Tina yells. She points to Castillo's office. "Get Castillo!"

Castillo emerges from his office. "What is it?"

"Me too." Ruiz lifts her phone in the air. "The Anchorage gate agent just called," she announces loud enough for both Tina and their supervisor to hear. "She went to her boyfriend's place after getting off work. And she confirmed seeing Liam inside Makayla's baby wrap when she boarded."

He's really on that plane. "I need you both to come see this." Stunned, Tina sits back down as Ruiz and Castillo stride toward her. When the agents reach her cubicle, her heart is still racing. Castillo comes to a stop beside her, leaning over her shoulder to look at her screen. Ruiz stands on the other side of Tina, folding her arms.

Tina gestures to her screen. "The passenger in seat 15H is deceased."

"What?" Castillo says from behind her.

"He had to have boarded with this guy's stolen ID. He died three days ago. The death probably hasn't been officially recorded yet, which is why it didn't get flagged by TSA when he went through security."

Castillo stands up straight. "Shit."

Tina swivels in her chair. "This passenger paid cash for his ticket two months ago. There's a woman seated next to him, Jemma Neilson." Tina pulls up the pretty, dark-haired woman's New York driver's license. "They purchased their tickets separately only one day apart. She used a prepaid credit card. And they selected seats beside each other despite it being a practically empty flight."

Ruiz places her hands on her hips. "She could have used a stolen ID too. I'll send a Long Island patrol unit to her address."

Castillo pulls out his phone. "Where's Pratt?"

Ruiz looks at Tina, waiting for her response before making the call.

Tina turns in her chair. "He went back to Jack Rossi's condo to interview him again. Rossi and Lionel Rothman both accused each other of fraud, and Pratt was worried that Rossi might've staged his son's kidnapping. Jack Rossi has a $20 million kidnap-and-ransom insurance policy that he failed to mention when we spoke with him earlier."

"I need to contact the flight," Castillo says. "Can you call Pratt and give him an update?"

"Yes," Tina says. "Jack Rossi called Pratt before he left and said Makayla didn't think the crew searched those two's luggage that thoroughly. They also have a pet carrier. We should make sure that gets checked too."

Castillo nods. "Thanks."

Tina's phone rings atop her desk. "It's the forensic accountant," she announces before the two agents leave her cubicle. "Analyst Farrar."

"Hey, it's Corban. Two outgoing transfers have just been initiated from a couple of Jack Rossi's accounts. Each for ten million. It looks like the money is headed to a foreign account, which I'm still tracking. But I wanted to let you know the transfers have been made."

"Thanks." She turns to Castillo after hanging up. "Jack Rossi has made two transfers for ten million out of his client accounts." A sinking feeling forms in her gut. "When we were in Rossi's condo earlier, Pratt heard a noise. Rossi tried to blame it on a remodel project in a neighboring unit until I reminded him it was the middle of the night."

Castillo holds her gaze, thinking about the danger Pratt might be walking into. "And Pratt went alone?"

"Yes. I'm calling him now."

She returns the phone to her ear. Pratt's cell rings four times before going to voicemail. "He's not answering." She lowers her phone, estimating how long it's been since Pratt left the office. "He must already be at Rossi's condo."

"I'm calling SWAT," Castillo says. "If this was a well-planned kidnapping, we have no idea what Pratt could be walking into. And it sounds like one of the abductors could have already been inside Rossi's condo when you were there."

"They won't get there in time." Ruiz strides out of the cubicle. "I'm heading there now. I'll send a unit from NYPD there to meet me. Can you call Long Island PD and send someone to Jemma Neilson's address?"

"All right—be careful," Castillo calls. "I'll still send a SWAT team to get there as soon as they can."

He turns to Tina. "How long ago did Pratt leave for Rossi's condo?"

She glances at the time on her laptop. "A little over fifteen minutes ago."

"Ruiz is right," he mumbles loud enough for Tina to hear when he pulls out his phone. "If there *is* someone in Rossi's condo, we're already way too late."

CHAPTER THIRTY-EIGHT

Makayla

As they start their descent over New York, the nose of the aircraft dips. Makayla's restraints keep her from being able to lift her window shade, but through a window on the other side of the plane, she can see that it's still dark outside. A flash of lightning in the distance illuminates the rain-streaked window.

She's gone over her time at Anchorage Airport several times in her head. She remembers everything: feeding Liam, then having to hurry to her gate. Rubbing his back by the window while he watched planes take off. She has no doubt Liam was with her. Up until the moment when she came out of the lavatory.

She stares at her phone in her hands. How could she have forgotten? She hurriedly unlocks the device with her fingerprint and opens her recent photos. There it is. A selfie of her and Liam in the food court at Anchorage Airport after she'd taken him out of her wrap. She meant to send it to Jack, but Liam had taken so long to drink his bottle that she rushed to the gate and forgot about it.

It might not convince anyone besides herself that Liam is on this flight, but it does prove that he was with her not long before boarding.

A new message pops up from Cori. I'm sure you must be terrified. But I have good news! The CEO got in touch with someone at the airline, and they are going to contact your flight and have them undo your restraints. I can't believe how they're treating you after Liam was taken while you were in the bathroom.

Makayla sets down her phone without replying. She prays they contact the flight soon and she's not stuck here until they land. Her eyes fall to Cori's text again before her screen goes dark.

Then it hits her. She doesn't remember telling Cori she was in the bathroom when Liam went missing. Her face grows hot. Had she forgotten?

She starts to scroll up through their texts, then stops, replacing her phone on her lap. *I had to have told her, and there's nothing wrong with my memory.* The hours since Liam went missing feel like a blur. Doubting herself isn't going to help find Liam.

She leans into the aisle, craning her neck to see what Chad and Jemma are doing. She can't see Jemma's bulky husband sticking out from his aisle seat anymore. Something about Jemma, and her coming up to speak to her, gnaws at her. If she was truly concerned and wanted to help, why not show Makayla the dog inside the pet carrier?

Makayla turns to the young woman across the aisle. "Hey."

The girl meets Makayla's eyes while keeping her head resting against her seat back.

Makayla flicks her head toward the rows behind her and lowers her voice. "What's that couple doing?"

Pink Headphones heaves a sigh and twists around. She looks back at Makayla. "Which couple?"

Makayla works to keep her frustration from showing on her face. *Could this girl be any less aware of her surroundings?*

"The only couple that's seated behind me. They're three rows back."

The girl looks again. "I don't see them. All the rows behind you are empty."

Panic hits her like a tidal wave. "What?" She strains to see behind her. "Where did they go?"

The girl shrugs.

"Did they take the pet carrier with them?"

The girl shrugs again.

Makayla leans back in her seat, her mind spinning. They wouldn't take the carrier on a walkabout of the cabin if it really had a fussy dog inside. They made such a fuss about not disturbing his precious sleep. It would still be there, under the seat.

So, if the carrier is missing from the row, that means she is right and the couple has Liam. This is her chance to find out.

"Hey. Hey! Unbuckle me."

Pink-headphone girl shakes her head.

"Please! Help me."

"I can't."

"Then go look and see if the pet carrier is there, under the seat." Makayla waits with pleading eyes for the girl to respond.

She purses her lips. "Okay, fine."

Makayla holds her breath while the girl gets up from her seat and retreats down the aisle. She steps into Jemma's row and crouches down.

"Well?"

No response.

Makayla lifts herself an inch off her seat, trying to see what's happening. "Is the carrier there?"

With a sinking feeling, she worries they took the carrier with them. *Then what are they doing with Liam? Hiding him somewhere else?*

An even worse thought enters her mind. *Oh, no. Please, God—no.* The young woman must've found Liam . . . and it's too late. *How else would Liam not have made any noise through all of this?*

"Hey! Can you hear me? Is it there?" But she's not sure she can bear the answer to her own question.

As she waits for a response, her thoughts run wild. An image of the young girl pulling Liam's limp, lifeless body from the carrier fills her mind.

After what feels like an hour, the girl reappears in the aisle, holding the pet carrier in front of her. Her eyes are huge, a mix of shock and horror. The door to the kennel hangs open as she approaches Makayla. It's empty inside.

Then Makayla sees it. In the girl's other hand is a small dog.

"I found this." When she lifts it closer to Makayla's face, Makayla sees that although the dog is very lifelike, it's not real.

Makayla's jaw drops. "Unbuckle me! *Now!*"

CHAPTER THIRTY-NINE

JACK

"How'd you get past the doorman?" Jack asks as he begins the final transfer.

The masked intruder's mouth lifts into a proud grin. "Easy. I got in through the back maintenance entrance by posing as a food delivery guy for the workers doing the repairs in the unit down the hall."

"How'd you get into my condo without a key card?" He hadn't noticed any signs of forced entry when he got home from work. Although he was distracted, consumed with facing life imprisonment if he didn't comply with Lionel's demands.

"Are you done yet? We're runnin' out of time."

Jack glances at his brown-eyed assailant on the barstool beside him as he types in the eight-digit amount to be transferred for the fifth time. "I'm going as fast as I can." His fingers hover above the keyboard before entering the foreign account number. "I want proof that my son is alive."

"I already told you—I don't have any." His mouth forms a frown in the reflection of Jack's laptop screen. "You're gonna have to trust me."

Jack swallows. He forces himself not to look at Sabrina's body on the floor. She had nothing to do with Liam's abduction. If he hadn't let her come up, she'd still be alive.

"As soon as I see that confirmation of the last transfer," the Brooklyn-accented man continues, "I'll call and let my colleague know that it's done."

The masked man leans forward. Jack smells his stale breath.

"But if you don't hurry up, you're not gettin' your kid back. Ever."

Terrified for his son, Jack slowly types in the account number from the printed page. If he *doesn't* comply, how the hell is Liam's abductor planning to get him off the plane once the FBI meets them at LaGuardia? They can't be that stupid to think the FBI is going to let all the passengers go with no questions asked.

Jack turns to the masked man at his right. "You won't get away with this. If Liam is still missing when that plane lands, the FBI isn't going to let anyone go until they find him."

The man stares back at him. Jack worries he went too far. He's going to shoot him, just like he shot Sabrina.

Instead, the man cracks a crooked smile. "There's more than one way off a plane."

Jack feels sick. "What the hell are you talking about?"

"Just keep going, and you won't have to find out." The man holds up his phone, wiggling it between his gloved fingers and thumb. "As soon as you make the last transfer, your son will be returned to your wife."

Jack refocuses on finishing the transfer. He has no other choice but to comply. A window pops up for Jack to authenticate the transfer with his log-in credentials. Jack types the first few letters of his passcode, and it strikes him that the man next to him is likely waiting to kill him as soon as he's done.

He can identify the man's eye color. And height. His Brooklyn accent. He was naive to think this guy was going to let him live just because he kept his mask on.

Could Lionel have orchestrated this without Sabrina knowing? Maybe he hadn't known that his daughter would come to Jack's condo. Unable to bring himself to look at Sabrina again, he pictures her lying dead on the floor. Would Lionel have his own daughter killed? Was he that much of a monster? But Jack realizes he never really knew him at all. And he's about to find out.

Jack presses Enter. Seeing the confirmation of the transfer, he closes his eyes.

Liam will never know him, even if his son survives. Jack's resentment for his father's absence runs deep. *How could I have allowed myself to do the exact same thing?*

A sharp rap on his condo door causes Jack's fingers to jolt off his keyboard. His assailant's head snaps toward the door.

"Who the hell is that?" he barks.

"I—I don't—"

"FBI! Open the door!"

The masked man turns to Jack, his mouth a snarl. "You called the police! *How?*" His eyes narrow at Jack's laptop screen.

"I didn't do anything. I swear. I—"

Three more raps. "FBI! Jack Rossi, I need you to open the door!"

Sabrina's killer shoves the end of the silencer against Jack's temple. "*Shut up!*" he hisses.

An explosive crack resounds through the quiet condo, making Jack jump. He opens his eyes, half-expecting to feel a bullet in his brain. Instead, his condo door bursts wide open, busted off one of its hinges.

The tip of the masked man's silencer appears in the corner of Jack's eye as Agent Pratt storms into his condo, his gun trained in their direction.

"FBI! Drop your weapon!"

"No!" Jack shouts. "Don't shoot!"

Over his own shouts and those from Pratt, Jack barely registers the soft hiss of the gun being fired next to his ear. Instinctively, Jack ducks, covering his head as he throws himself off his barstool.

"*Stop!*" Gunshots blast through the condo, drowning out his voice, as Pratt returns fire.

Beside Jack, the masked man flies backward, his head jerking as his chest recoils from the impact from two shots to the chest. His gun arm swings to the side. Glass shatters behind them. The masked man falls to the floor and lies still, his gun clamoring on the hard wood beside him.

Heavy footsteps trudge toward them as Jack lifts his head.

"*Noooo!*" Jack reaches for his assailant, who lies unmoving on the floor. "Hey!" He gets to his knees and crawls toward Sabrina's killer, trying to shake him back to life. His hand slips on something wet when he gets to the man's side. *Blood,* Jack realizes with horror. He grasps the masked man's shoulder. He shakes it but gets pulled back by Pratt.

"*What have you done?*" Jack fights to free himself from the agent's hold.

Pratt shoves him in the chest with his palm.

"Stay back!" Jack looks up to see a uniformed NYPD officer standing over him. She raises her weapon at Jack's torso.

Jack lifts his hands in the air. "He has to make a call, or we won't get Liam back!"

"Put your hands on your head!" Pratt orders, aiming his gun at Jack's chest.

"Did you hear me?" Jack complies, pressing his palms into the back of his head.

"What happened here?" Pratt keeps his pistol trained on Jack. "Do you know this man?"

Jack turns from Pratt to stare into the man's lifeless eyes as the NYPD officer crouches beside him and puts two fingers to the man's neck.

Jack's heart beats in his throat. This can't be happening. "He has to make a phone call! He's working with Liam's abductors on the flight! They're waiting to hear from him. If they don't . . ." He can't bear to think of the alternative.

"It's too late for that." The officer plucks the man's pistol and silencer off the floor.

"Are you hurt?" Pratt asks, lowering his weapon.

Jack grabs a fistful of his short hair. He stares at the dead man in disbelief as the FBI agent pulls off the man's balaclava. His head is shaved, exposing a spiderweb tattoo above his ear.

In Jack's periphery, the NYPD officer crouches beside Sabrina's body and feels her neck for a pulse. "This is Officer Tate," she says into the radio clipped to her vest. "We've secured the condo. Requesting immediate medical assistance for two shooting victims. Both unresponsive."

"Unlock his phone," Jack says as Pratt lifts the device from the floor. Jack's pulse races. "We can still send a message saying the transfers are complete."

Pratt holds up the phone for Jack to see. "We can't. There's no fingerprint sensor. It's asking for a passcode."

Jack's chest wall tightens. From beyond Jack's shattered condo window, thunderclaps. Rain blows into his living room when he glances toward the sound.

Pratt motions toward the phone, taking a closer look. "It's probably a prepaid. Did he have another one on him?"

"No. Not that I saw." Jack gapes at Pratt in disbelief as the agent searches the front pockets of the dead man's jeans. Pratt turns the man on his side to feel his back pockets and withdraws a gray key card, identical to Jack's.

"That must be how he got in. He said he posed as a food delivery guy for the contractors doing work on the unit down the hall. Our building's maintenance workers have master keys to all the units." Jack's veins constrict as his shock morphs into rage. "I did everything he asked." He glares at Pratt. "Did you call the flight about the couple with the pet carrier? Tell me they found Liam."

Pratt shakes his head. "My squad supervisor contacted the flight while we were en route. But I haven't heard anything back yet."

Jack grits his teeth. "He was just about to call whoever has Liam on that plane. One more minute and Makayla would've gotten Liam back." Jack sinks lower to the floor. "Shit, I can't even believe this."

Pratt stares at the dead man. Jack follows his gaze. He was so close to getting Liam back. *How did this all go so wrong?* Now, they're back where they started.

"He said something earlier," Jack says. "That there's more than one way to get off a plane." Jack turns to the agent. "What the hell do you think he meant by that?"

CHAPTER FORTY

ANNA

A sound like a doorbell chimes over Anna's headphones.

"Looks like company is calling." Miguel selects the number two radio. "Dispatch, Flight 7038."

"Flight 7038, dispatch. I've got the FBI on the line requesting to be patched through. Are you available to speak with them?"

Anna casts a look of frustration at Miguel. With their arrival into New York airspace, they don't have time for this.

"This is Flight 7038," Miguel says. "We are starting our descent over New York, but I can speak briefly with the FBI if you patch them through."

"Roger that, Flight 7038. Stand by while I patch them through."

Anna sits tall, gazing out at the darkness through the windshield. Miguel already spoke directly with an FBI agent earlier. They must have some very pertinent information to call again now, when they're less than an hour from landing. The FBI wouldn't be calling the cockpit just to get an update. They know that if they found the baby on the plane, they would communicate that immediately.

When the agent called earlier, he said they were working to confirm the baby had gone through TSA with his mother.

"Flight 7038, this is Special Agent Castillo."

Anna recognizes the man's voice from the last time he was patched through.

"One of our intelligence analysts discovered that the passengers in seats 15H and 15J boarded using stolen IDs."

Anna and Miguel exchange glances. The shock in his eyes mirrors her own.

"We're still working to confirm their real identities. In the meantime, we'd like your crew to search their luggage again. But advise them to be careful—we don't know exactly who or what we're dealing with. They may need to enlist the help of some of the passengers in case these two put up a fight. According to Makayla Rossi's husband, his wife is suspicious of these two and raised concerns about them having a pet carrier. The carrier should be checked again too."

"Roger that," Miguel says. "We're on our descent into LaGuardia, and we're going to have our hands full landing in this weather, but I'll instruct the crew to check that right away. We may not be able to contact you again, however, before we land."

"Understood," the agent says. "I'm sending a task force to meet your plane when you land at LaGuardia. Thank you."

As Miguel signs off with the FBI agent, Anna stares at the sleet and rain hitting the windscreen, illuminated by the flashing of the wing strobe lights.

"Shit." Miguel swipes the flight deck phone from the receiver, interrupting her thoughts. "This is bad."

CHAPTER FORTY-ONE

MAKAYLA

Makayla's eyes are glued to the fake dog in the girl's hand. Jemma acted like she was helping her, but the whole time she had Liam hidden in a dog carrier. "Unbuckle me!" she repeats.

The girl hesitates. "I'm not sure that I—"

"Just do it!" There's steel in Makayla's voice when she shouts. "Where are they?"

"I don't know; I didn't see them get up."

Britt appears beside the lavatories at the back of the cabin. Seeing the empty pet carrier in the girl's hand, her mouth falls open. An alarmed expression comes over the attendant's face before her eyes snap toward Makayla.

"They have Liam!" Makayla writhes beneath her restraints, her eyes pleading with Britt. "And now they're gone!"

Britt glances at Chad and Jemma's empty row. "We need to find them," she says. "The captain just called and said they boarded with fake IDs."

The couple in the middle row stand from their seats, their petrified gazes scouring the cabin.

"Oh, my!" the woman clasps a hand over her mouth before following her husband into the aisle.

Aubrey swings open the curtain to business class, her eyes moving from Makayla to the girl standing in the aisle. "I just heard from the captain. What's going on?"

Makayla fights against her restraints. "Unbuckle me! My baby was inside that pet carrier! They had a fake dog inside. We need to find that couple from row fifteen!"

"Did you see anyone come into the front cabins?" Britt asks Aubrey.

Aubrey shakes her head. "No, but I'll double-check."

"Let me up!" Makayla pleads. "Please." She extends her wrists toward Aubrey. "Undo these first."

"It's okay; let her go," she hears Derek say.

Makayla twists to see him standing behind the girl, the worry lines on his forehead belying the calm in his voice.

The young woman stands frozen in the aisle, holding the pet carrier and fake dog, as Aubrey reluctantly withdraws a pair of scissors from her blazer pocket and snips one of the zip ties free. Makayla tears off the seat belt around her arms and waist, leaving the other zip tie around her wrist.

"I'll check the back," Britt says as Aubrey turns for the front of the plane.

When she gets up, Makayla drops her phone into her diaper bag, then sees Derek follow Britt toward the rear. "I'll check the crew compartment," he says.

Makayla pushes past the girl in the aisle, studying the pet carrier in her hand. Liam must've been in there, only three rows behind her, this whole time.

The carrier has mesh sides, so at least Liam should've been able to breathe normally. He was in such a deep sleep when she went to the bathroom. She prays the reason he hadn't made any noise was because he hadn't woken up—not because he couldn't.

Makayla rushes down the aisle, pausing beside the retirement-aged couple in the center row, both wearing the airline-provided headphones while watching the small screens in front of their seats. "Did you see them get up?"

The woman looks up from her movie, startled at the sight of Makayla up from her seat. She lowers her headphones and turns her head in the direction of Makayla's pointed finger before warily shaking her head. "No. Sorry."

"They aren't up front," Aubrey announces from the divider to business class.

After reaching the back of the rear cabin, Britt turns to Derek and Makayla. "I don't see them anywhere."

Makayla wants to scream, rip her hair out. *How can people keep going missing on this plane?*

"Check the lavatories!" Makayla yells.

"I'm looking!"

Makayla watches Britt push open the lavatory doors on either side of her. In her seat across the aisle, Rose startles awake from the commotion, her white hair flat on one side as she gapes at Makayla. The lavatories behind their section are unoccupied. Makayla checks them both anyway.

She peers inside the bathroom she used when Liam was taken. *Had* she told Cori she was in the lavatory when Liam went missing? She didn't have a chance to look back at all of their texts. She left her phone on her seat, but she's almost certain now that she didn't.

Jack's question from earlier replays in her head. *You did meet her, right?*

She thought she had, although she doesn't specifically remember. When Cori first messaged her through the mother's group's social media page, saying they'd met the day before at the gathering at Rockefeller Park, Makayla didn't question her. She'd met so many new faces that day—more than a dozen—and she couldn't remember all the names. Makayla had hardly slept in those first three weeks after Liam was born.

And Cori's profile photo, a tall blond holding a baby girl, looked familiar. She could've been one of several mothers at the gathering, all wearing sunglasses. Some wore hats too.

Makayla recalls how inferior she felt to all the other Tribeca mothers at the time. When Cori reached out the next day, Makayla felt flattered that someone from the group wanted to befriend her.

She moves into the rear cabin and runs past the empty middle row to the other side of the plane. When Cori shared that her mother was romance novelist Snow Browning, Makayla felt an instant connection. None of her other friends knew what it was like having a famous parent. But Cori did.

After losing her mom, Makayla found it even harder to open up to people. Even though she'd lived in New York for over fifteen years, she still felt like an outsider, especially in Tribeca. She'd often wondered how it could be so hard in a city of eight million people to fit in, but it was.

All the other mothers from her prenatal group seemed too busy for a friendship with her. She always felt understyled and underdressed. But she and Cori clicked and became fast friends. There was an easiness in her friendship with Cori that Makayla hadn't felt in a long time. *Was that because it wasn't real?*

She glances over her shoulder at Jemma's empty row. *Could Cori somehow be involved in this? Had she been in contact with Jemma and Chad this whole time?*

The middle lavatory is vacant, but the other is lit up as OCCUPIED. Makayla bangs on the door. "Come out right now!"

She slams her fist against the flimsy door, making it rattle with each rap. "Open up! I know you have my son!"

Britt rushes toward her from the rear of the plane with Derek on her heels. Makayla throws her shoulder against the door.

"Stop!" Britt puts her palm in the air when she reaches her. "We don't know it's them."

There's no answer from inside, not even a cry from Liam. When Makayla swallows, it feels like there's a knife in her throat.

"It has to be them." Makayla steps back. "Open the door."

Britt doesn't move, and Makayla motions to Derek. "Open it!"

The buzz of an electric tool comes from inside the bathroom as Derek moves forward. He lifts the **Lavatory** sign and slides the lever to the left, turning the window below it from red to green. Derek pushes against the door, but it doesn't budge. The electric hum coming from inside morphs into an ear-piercing drone.

Makayla gapes at the door in terror. *"Push harder!"*

Derek slams his shoulder against the door. This time it cracks open an inch before someone shoves it closed from the other side.

A passenger jumps out of his seat a few rows back. "What's happening?"

"Hurry! Open it!" Makayla screams.

She throws herself against the door beside Derek.

Another passenger stands up in the rear cabin, alarm written on her face. "*What's going on?*" she yells. "What's that noise?"

Britt stares at the door in horrified confusion. "What are they doing?"

A loud *whoosh* sounds from inside the bathroom as air escapes from the plane, muffling the electric whir. Realization floods the attendant's face when oxygen masks drop throughout the cabins. Panicked shrieks and wails erupt from the scattered passengers, but none as loud as Makayla's.

Derek steps back and prepares to throw himself against the door. "They're sawing through the wall of the plane!"

CHAPTER FORTY-TWO

ANNA

Miguel checks his phone as Anna initiates their descent. After dropping his phone back into his shirt pocket, he grins at her. "My wife just texted me. She's in labor and heading to the hospital."

"Oh, wow." Anna glances at their flight path. They'll be landing in less than an hour. "I hope you can make it there in time."

"I hope so too."

"Do you know what you're going to name her?"

The entire cockpit rattles as they encounter more turbulence. The nose drops, lifting her off her seat, and Anna's stomach churns. The nose pitches upward. As she's jerked against her seat back, she wishes she would've eaten something with her coffee. The last time she felt airsick was during pilot training in the air force.

"We're getting bounced all over the place," she says to Miguel. "Didn't dispatch say there should only be light turbulence on our descent?"

"Yeah. This is much more than that. We must be on the edge of that—"

The ding-dong sound of the SELCAL interrupts Miguel's sentence. **COMPANY CALL** appears on a screen on the instrument panel. Miguel switches to the number two radio.

He keys his microphone switch. "Flight 7038."

"7038, dispatch, the weather for the New York/Newark area is deteriorating rapidly. Wilmington International, India Lima Mike, is your new alternate. Fuel required is eighteen decimal two. What is your fuel remaining at this time?"

Miguel looks at the lower ECAM display. "Fuel remaining right now is seventeen decimal five."

He checks the flight plan and turns to Anna. "We don't have enough fuel for that. I don't think dispatch realizes our weather deviation used up our extra fuel."

He keys the microphone switch again. "Dispatch, Flight 7038. Uh, we don't have the fuel for that, due to an extensive weather deviation earlier. Unless we head there right now."

"Roger, Flight 7038, I'll see what I can come up with. I'll let you know via ACARS."

"Flight 7038, roger." Miguel punches the radio button back to the number one radio. "Sounds like dispatch might have dropped the ball on keeping track of our fuel."

The radio blares before Anna can reply.

"Pacific Air 123, things are getting backed up at New York Approach. I have holding instructions for you; advise ready to copy."

"Shit," Miguel mutters, pulling out his pen and grabbing the paper flight plan. "Pacific Air 123, ready to copy, go ahead."

"Pacific Air 123, roger, hold northwest of CYPER on the three zero seven-degree radial, right-hand turns. Length of legs your discretion; expect further clearance at time zero four two seven. Descend and maintain flight level one niner zero."

Miguel reads back the clearance as Anna dials in nineteen thousand in the altitude window.

"This isn't good," Miguel says as he prints out the latest weather observation for LaGuardia. "Unless we divert to Wilmington now, we'll have only Newark or JFK as alternates, and their weather is going down the toilet fast."

A wave of disappointment washes over Anna. She won't see Joel now. She instantly regrets her selfish thought at the expense of everyone's safety on board, knowing in her gut that she shouldn't be seeing Joel anyway.

She thinks of that night in LA at the start of summer, seated across from Joel at her hotel restaurant after bumping into him at LAX. Their paths had only crossed a few times since their air force pilot training in Oklahoma over ten years ago, but that evening in June, they reconnected so easily.

Joel made her laugh harder than she had in years, bringing tears to her eyes at the restaurant. Several hours later he opened up about his divorce. Tired of feigning happiness about her own marriage, she told Joel about her own relationship struggles. She immediately regretted it, feeling a sense of betrayal to her husband. But it was also a relief to say it out loud.

Anna recalls the kiss they shared a month later, in Joel's hotel lobby, after trading trips to be in Chicago on the same night. It had felt so right and so wrong at the same time. When Joel invited her up to his room for a drink, it had taken all her willpower to say no, knowing what would happen if she did.

That kiss was three weeks ago. When Joel said he was coming to New York for thirty-six hours, she couldn't stop herself from fantasizing about all the ways they could fill the time. It strikes her that she and Joel got to this place the same way she and Carter morphed from happily married to passionless roommates. Gradually. In both cases, by the time she sensed what had happened, it was too late. Now, Joel is asleep in his downtown hotel room, where she's promised to meet him as soon as she lands.

She glances at their fuel quantity display and knows what Miguel is going to say before he responds.

"New York Center, Pacific Air 7038. It looks like we don't have any holding fuel, so if we don't get a clearance to continue the arrival at CYPER, then we will be requesting to divert to Wilmington, India Lima Mike," Miguel says with urgency in his voice.

"Pacific Air 7038, New York Center. Roger, I have your request."

A bright lightning flash accompanied by a boom so loud it muffles the last few words from New York Center startles both pilots.

Anna steals a glance at Miguel's grim expression as the airplane takes a hard bounce several times in the turbulent air. She instinctively puts her hand on the control stick to her right, just in case the autopilot can't keep up with the rough ride.

The map display shows several large thunderstorms along their route, but so far the red and yellow danger zones it depicts are clear of their intended path.

"The storms are really closing in around us," she says.

Above them, a strobe of lightning flashes, brightly illuminating the sky and the rain streaming down their windshield.

The turbulence intensifies. Anna notices Miguel's hands around his control stick too. The autopilot struggles to maintain control but somehow remains engaged.

"Damn. I should've gotten more sleep for this," Miguel says. "I thought I was going to finish my book tonight. You'd better lock your shoulder harnesses. I think it's going to get pretty rough."

Anna presses down on the lever beside her seat, locking her harnesses in place. Feeling the aircraft tossed about by the storm, she's fueled with adrenaline.

"Should I disconnect the autopilot and hand-fly this?" She works to keep the nervousness out of her voice.

"No, it can probably do a better job than either of us can right now, and when we get handed off to New York Approach Control in a few minutes, we're going to get really busy."

Anna notes the concern on Miguel's face but tries not to let it feed her own rising panic.

A rapid dinging sound fills the cockpit. Beneath her headphones, Anna feels a pressure change in her ears and hears a momentary loud rush of air. Her eyes dart to the lower ECAM screen. **CAB PRESS** is displayed in bold white letters. *What the hell just happened?* The cabin pressure numbers are now red, showing the cabin altitude at eighteen thousand feet.

Miguel pushes a button to silence the steady dinging sound and yells, "Cabin press, cabin altitude, masks on, emergency descent!"

Anna squeezes the red grips on the oxygen mask stowed in her side panel and whips it out. After slipping it over her head, she releases the red grips. With a loud whoosh, the mask seals against her face.

A high-pitched triple beep blares from the forward panel.

"The autopilot is disengaged!" Anna shouts.

The nose pitches forward. The weight of Anna's torso presses against her shoulder harnesses. She grips her side stick to take control of the aircraft.

"Something's not right with the pitch control!" she yells over the rush of oxygen blowing against her face. "It's responding *really slow*. I can't get it to settle down."

The airplane continues to pitch up and down as she fights to maintain the descent with her control stick.

Miguel shoots a glance at Anna struggling with the control. "Just do the best you can; I need to go through this checklist," he says into his mask's microphone.

Miguel reads the checklist off the ECAM screen. Anna's body tenses as it crosses her mind that they might not make it. She's surprised to find herself thinking of Carter. Anna forces the thought aside as she continues to fight with the pitch control.

Miguel announces over the cabin PA system, "Emergency descent, emergency descent!"

Seeing that the cabin altitude is above fourteen thousand feet, he presses the "Mask Man On" button to ensure the oxygen masks have dropped out of the overhead compartments for the passengers.

Anna is sucked against her seat before lifting away from it, feeling weightless as the nose pitches up, then down. "There's definitely something wrong with the controls!"

CHAPTER FORTY-THREE

Makayla

The floor tilts to a steep angle. Makayla stumbles sideways down the aisle and grabs a seat back to stay upright. A sharp crack comes from the rear of the plane, followed by a loud rush of air that sends a knife into her ears. Screams and panicked cries resound through the cabin over the loud rush of air coming from inside the lavatory. Britt rushes into the rear cabin as the standing passengers scramble for their seats to put on their oxygen masks.

Makayla runs up the sloped aisle and hurls her side against the lavatory door.

"Liam!" Makayla screams.

The door budges an inch before someone on the other side shoves it closed. The floor drops, throwing Makayla—and every standing passenger—into the air. Her head hits the ceiling with such force that her whole body rolls upward, smacking her spine. She hits the aisle floor face down. Derek lands beside her as screams of terror erupt throughout the plane.

She claws at the closest armrest and drags herself to her feet. As Derek gets to his knees, blood drips from a gash on his temple. Makayla throws herself against the lav door.

"Help me get it open!" she shrieks at Derek.

Derek stumbles backward after standing. He pushes against the bulkhead wall to regain his balance and yanks her away from the door. "You need to get an oxygen mask on!" he yells.

Britt scurries toward them from the rear, wearing a clear plastic mask over her mouth and nose, carrying two portable oxygen tanks. She stops to pull a dazed passenger to his feet and help him into the nearest seat while he frantically grapples for the dangling oxygen mask. When she reaches them, Derek releases Makayla's arm and takes one of the tanks, pulling a mask identical to Britt's over his face.

Makayla shakes her head. "Not until I get Liam!"

An overhead announcement drowns out Makayla's voice.

"Ladies and gentlemen, this is your captain speaking. We experienced a sudden loss of cabin pressure and are making a rapid descent to a lower altitude. We are in full control of the aircraft, but it appears our left elevator is not functioning properly, so our pitch control may cause it to be more bumpy than normal. Please don your oxygen masks, fasten your seat belts, and comply with the crew's instructions."

Makayla throws herself against the door again. It shakes without opening.

She turns to Derek, yelling over the shrieks and cries of several passengers. "I need your help!"

Derek swipes his hand through the air. "Move aside."

Makayla retreats as Derek charges at the door, slamming his shoulder into it with the full weight of his body. The door flies open. Derek falls forward, disappearing into the lavatory.

Makayla rushes inside behind him, eyes bulging in terror at what she sees. *"Noooo!"*

The floor is wet, causing her to slip before she catches herself. The temperature has dropped significantly, but Makayla barely notices. She stands frozen in horror, unable to move, gaping at Derek's head hanging out of a large hole in the wall above the toilet, exposing a thin layer of plastic and aluminum inside the wall of the plane.

Oh, God. No. Please, no. Let this not be happening. Let them not have taken Liam with them. Suddenly, the plane dips, lifting Derek's feet off the floor. Makayla lunges for his ankle. Rain blows against them through the opening like a sprinkler.

Derek screams something that Makayla can't make out over the roar of wind. He presses his hand against the sawed side of the hole. The plane lurches. His hand slips. He's sucked forward, his head and shoulders disappearing out the side of the plane. His legs slide forward, pulling Makayla with them.

Britt pushes into the bathroom behind her.

"I can't hold him!" Makayla cries.

The plane tilts to the left, and Makayla topples toward the opening. The wind howls in her ears as the force of the suction—and Derek's weight—drags her toward the hole. Britt's hands encircle Makayla's upper arm, but she's not strong enough to hold Makayla back against Derek's weight. Both women's feet slide across the floor, wet from the rain.

"Let go!" Britt screams in her ear as the weight from Derek's ankle jerks Makayla's hands outside of the plane.

The floor shakes beneath them. Britt releases Makayla's arm. Instead, she grabs her waist and tackles Makayla to the ground as Derek's leg slips from her grip.

"Derek!"

She and Britt fall against the lavatory door, pushing it open. Makayla gapes at the hole and the dark sky beyond.

"You couldn't have saved him!" Britt yells. "If you'd held on any longer, you would've gone too."

Makayla grabs a bar on the wall and pulls herself up as the plane plummets in altitude. She ignores Britt screaming at her to stay back and shoves herself off the edge of the sink to stand on the angled floor, climbing over Britt to get to the hole. A six-inch saw blade attached to what looks like an electric shaver protrudes from the waste bin beside the lavatory sink. The shaver is wedged firmly through the waste bin's spring-loaded lid. A cord waves wildly as the winds buffet it, barely connected now to an electrical outlet.

She kneels on the slick toilet seat cover and grips the sheared thin layer of plastic. Loose strands of wet hair from her ponytail blow wildly in front of her face, impeding her vision along with the rain. She starts to lean her head out of the hole and is sucked forward by the force of the wind. Instinctively, she draws her head back inside the plane, leaning back to combat the suction, but doesn't move from the hole.

"Derek!"

Britt's hand clutches her lower leg. Makayla shakes her off, blinking rapidly to see through the gust of rain and cold wind.

"Liam!"

Britt tugs on her sweatshirt. "Stay back!"

The floor tilts, and Makayla falls backward. She twists to shove the flight attendant away. "I have to see if they took him!"

Makayla lunges forward, trying to lean her head out the gaping hole a second time, her eyes filling with tears from the blast of frigid wind. The aircraft vibrates, and Makayla grips the sawed aluminum on the edge of the opening, ignoring the pain in her palm as it cuts into her flesh. There is only the faintest amount of daylight, and she strains to see below. To her lower right, lights flash on the end of the large wing, strobes of red and white reflecting off the heavy rain and patches of clouds that whiz past.

Just imagining Liam going out of the plane, falling to the ground amid these severe elements, makes her dizzy.

Below, all she can see is the glow of scattered lights in the distance among a blur of darkness. No sign of Derek. Or her baby.

"Liam!"

The force of the wind drowns out her voice. She gulps for air. How long would they have until they hit the ground? Would they feel anything? Were they already dead? She imagines the gut-wrenching terror Derek must've felt while free-falling to the ground. At least little Liam wouldn't know what was coming. The thought of him falling from the sky fills her with so much panic it feels like it might kill her.

In the distance, a bolt of lightning lights up the sky. Britt grabs her arms and tugs. Makayla grips the sheared aluminum, resisting her weight. Britt yanks harder. Makayla tightens her grip on the wall opening, the metal slicing into her wrist. Blood seeps from her palm. The plane bounces and her hand slips. She tumbles forward as the nose of the plane lifts. Britt's arms wrap around her middle. The plane tilts to the right, raising the left wing toward the sky.

Makayla's knee slides off the toilet seat cover as she's thrown backward, landing on top of Britt in the open doorway to the lavatory.

Britt keeps her arms cinched around Makayla's waist as they're propelled against the floor from the g-forces of the aircraft's steep climb. The plane drops suddenly before leveling out. Makayla struggles to free herself from the attendant's hold, but her strength seems to have left her body.

"Let go—I have to help him! He's my baby!"

"We don't know that your baby was with them."

Makayla spins to face her. *Yes, we do!*"

Britt doesn't argue. She knows that Makayla's right. "Okay, but you can't help him if you're dead."

The floor spins. Makayla takes quicker breaths to try and steady herself. Britt releases Makayla, and she slowly gets to her feet.

Makayla falls against the opposite lav door, and Britt grips her by both shoulders. "You're going to pass out. Come get an oxygen mask on."

Makayla digs her heels into the floor when Britt tries to lead her up the aisle. "I can't. Not yet."

Britt brings her face toward Makayla's. "There's nothing more we can do now!"

Despite the flight attendant's proximity, Makayla can barely hear her over the roar of wind blowing into the lavatory.

She shoves Britt's shoulders and pivots for the hole in the wall, catching a blurry glimpse of herself in the lavatory mirror. *Maybe they had parachutes. This was obviously very planned out.*

"I just need to look again."

As her vision dims, she sways on the unsteady floor. She blinks repeatedly, falling against the wall. Her heart crashes against her chest. She breathes faster, staring at the blurred hole in the plane.

My baby. Liam. Gone.

Pain stabs at the front of her skull. *Breathe. Just breathe.*

The floor rolls beneath her like a wave. *Please, God, let my baby be alive. Let him—* The lavatory spins. She stumbles forward.

A pair of arms wrap around her waist, dragging Makayla backward until she smacks her head on the opposite lavatory door. The plane nose-dives toward the ground, and Makayla slides to the floor, her head coming to rest between Britt's navy heels. She fights to get up, but her body isn't responding to her commands. Britt crouches over her.

Through her darkened vision she can see the attendant's lips move like she's yelling, but she can't understand what she's saying. She turns her head toward the lavatory. *I have to go back and look again. Help me up!* But the words won't reach her lips.

She reaches toward the accordion lavatory door, which is flapping wildly from the wind howling through the hole in the side of the plane, as everything goes black.

CHAPTER FORTY-FOUR

Anna

Miguel keys his microphone. "New York Center, Pacific Air 7038. We are declaring an emergency. We've lost cabin pressure and are in an emergency descent to ten thousand feet."

"Pacific Air 7038, New York Center. Roger, the Rockdale altimeter is two niner niner three."

Anna pushes against the side stick with greater force. It doesn't feel right. "Something's wrong!" she repeats to Miguel. "I barely have pitch control."

As the nose continues to pitch up and down, she's lifted off her seat.

"Easy!" Miguel yells. He grasps his control stick. "I've got the airplane." He grimaces. "I see what you mean," he says after maneuvering his stick.

Anna points to the lower ECAM flight control screen. "Look, the left elevator isn't moving, but the right one is. It must be jammed for some reason. That's why the autopilot kicked off." She sees the altitude is at 10,500 feet. "Approaching ten thousand," she announces.

Miguel attempts to level the airplane, but dips below and then back up to ten thousand feet.

"This is going to make our approach interesting!" he says while struggling to keep the airplane level. "We're at ten thousand feet. Oxygen masks can come off."

Miguel struggles to maintain altitude. Anna notes the look of intense concentration on his face.

"Look," Miguel says without taking his eyes off the instruments. "I know you are very capable of flying this approach, but given the emergency situation, I would feel better if I flew this one myself."

Anna tries not to show the huge relief she feels on hearing this. "No problem. I think that's a good plan. And I would feel better about it knowing you have a lot more experience than me."

"Not with anything like this!" he exclaims.

The nose pitches up again in the turbulence. Miguel fights to bring the airplane back down to ten thousand feet.

"We should check on how they're doing in the back. But first, tell Approach—"

The flight attendant call buzzer sounds through the cockpit.

Anna pulls off her mask and selects "ATT" on her interphone panel. "This is Anna!"

"Anna! It's Aubrey."

Anna presses her headphones tight against her ears with both hands, straining to hear the flight attendant on the other end through the background noise. Aubrey sounds muffled. It must be her oxygen mask.

"The passengers . . . row fifteen . . . hole in the lavatory. And jumped! Derek . . . he fell. And—" Aubrey's voice cracks.

"Can you repeat that?"

"The passengers in row fifteen sawed a hole in the lavatory wall and jumped out!"

"*What?* How could anyone saw a hole in the side of the plane?"

Miguel shoots her a wary glance. He's still wearing his mask. Anna's not sure if he heard what she said over the flow of oxygen.

"We found a saw blade in the lavatory attached to what was made to look like an electric shaver. But that's not all. Derek fell out while trying to help the mother of the baby get inside. He's . . . he's gone."

Anna's stomach churns as she looks to Miguel with wide eyes. "Did the mother fall out too?"

"No. Just Derek."

Anna moves to cover her mouth with her hand, but it hits her boom microphone instead.

"We've closed the lavatory door, and all other passengers are safe in their seats."

Miguel toggles his transmit switch. "Make an announcement for passengers to prepare for an emergency landing. It's going to be a very rough descent. We'll make an announcement from the cockpit when we can. Also, we've reached a safe altitude, so oxygen masks can come off."

"And Aubrey?" Anna asks before ending the call. "Did you find the baby inside the pet carrier?"

"No. It was empty. We still haven't found him."

Anna hangs up without another word. The probability of the baby being taken out of the hole in the plane with his kidnappers floats in her mind. She thinks back to their altitude when the cabin pressure alarmed. If they were at eighteen thousand feet when they started to cut the hole, they probably jumped around fifteen to sixteen thousand, given how rapidly they descended. Low enough to make the jump without oxygen.

If the kidnappers have parachutes—and survive the jump—they might actually get away with the baby. She envisions the infant, strapped to his abductor's chest as they jumped from the plane. And the poor mother in the back who may never see her child again.

A bolt of lightning flashes, much closer than she's ever seen from inside an aircraft, momentarily illuminating the rain pelting against the windshield. Turbulence continues to toss the plane about.

As Anna switches her intercom panel back to the number one radio, she thinks of Derek, free-falling to his death. It's almost too horrific to imagine. She sees Miguel change the frequency before she can find the words to tell him.

He tosses his mask to the side. "New York Approach, Pacific Air 7038. We are declaring an emergency. We've had a decompression event, and one of our elevators is jammed. We have reduced pitch control, and we'll need a long runway. Requesting a divert to JFK."

"Pacific Air 7038, New York Approach. JFK is reporting a thunderstorm directly overhead with lightning strikes on the field. Aircraft are diverting to their alternates."

"How about Newark?" Miguel asks.

"Newark's wind is two eight zero at twenty-three gusts to thirty-five, and they are circling to land on runway 29."

Miguel looks at the airport diagram for Newark and turns to Anna. "That runway is shorter than LaGuardia's, and I hate that circling approach, so looks like LaGuardia is our best bet now. At this altitude, we don't have the fuel to go anywhere else now."

"I agree," Anna says reluctantly, her mind still filled with the image of Derek falling from the plane.

"Miguel?"

He cocks his head to meet her gaze.

She debates whether to tell him about Derek. They need to focus. But he also needs to know. She gives him a short, horrific version of what happened in the main cabin.

Miguel's eyes double in size. "Shit."

"And the baby?" he asks.

"They haven't found him."

Miguel stares out the windscreen. "Dear God." He closes his eyes, pinching the bridge of his nose with his thumb and forefinger. After a moment, he lowers his hand, exhaling. "Tell New York Approach that we'll be requesting an approach to LaGuardia. With this wind, looks like runway 31 will be the best."

"Okay." She tries her best to erase from her mind the image of Derek—and the baby—falling out of the side of the plane. There are still forty souls on board, and right now, she has to focus. She keys her microphone but takes a steadying breath before she speaks.

When they discovered the elevator was jammed, she recognized the fear in Miguel's eyes. Even with a fully functioning aircraft, it was going to be a tough landing in this storm. Without the left elevator to control the up and down pitch of the aircraft, it's damn near impossible.

Her thoughts are interrupted by the sound of a single chime and an amber **FUEL L+R WING TK LO LVL** warning that pops up on the lower ECAM screen, signaling their fuel supply is running dangerously low.

"Shit!" Miguel exclaims. "We've got to get this plane on the ground, *now*!"

CHAPTER FORTY-FIVE

TINA

After hanging up with Ruiz, Tina returns to her cubicle, leaving Castillo alone in his office to try and contact the flight again. Tina had the call on speaker as Ruiz recounted to her and Castillo what went down at Jack Rossi's condo, and Makayla's suspicion that her son is hidden in a pet carrier on board.

Pratt could've died. Her thoughts shift to Lionel Rothman's daughter, who wasn't so lucky. *What was she doing at Jack Rossi's condo?*

Tina imagines the look on the wealthy financier's face when he receives the news about his daughter's death. All that money wouldn't do anything to ease his heartbreak.

Tina zooms in on the security footage from Anchorage TSA, forcing herself to focus on the task at hand. She leans closer to her screen. Even with the enlarged image, she still can't make out the face of the woman who boarded as Jemma Neilson. So far, both she and her male counterpart have done an expert job of keeping their heads down and away from the camera.

She double-checks the time on her laptop screen. The flight is due to land in less than an hour. They likely won't know who those two passengers are until they arrest them.

She lifts her coffee mug to her lips before realizing it's empty.

"Find anything?"

She turns to Castillo standing behind her.

"No." She sets down her mug. "Nothing we can use for facial recognition anyway. Both passengers in row fifteen managed to keep their faces away from the camera." She glances at her paused screen. "But I'm still looking."

"Long Island PD just called. Jemma Neilson was at home asleep when the officer went to her home. He said it looked like the same woman from her driver's license photo. She was able to produce her license, but the officer thinks it's a fake. She agreed to be fingerprinted to confirm her identity, so the officer's taking her to the nearest precinct. I'm dispatching an agent to meet them there, but the patrol officer said that Jemma Neilson has no idea how her ID was stolen and replaced with a fake. She works at Saint Anthony's Hospital and keeps her purse in a locker during her shifts. Her ID could've been stolen there and replaced with a fake without her knowing. And she doesn't know Chad Wickham, which makes sense since their IDs were likely stolen based on their appearances."

"Have you heard back from the flight?" Tina feels sick at the thought of the baby inside the pet carrier, not making a single sound since he was taken.

"Not yet." He checks his watch. "But hopefully soon. I'll let you keep looking through that footage. Let me know if you find something."

Tina turns back to her desk as Castillo strides toward his office. She restarts the video and watches the woman posing as Jemma Neilson make it all the way through security without giving the camera a glimpse of her face. Tina grabs her empty coffee mug off her desk, rubbing her eyes after the woman disappears from the camera's view.

She checks her phone before standing to make sure she hasn't missed any messages. Felicity hasn't called again or texted, which she takes as a good sign. A lump forms in her throat as she heads for the break room, thinking about Makayla Rossi restrained on that flight—treated like a criminal—after her baby was taken.

Bringing up Lydia Banks's memory disorder just slowed them down, and a pulse of regret moves through her. Would they have found Liam sooner if she hadn't suspected his mother? She swallows the thought. Right now, she needs to stay focused on finding Liam and bringing his kidnappers to justice. There will be time to reflect on her decisions later.

She imagines Makayla, restrained in her seat, not knowing where her baby is. After Felicity called tonight about Isabel's nightmare, Tina felt sick to her stomach, knowing she couldn't comfort her daughter like she wanted to. It was nothing compared to what Makayla Rossi is going through on that flight. To not know where her baby is. Whether he's safe.

She reaches the break room and goes straight for the half-filled pot of coffee. She fills her mug, recalling the news from Pratt about Lionel Rothman's daughter. She thinks of the renowned investor she met earlier tonight and his seeming concern over Liam's kidnapping, not knowing that he would be getting the worst news of his life—his only child's death—later today.

She replaces the pot and heads for the door, taking a careful sip of coffee as she walks. She nearly collides with Castillo, who seems to appear from nowhere when she reaches the doorway. She extends her mug to the side as brown liquid sloshes over the top.

"Oh!"

Castillo throws up his hand, his phone gripped in his palm. "Sorry. I just spoke with Flight 7038's dispatch." His face has gone as white as his hair. "While they were making their descent over the Finger Lakes, the couple from row fifteen sawed a hole in the lavatory wall—and jumped. They might've parachuted, but we don't know for sure."

Tina gapes at him. "*What?* How did they get a power tool like that on board?"

Castillo shrugs, and Tina knows at this point, his guess is as good as hers. And what matters right now is finding Liam.

"The flight had to make an emergency descent due to the loss in pressure, and they've also reported a mechanical failure. A jammed elevator, the dispatcher said."

"What does that mean?"

"They said it's the control on the tail that makes the plane go up and down. So it's no longer flying like a normal aircraft, making it much harder for the pilots to control. The flight has been cleared for an emergency landing at LaGuardia, and they're making a rapid descent." He glances out the window behind her. "The thunderstorm that was supposed to hit north of Chicago is hitting us instead, along with flash flood warnings, but the flight doesn't have enough fuel to divert anywhere else."

Tina follows his gaze. Rain beats against the window from the force of the wind, and she thinks of the passengers still on board the plane. She crosses the room to peer twenty stories down. A few inches of water have already puddled onto the street, sloshing onto the sidewalk with each car speeding past.

A few years ago, a flight coming into Boston lost all hydraulic power and, upon landing, flipped upside down, killing over half of the souls on board. *This is different,* she tells herself. That flight clipped its wing on the runway after losing all hydraulic power, which caused the plane to flip. From the sound of it, Makayla's flight shouldn't have that issue if it's only the up and down they're fighting to control. Thunder roars above their building. Although that Boston flight wasn't flying through a storm. Surrounded by water on three sides, they wouldn't have to miss the runway by much to end up in the East River.

"Call Pratt and let him know. I'm going to have Ruiz meet the flight at LaGuardia with a team to search the aircraft and see if we can lift any fingerprints to ID the two abductors on the flight. Then I've got to organize a search of the entire Finger Lakes area. I'm not very familiar with that part of the state." Castillo glances out the window behind Tina. "At least it's getting light out."

"My parents have a cabin up there, on Seneca Lake. They were both teachers, and we spent every summer there growing up." She spins around. "What about the baby? Was he in the pet carrier?"

Castillo shakes his head, and Tina realizes this is why he looks so grim.

"No. They never found him."

CHAPTER FORTY-SIX

JACK

"Have you ever seen this man before?"

Jack tears his eyes away from Sabrina's body. Pratt motions toward her killer. Jack shakes his head, staring at the man's bony cheekbones and shaved head.

"No. But what about my son?"

Pratt folds his arms across his chest. "My supervisor had to contact the flight, and we'll have to wait to hear back from them. He'll call me if they get any new information."

"They're in here!" A female FBI agent posted at Jack's open doorway steps aside as a team of medics enters his condo.

A tall medic in front rushes in, carrying a large bag while the two behind him push a stretcher toward Sabrina's body. Pratt approaches the one carrying the bag.

"Both victims are pulseless and unresponsive. The woman was shot first. Looks to be a single shot to the head." Pratt points to the man lying a few feet away. "We returned fire on the shooter. He's got two bullet holes to the chest."

The medic kneels beside Sabrina, unzipping his bag. "How long ago was she shot?"

Pratt looks at Jack.

"Um." Jack's eyes linger on Sabrina's blood on the floor. "I'm not sure." Time seems to have slowed down ever since the FBI showed up at his door. "About thirty minutes. I think."

Another medic starts compressions, while the tall one places leads on her chest connected to a cardiac monitor. Jack looks away as Sabrina's lifeless body jerks with each pulse of electricity.

"There's a second medic unit en route," one of them says to Pratt.

"Okay, good." Pratt's phone rings in his hand. "This is Pratt."

While the medic spouts off orders to the other two working on Sabrina, Jack goes still, his senses on full alert as he strains to hear what's being said on the other end of the call.

"She's still pulseless," the medic announces.

Behind Pratt, a medic pauses compressions for the other two to roll Sabrina onto a board before lifting her onto the stretcher.

"They *what*?" A look of surprise washes over Pratt's face.

Jack goes still. "What is it? Have they found him?"

Pratt turns away, plugging his other ear with his finger. Jack's heart thumps against his ribs. He stares at the back of Pratt's head as the medics rush Sabrina out of his condo on the stretcher. A second medic team rushes inside, moving in between Jack and Pratt to work on Sabrina's killer.

Jack steps to the side to keep Pratt in his view. Finally, Pratt lowers his phone. When the agent turns around, Jack studies his face.

"It appears your wife was right about your son being hidden in the pet carrier aboard the flight."

"Did they find him?"

"The carrier was empty. A passenger found a stuffed animal dog nearby." Pratt's chest lifts with a deep inhale. "The flight is coming in for an emergency landing at LaGuardia as we speak."

"So, Liam's alive?"

Jack's heart stills as he registers the look of shock on the agent's face.

"The couple who took him sawed a hole in the side of the aircraft in one of the lavatories and jumped out while the plane was making its descent south of Rochester. We're sending out a team to search the area."

Jack feels the floor sway beneath his bare feet. Pratt clears his throat while Jack's tightens.

"We believe they took your son with them."

CHAPTER FORTY-SEVEN

Makayla

At the sound of a woman's shriek somewhere behind her, Makayla's eyes snap open. The plane abruptly tilts forward at a steep decline. Makayla's lifted off her seat and grips her armrests, her hips pulled taut against her seat belt. Her forehead comes within an inch of the locked tray table rattling against the seat back in front of her. Cold air blows against her mouth and nose through the yellow mask strapped to her face. The scattered heads in the surrounding seats sway simultaneously with the aircraft as it rocks in jerky motions from side to side.

She struggles to remember how she got here. She's in the last row of the main cabin, on the side of the plane opposite her seat. The gray-haired man seated in front of her looks familiar, and she realizes he's the passenger who was reading on a tablet right after Liam went missing. Then she remembers collapsing outside the lavatory, and her horrific reality comes flooding back.

Someone must've moved her here. Out the window, all she can see is the wing. A loud roar still emits from the hole in the aircraft behind her. Her heart aches. *Liam.*

"Flight attendants, prepare the cabin for emergency landing."

To her right, movement catches her eye. She turns to see Rose removing her oxygen mask with a trembling hand before shakily getting to her feet. The twentysomething flight attendant appears at the front of the cabin, running one hand along the overhead compartments, with the other holding a portable oxygen bottle attached to a clear mask strapped over her mouth and nose. She sees Rose stumble into the aisle and hurries toward her. Makayla watches her grab Rose by the shoulders and coax her back into her seat, pulling the woman's oxygen mask over her face and clipping Rose into her seat belt.

Beyond them is Jemma and Chad's empty row. Makayla's chest tightens. The nose lifts, throwing Makayla against her seat. Multiple screams fill the cabin as the g-forces of their climb suction her against her seat cushion.

"Why are we climbing?" someone yells.

As the nose comes down, the plane tips to the left. The young flight attendant stumbles sideways, her head cracking against an overhead bin before she disappears into the rear cabin. Makayla removes her seat belt and slides toward the window that's blurry with rain. She leans forward, spotting the Hudson River up ahead. Even from their altitude, she can make out the divots on the surface from the downpour.

At the thought of Liam going out the hole in the side of the plane with his abductors, bile rises to the back of her throat. It's so painful she can hardly allow herself to accept it. *God, please let Liam be alive.* They cross the Hudson, and she studies the buildings below as they fly low over Harlem. *Where is he now?*

"Ladies and gentlemen." A shaky flight attendant's voice blares over the loudspeaker, making Makayla jump. "The captain has advised that we will be making an emergency landing at LaGuardia Airport. The instructions I am about to give you are extremely important, so I ask that you pay close attention." The flight attendant speaks fast, and there's no masking the tremor in her voice. "There are eight emergency exits on this aircraft, two door exits in the front, four in the middle section, and two in the rear. These exits are equipped with slides, which can be used as rafts."

The floor drops. As she's lifted off the seat, Makayla feels weightless. She flails her arms for something to grab on to before she's slammed against the seat cushion. Screams erupt all around her, muffling the next few words of the attendant's announcement.

"Take a moment now to locate your closest exit. Note that the closest exit may be behind you. Immediately prior to landing, the captain will announce 'brace, brace, brace' over the intercom. At that time, place your arms and head against the seat back in front of you. If there is not a seat back directly in front of you, lean as far forward as possible, with your head straight down between your legs, and tightly grasp your legs or ankles. Remain in this position until the aircraft comes to a complete stop or until directed by your flight attendants. At this time remove from your pockets your glasses, earrings, piercings, and anything sharp, such as pens or pencils."

Makayla looks away from the window and lifts her head toward the compartment above Jemma's seat. No one searched the compartment after they jumped out of the plane. There's a chance Liam could be up there.

"And you may now remove your oxygen masks, as we have descended to a safe altitude and oxygen is no longer required," the flight attendant adds.

Makayla pulls off her mask and gets up. Rose gapes at her with wide eyes as she staggers through the middle row in front of her. Makayla reaches for the storage bin's lever when a cold hand closes around her forearm. Britt lowers Makayla's arm.

"Sit down!" she yells.

Makayla twists out of her grip. "I have to check! Liam could be in there!"

Britt slaps her palm against the compartment. "We already checked. He's not in there! And there's no time!"

"I need to make sure!" She lifts the lever and tugs, but Britt pushes the bin closed.

Makayla suddenly realizes something. She grips Britt by both shoulders. "You checked their bags! Were there parachutes inside?"

Britt glances at the overhead bin. "No." She looks pensive when she meets Makayla's eyes. "Wait. They each had a backpack inside their carry-ons. They told me they'd been backpacking outside of Anchorage. I didn't have any reason not to believe them. At that point, I was only looking for a baby . . ." Her voice trails off as she eyes their empty row.

Makayla brings a hand to her forehead. "There must have been parachutes! Help me check!"

When Makayla reaches for the compartment, the nose lifts, and the plane turns. She falls into Jemma's empty seat. When she tries to get up, Britt extends her arm.

"Stay seated!" Britt reaches across her waist and buckles her seat belt.

"I have to know!" Makayla shouts.

"You can check as soon as we land. Get in the brace position." She lowers her head toward Makayla's. "Do *not* get up."

The front of the plane plunges toward the ground. Makayla shoots forward, her forehead hitting the tray table in front of her. Britt stumbles backward down the aisle, grabbing a seat back on either side. Makayla rubs her forehead.

Britt grips the tops of the aisle seats as she climbs toward the rear. The front of the plane continues to plunge. Makayla unbuckles her seat belt and tries to get up. The plane bounces, pulling Makayla against her seat. The nose suddenly dips, and Makayla is thrown against the seat back in front of her. Several passengers cry out.

Makayla pushes herself to her feet and steps into the aisle. When she reaches for the overhead bin, the floor drops. Her back hits the floor of the aisle with a thud, knocking the air from her lungs. Makayla fights against gravity to sit up and crawl back to her seat, barely managing to buckle her seat belt before the angle of the floor steepens. She begrudgingly leans her head and arms against the seat in front of her.

While in the brace position, Makayla cranes her neck to peer beneath the seats. The empty pet carrier and stuffed dog are tucked under one of them. Makayla watches them slide forward on the sloped floor. Aside from that, the floor is bare.

She thinks of the compartment above her head, replaying Britt's words. *He's not in there.* She closes her eyes, grappling with the probability that Britt is right.

CHAPTER
FORTY-EIGHT

ANNA

"You never told me what you're naming your daughter," Anna says.

It's no time for small talk, and any non-flight-related talk below ten thousand feet goes against FAA regulations—especially in a situation like this—but if she doesn't talk about something normal, she's afraid she'll throw up. As they descend through thick, gray clouds and the blur of heavy rain, the visibility outside is next to nothing, but after taking off her full-face mask, she's glad to have her peripheral vision back.

"Scarlet," Miguel finally says.

"That's beautiful."

As they descend beneath the lowest patch of clouds, the lights of the Manhattan skyline come into view. The city is a gray blur beneath the downpour. She spots a dark patch where there are no lights and makes out the Hudson River.

"Pacific Air 7038, how long of a final do you need at LaGuardia?" the New York Approach controller asks.

A gust of wind hits the airplane, raising the nose. Miguel pushes forward on his side stick. Anna glances at Miguel's knuckles turning white as he tightens his grip on the stick once he gets the airplane back on the assigned altitude.

"Tell him twenty miles," Miguel says to her through the interphone.

"Altitude!" Anna exclaims, seeing the altimeter dip three hundred feet below their assigned altitude of three thousand feet.

"I'm trying!" A bead of sweat drips along Miguel's jaw beneath his headphones as the nose of the airplane slowly responds to his control inputs.

Anna keys her microphone. "Pacific Air 7038, we're requesting a twenty-mile final."

"Pacific Air 7038, roger. Turn left heading one five zero, I'll bring you in about ten miles outside of CHALN."

"Left, heading one five zero," Anna replies.

The airplane bounces in the turbulence as they make the gentle left-hand turn around the lighted skyscrapers of Manhattan Island. Anna cross-checks their altitude. Three thousand feet. *Good.*

Wondering how Miguel is possibly going to be able to keep the airplane under control in this wind makes her pulse race. The pitch of the airplane seems to be totally at the mercy of the storm, which gives her no confidence. She strains to see LaGuardia through the wet, gray blur from the storm. A ripple of fear runs down her spine.

She feels the sudden urge to call Carter, aware of her phone in her pocket. It strikes her that last month, he had a rare three days off in a row. He suggested they go to their favorite pizza place in Hell's Kitchen. Had she planned for it, they could've been off together. Instead, she traded for a trip to meet Joel in San Fransisco.

What the hell was I thinking? She's assaulted by the thought of all that she'd lose if she goes through with her affair. It strikes her how little she even knows Joel.

Carter isn't the only one to blame for their drift apart. She longs to hear his voice—just in case—but there's no time. It's going to take their total focus to attempt a safe landing.

"I was planning to have an affair," she blurts into her mouthpiece. "Today. I was going to meet with another pilot after we landed while my husband is at work."

Miguel's eyes meet hers for a moment before he refocuses on the control panel.

"Now all I can think about is my husband. There are things I wish I could tell him." Her voice cracks.

He turns to Anna. There's a hyperfocused intensity in his eyes now, but no trace of the fear she saw in them earlier.

"You can tell him in person after we land," he says, then adds, "and I'm going to the hospital to see my daughter be born."

"Pacific Air 7038, New York Approach. You're ten miles from CHALN. Turn left to zero two zero. Maintain two thousand until established, cleared for the RNAV Zulu 31 Approach. You can contact LaGuardia Tower now on one one eight decimal seven."

"Roger," Anna responds. "Left heading zero two zero, two thousand until established, switching to tower now. Pacific Air 7038."

She flips the switch to the tower frequency she'd already placed in the standby position of the radio. "LaGuardia Tower, Pacific Air 7038 is with you, emergency aircraft; please have the equipment standing by."

"Pacific Air 7038, LaGuardia Tower, roger your emergency. The equipment is standing by. The wind is two niner zero, variable three three zero, at twenty-five gusts to thirty-two. You are cleared to land runway 31."

"Cleared to land runway 31, Pacific Air 7038," Anna acknowledges.

She's barely able to make out the runway lights at LaGuardia as Miguel continues to struggle with the controls. He reaches up and switches the windshield wipers to slow and holds the "Rain Repellant" button.

"Ah, that's much better," he announces as the runway becomes clearly visible ahead.

Anna decides to do the same. "Yes, much better. Runway in sight."

"Coming up on CHALN. Landing gear down. Landing checklist," Miguel commands through the interphone.

Anna reaches forward as another gust of wind lifts the nose of the airplane, making it difficult for her to grasp the landing gear lever. After a short struggle, she places it in the down position and feels a slight bump when the nose gear drops into position.

"Landing checklist," Anna repeats as she reads off from the list. "Cabin crew—advised. Auto Throttle—off. Autobrake—medium set. ECAM MEMO—landing, no blue. Signs—on. Cabin—ready. Landing gear—down. Final flaps. Standing by final flaps."

"Flaps full," Miguel says.

Anna places the flap lever to the full position and continues with the checklist. "Flaps—landing. Speed brake—armed. Landing checklist complete."

Miguel strains to maintain the glide path, constantly moving the thrust levers forward and back to try to maintain the approach airspeed. Their speed drops below the target speed.

"Airspeed!" Anna yells.

Miguel slides the thrust levers forward. "Correcting!"

The engines howl as they speed up in response. The airplane pitches in wild movements. Anna's heart races with adrenaline amid the rush of the wild approach. Miguel fights to maintain the glide path to the runway.

"Five hundred," the loudspeaker announces when they pass below five hundred feet above the runway.

Rain pounds against the windscreen, blurring their visibility again.

"Turn my wipers to fast!" Miguel yells.

Anna reaches over and switches his wiper setting. The whir of the wipers is distracting, and their visibility barely improves. Beyond the windscreen, the runway lights are still a bright blur.

The nose pitches up and then down as Miguel struggles not to overcontrol.

"One hundred," the computer voice announces as the nose drops. "Sink rate, sink rate!" blares over the speaker.

Anna notes the vertical speed indicator. "Sinking eight hundred, sinking nine hundred!"

Miguel gives a sharp pull on his side stick, slowing their rate of descent—but not enough.

CHAPTER FORTY-NINE

MAKAYLA

With her head against the tray table, Makayla's thoughts remain focused on the compartment above her seat. If those backpacks *were* parachutes, it would mean there's a chance Liam is still alive. But the kidnappers would've needed something to strap Liam onto one of their chests.

The nose plummets. A scream escapes her own lips as the weight of her body is propelled against the seat back in front of her. Makayla's seat belt digs into her stomach as she stares at her sneakers on the floor angled beneath her at nearly forty-five degrees. As she looks down at her shoes, Jemma's words from earlier pop into her head. *This will all get sorted out.*

Hadn't Cori used that same phrase in one of her texts? She strains to remember as her head is forced against the locked tray table.

"We're gonna die!" a man shouts.

This is it, Makayla thinks. *We're not going to make it. And I'll die without knowing for sure what happened to Liam.*

She holds her breath, envisioning Jack getting the news of their downed plane. Losing his infant son and wife on the same day. She exhales, closing her eyes.

She hears Rose vomit in the middle aisle. The nose lifts, and the scattered passengers around her grow eerily quiet.

Makayla braves a glance out her window. They're flying low over the East River. Even with the nose lifting, they appear headed straight for the dark water. Through the heavy rain and early-morning light, she can make out the large whitecaps on the river and the headlights from cars on the Rikers Island Bridge.

The nose keeps lifting, so much so that when they soar over the break wall at the edge of the runway, they angle slightly up. Makayla's eyes widen when they cross over the runway. *Why aren't we coming down?*

A man's voice blares from the PA speakers. "Brace, brace, brace!"

Makayla tilts forward, pressing her forehead against the seat back seconds before the nose drops. They slam against the ground, impacting with a metallic groan from the belly of the aircraft, along with a high-pitched screech and several screams throughout the cabin. The aircraft bounces back into the air.

Makayla's forehead smacks the hard plastic of the tray table as several overhead bins fly open. Luggage flies around the cabin as the plane lifts into the air. They come down hard a second time, the landing gear slamming against the runway.

Makayla's head smacks the tray again. A passenger swears in the middle row while someone cries out in the rear cabin. But all Makayla can think about is Liam as she leans into the aisle from the force of the plane's turn. Her gaze darts out her window. They slide sideways, crossing over bright lights on the side of the runway, speeding onto puddled grass, heading straight for the whitecapped East River.

CHAPTER FIFTY

Anna

When the landing gear slams against the waterlogged runway a second time, Anna is jolted against her shoulder harnesses, although this impact is not as hard as the first. The aircraft stays on the ground, but the tires skim across the surface of the wet tarmac as the anti-skid braking system begins cycling continuously. The engines roar when Miguel pulls the reverse thrust levers back to maximum thrust.

A strong gust of wind swings the nose to the left. Anna is jerked to the right, her harness cutting into her neck as the back of the plane starts to fishtail. She knows Miguel must be pushing hard on the right rudder, but the nose continues to swing left. Anna places her hand on the glareshield to brace herself as the airplane slides sideways. Miguel reduces the reverse thrust on the left engine, she realizes, as a last resort. Sliding sideways at over one hundred miles an hour, Anna fears they will tip over.

"I can't hold it!" Miguel yells as the nose swings toward the grass separating them from the passenger terminal. "Help me with more right rudder!"

Anna presses hard with her foot on the right rudder, trying to help steer the plane back toward the runway. But the nose keeps turning left. A thumping fills the cockpit as the nose gear strikes the runway edge lights.

Her eyes widen with panic as the nose continues its trajectory. Now they're sliding backward at over eighty miles an hour—the tail of the airplane headed directly for the East River. Miguel must realize the reverse thrust is speeding the airplane toward the river, and he pushes the reverse thrust levers full forward.

Anna sends a panicked glance at Miguel, worried that if he keeps applying pressure to the brakes, the airplane will tip onto its tail, and they'll lose control of the plane.

"Ease up on the brakes!" she yells, and he lets up the pressure on his brake pedals.

At the same time, he pushes the thrust levers full forward to their stowed position. The engines roar as they accelerate to full power, but the airplane starts to slow.

Heart pounding, Anna stares out the windscreen. The runway lights are flashing past more slowly.

"We're slowing down!"

The airplane comes to a halt with the tail hanging precariously over the edge of the break wall, but the main wheels remain on the concrete at the end of the runway. Miguel draws the thrust levers back to idle. The roar of the engines quiets as he presses his feet against the brake pedals. They both sit in silence for a few seconds, assessing their status.

"You okay?" Miguel asks.

Anna nods, feeling a bead of sweat trickle down the side of her neck. "I'm good."

"Let's hope the rest of the passengers are too. It was an honor to fly with you, Anna. I was happy to have such competent help tonight in the flight deck."

"Thank you." She gives him an exhausted smile. "You too."

"You're going to make one hell of a captain."

She flashes him a grin. "If I don't quit after today."

"After today, you'll be able to handle anything." Miguel grabs the PA microphone from the rear pedestal. "Remain seated, remain seated, remain seated!"

He lowers the microphone and clears his throat before continuing his announcement. Anna's chest constricts as she thinks of Derek falling out of the side of the plane while trying to help the mother of the missing baby. She guesses Miguel is thinking of him too. Derek couldn't have been more than thirty-five.

Miguel wipes the side of his cheek. "I can't believe we lost one of our own tonight."

"Me neither." She's never lost anyone on a flight before, let alone a crew member. At least Derek didn't suffer, she thinks; he would've been killed instantly upon impact. Still, she shudders to imagine his free fall to the ground. It would've been terrifying.

Her thoughts shift to the missing infant as Miguel finally lifts the intercom toward his mouth. She looks out her side window at the small waves forming on the East River in the first light of morning.

Landing without the baby, and knowing he'd been on the plane this whole time, she can't help but feel that they've failed.

CHAPTER FIFTY-ONE

MAKAYLA

Heart thumping and forehead throbbing, Makayla sits straight to see that beneath her window is the start of the runway, and the water's edge is not far behind them. She looks around. Rose looks to be unconscious, her head hanging slack, with her oxygen mask tangled in her mess of white hair. Makayla searches for signs of life until she spots a reassuring rise and fall of her chest.

She scans the rest of the passengers in the cabin, their faces in various states of shock and disarray.

"Ladies and gentlemen, this is your captain speaking," Miguel breathes into the intercom. "We've managed to come to a stop at the end of the runway but will require a tow to pull us to our gate. In a few moments, we are going to have our ground crews come out and inspect the airplane. If all is normal, they will tow us to the gate. I ask that you all remain seated, and we should have you to the gate in the next ten minutes or so. At the gate there will be some law enforcement officials coming on board to take care of another matter. All passengers must comply with their instructions. We appreciate your cooperation."

Makayla unbuckles and stands up. She kneels beside the roller bag that fell into the aisle from the overhead compartment above her and unzips the sides. It's obvious as soon as she opens it that Liam isn't inside.

It's only half-full. A red dog leash lies on top of a few pairs of clothes, all of which look brand new. No backpack. *Thank God.* Makayla empties the bag and tosses the clothing items onto a seat. *He's not here,* she thinks, echoing Britt's words from earlier.

Makayla is rocked backward as the plane begins to move. She stands and withdraws a duffel bag that managed to stay in the opened compartment. She can tell right away that it's too light to contain Liam. She sets it on Jemma's seat and tears the zipper open. It's mostly empty, aside from some men's clothes. She stares inside the bag, her relief that the parachutes Britt may have seen earlier are missing quickly replaced by a numb sense of helplessness. Even if Liam *was* secured to one of the parachuters, it doesn't mean they survived.

"FBI!" she hears a woman call out from the opened exit door at the front of her cabin. "We need everyone to remain in their seats while we search the aircraft!"

Britt steps aside for the dark-haired woman holding a gun to enter the aircraft. A white-haired man enters behind her, wearing a matching FBI jacket. A uniformed officer who Makayla guesses is airport police appears next. He stands guard at the exit door as two uniformed medics climb on board. The woman's eyes sweep the cabin until they land on Makayla, who's the only one standing.

Makayla points to Rose. "This woman's unconscious. She needs medical attention!"

The FBI agent strides toward her, gun outstretched. "Ma'am, I need you to put your hands in the air and sit down."

A couple seated in the middle row turn toward Makayla. So does Pink Headphones, looking dazed, with a bright red gash on her cheek.

Makayla does as the agent says, lowering herself into Jemma's seat.

"I'm his mother!" Makayla says as the woman approaches. "I'm just looking for my son." She gestures to the seat beside her. "Making sure he wasn't inside that bag."

A second man, younger than the first and also wearing an FBI jacket, strides toward them from the front of the aircraft. He sweeps each row with his gun outstretched toward the floor as the two medics rush to Rose's row.

The FBI woman eyes the opened bag. "I'm Agent Ruiz. We're here to help find him." She points to the bag. "You leave this to us. This plane is a crime scene, and you're tampering with what could be evidence."

"I need every overhead compartment opened that isn't already," the white-haired FBI agent calls out to Britt. "Where's the hole they escaped out of?"

Makayla watches Britt lead him toward the lavatory before turning to Agent Ruiz.

"Have you found the kidnappers?" Makayla asks. "Did they have parachutes?"

The woman's facial expression softens. "We don't know yet."

Makayla collapses against the back of her seat, vaguely aware of the tears streaming down her face.

The agent glances above Makayla's head. "This isn't your seat."

"No. I moved here before we landed. I was looking for Liam. This is where his kidnappers were sitting."

A loud beep sounds behind Makayla's seat and she turns to see the white-haired agent holding a radio to his mouth.

"The aircraft is secure. Tell CSI it's safe for them to come aboard."

Another beep sounds before a voice crackles through the radio. "Got it."

"Come see what we found in the lavatory," he says to Ruiz.

"Ladies and gentlemen, this is your captain speaking. We've just been instructed by the FBI that when you deplane, you must leave all of your belongings on the aircraft."

Makayla watches Ruiz follow after the white-haired agent.

The captain continues, "And you will be escorted by airport police to a secure waiting area where you will be required to remain while the FBI searches the aircraft. In addition to the emergency crews, Pacific Air has people standing by inside the terminal to give you any assistance you may need."

Makayla stares at the agents in the doorway of the lavatory as she stands and follows the other passengers toward the exits. She spots Liam's diaper bag on the floor of an empty middle row, then crosses the aisle to reach into the side pouch, glad to find her phone still tucked inside. Her breath sticks in her throat when her eyes catch the empty bassinet and Liam's blanket lying on her seat.

The reality of Liam going out the side of the plane with his abductors nearly causes her knees to buckle.

CHAPTER FIFTY-TWO

Tina

Castillo is on the phone when Tina reaches his office.

"Okay, thanks." He lowers his phone and pushes his chair back.

Tina steps inside the small room, holding her opened laptop in front of her chest, her pulse racing. "I think I've found the identity of the male passenger traveling as Chad Wickham."

Castillo remains seated as Tina strides toward him and sets her laptop on his desk.

"I ran the deceased intruder at Rossi's home through our database using the driver's license Pratt found on him and learned that he spent the last four years at Otisville Federal for internet crime. He was released earlier this year." She crosses her arms. "So I went through every Otisville prisoner released this year and compared their photos to Chad Wickham's driver's license." She nods toward her laptop screen. "And I found him. Conner Abrams. He was let out from his three-year sentence for third-degree robbery last March and could easily pass for Chad Wickham. He served in the navy for six years, from 2005 to 2011, and was a Navy SEAL for the last four. Both men are five eleven, have brown eyes, brown hair, and very similar facial features." She pivots to face Castillo. "I think this is who we're looking for."

"Good work. Send me his photo, and I'll get it out to our search team. Get me his address, too, and I'll send a patrol car to make sure he's not home." He stands from his chair. "The search team up north just found the female passenger's body suspended in a tree near Otisco Lake. She had a parachute but sustained severe head injuries from her fall and was impaled by a tree limb through her broken neck. They cut her down and declared her dead at the scene."

She cringes, envisioning the woman's mangled body dangling from the tree. She swallows, wondering how her male conspirator fared—and baby Liam.

Conner Abrams's Navy SEAL training would make him an expert parachuter. If he has Liam, and he kept hold of him during the jump, there's a chance the boy is alive.

Tina covers her mouth with her hand. "Did they find the male passenger? Or the baby?" She braces herself for the answer to her second question, unsure if she can stomach the answer.

Castillo presses his lips into a hard line. "No. Not yet. Ruiz called before I got the news about the female parachuter. They've done a preliminary search of the aircraft, and there's no sign of the missing infant." He points a finger toward her. "You know the Finger Lakes area well from your time there as a kid?"

Tina nods. "Very well."

He reaches for the bulletproof vest hanging on the wall beside his desk and dons it over his head. "Our Black Hawk is taking a SWAT team up north to join the search. The pilot wasn't too excited to be flying in this weather, but the visibility has improved enough to go. It's a good thing our chopper was already parked on the roof, because the pilot said it will be much easier to take off than it would have been to land. I'm going with them. I want you to come too."

"What?" *Has he forgotten I work behind a desk?* Just the thought of flying through a storm in a Black Hawk with a SWAT team makes her heart race. "I don't know that I'm—"

"I need someone with us who's familiar with the area." He strides past her. "Send me that info, and I'll find you a bulletproof vest. Then meet me on the roof. We're leaving in five."

Speechless, Tina lifts her laptop and hurries back to her cubicle.

The floor is now brightly lit and bustling with activity: phones, people talking, fax machine beeps, and the chatter of keyboards as she passes several colleagues on her way to her desk. But all she can hear is her pulse pounding in her ears.

When she reaches her desk, she sets down her laptop and sends Conner Abrams's information to Castillo without sitting down.

"Here you go."

She turns to Castillo standing behind her, holding out a bullet-proof vest.

"It's just a precaution," he adds, seeing the fear in her eyes.

She pulls it on, surprised by how heavy it is.

"Let's go." Castillo is already heading for the elevators.

Tina hurries after him, her pulse spiking at the rain pelting against the windows.

"You been on a chopper before?" he asks.

"Never."

"Today might be a bit of a rough ride."

When they reach the top floor, she hears the whir of the Black Hawk's blades and the drone of its two jet engines. During their elevator ride, Castillo explained they'd be using a thermal camera attached to the helicopter to search the forested area surrounding the Finger Lakes. As she follows Castillo onto the roof, she's hit with a rush of wind, unsure if the gust is from the storm or the chopper.

Adrenaline courses through her as she climbs inside the long, black helicopter and takes a seat beside Castillo, facing the tail. Across from them, a SWAT member hands them each a black-and-mint green headset.

"Put these on!" he yells.

Tina's hand trembles as she dons the headset. The door beside her slides closed, and they lift away from the building. When the tail elevates into the air, she's forced against the back of her seat and grips Castillo's arm.

He turns, looking startled, and she releases her grip.

"Sorry," she says into her mouthpiece. But her voice is drowned out by the rhythmic thump of the blades spinning overhead.

CHAPTER FIFTY-THREE

MAKAYLA

Makayla scrolls through her seemingly endless text conversations with Cori. An airport police officer stands guard at the door to the large room where Makayla and the rest of the passengers have been sequestered for the last hour. Makayla's gaze darts to a middle-aged man who gets up to stretch.

Every time she spots movement out of the corner of her eye, she looks up—unable to keep herself from clinging to the false hope of one of the FBI rushing in carrying Liam. The image returns, as if on a loop, even though she knows in the pit of her stomach that Liam went out the sawed opening of the plane along with his abductors.

Her leg jiggles nervously as she returns her attention to her phone. She texted Cori after getting off the plane but still hasn't gotten a reply. Throughout their exchanges, Cori has always responded right away. Her sudden silence is damning.

She stops scrolling, seeing a text Cori sent three weeks ago. I can't wait to catch up when I get home from the Hamptons! What are the dates of your Alaska trip again?

Makayla scrolls down to Cori's reply after Makayla gave her the dates. **Perfect! I'll be back on the 6th. Is your flight nonstop? What time do you get in on the 7th?**

Makayla lowers her phone, the taste of betrayal fresh on her tongue. She told Cori all about this trip, not long after they "met." Since then, Cori had asked her about the trip a few times, probably needing to make sure her trip was still on as planned. Naively, Makayla gave Cori all the details. Cori had been playing her all along.

Pacific Air is the only airline that offers a nonstop flight from LaGuardia to Anchorage. They started doing the route earlier this year when Makayla booked her ticket. There is only one flight a day, so Cori would've known her flight number from what Makayla told her.

Her phone rings in her hand, startling her. It's Jack. She called him on the way to the waiting area, but he hadn't answered. She wonders if he knows about Liam's abductors jumping out the side of the plane.

"Makayla? Have you landed?"

"Yes." She swallows. "But Jack, there's something I need to tell you."

"I know about the kidnappers jumping out of the plane."

She leans forward, relieved she doesn't have to say those words out loud. She brings a hand to her temple. "Have you heard anything more from the FBI? Have they found him?"

"Not yet. But the FBI is here. A man broke into our condo. I'm not sure when, but he was already inside when I got woken by the FBI earlier. He held me at gunpoint and threatened to kill Liam if I didn't transfer money from my biggest client accounts. You were right. Liam was taken for a ransom because of my job."

Makayla drops her hand to her mouth.

"I did everything he asked." Jack breathes into the phone. "But the FBI barged in and shot him before I could finish the last transfer." His voice cracks. "If I'd had a little more time . . ."

Makayla lets his words sink in. "It's not your fault, Jack."

"Sabrina's dead."

"What?"

"The guy that broke in, he shot her in the head."

Makayla sits up straight. "What was Sabrina doing in our condo? And in the middle of the night?"

A few heads turn in her direction as she waits for Jack to respond, knowing there could be only one reason Sabrina was at her home in the middle of the night.

A barrage of questions swirl in her mind. How long had it been going on? Had there been something between them the whole time they'd been married? And how could she be so stupid not to have suspected something sooner?

"You were having an affair." More heads swivel toward her. Makayla ignores them, her gaze dropping to the floor after finally verbalizing the thing that's been haunting her for months.

"No! Of course not. The FBI interviewed Lionel after coming to see me. He told Sabrina, and she called me from our lobby, wanting to come up after hearing the news. I didn't realize," he breathes into the phone, "that a man with a gun was already in our condo."

Makayla watches a plane take off out the window to her left as she absorbs what Jack said.

"Are they sure Liam went out of the plane with his kidnappers?" Jack asks.

Makayla's lower lip quivers, wishing she could say no. "Yes."

The door to the waiting area opens. Agent Ruiz marches inside, heading straight for Makayla.

"I have to go. I'll call you back," she says to Jack, lowering her phone.

Ruiz stops a foot in front of her. "The female kidnapper's body has been found suspended in a tree near one of the Finger Lakes. She was wearing a parachute, but she didn't survive."

Makayla stands, flooded with relief and terror at the same time. "What about Liam? Did they find him?"

Ruiz shakes her head. "Not yet. But we're still looking. And we have a good idea of the area where he should be now."

Makayla squeezes her phone in her palm.

"I'd like you to come back to our field office with me to answer some questions while we wait to hear more from the search. CSI is still processing the plane, but there's no sign of Liam still being on board."

Makayla nods and follows the agent out of the room and into the terminal.

She keeps stride with Agent Ruiz as they move through the busy terminal, her relief over the parachute dissipating with each step. *If Jemma didn't survive, what were the odds that Liam did?*

CHAPTER FIFTY-FOUR

ANNA

After being towed to their gate and briefly questioned by the FBI, Anna and Miguel step off the shuttle bus that dropped them at the crew parking lot, pulling their roller bags side by side. After they got to their gate, maintenance informed them of the cause for their jammed elevator: a piece of aluminum from the plane's outer skin, after being cut free from the plane, had flown back and jammed between the elevator and fuselage, immobilizing it.

They didn't say much afterward as they moved through the terminal and rode the employee bus. Derek's death, and not knowing what happened to the baby on board, has left them both feeling somber.

"I hate leaving not knowing what happened to the baby," Miguel says as they cross the street, echoing her own thoughts.

"I know. Me too." She can only imagine what his mother is feeling right now.

She turns to Miguel, suddenly remembering. "Has your daughter been born yet?"

"Not yet." He cracks a slight smile. "I think I'm going to make it."

"That's great."

When they reach the parking lot, Miguel looks over his shoulder at her before going in the direction of his car, the collar of his trench coat pulled up around his ears. "I know it's none of my business, but I think you should tell your husband what you were wanting to tell him before we landed. If not, you might regret it.

"Bye, Anna," he adds, casting her a final smile before speed walking away.

"Goodbye," Anna calls. She watches him duck out of the rain and into his car, grateful to have been paired with such a capable pilot on their flight from hell.

She turns in the opposite direction, toward her car, and pulls out her phone. She has a missed call from Joel along with a text. She reads his message as she walks. Knowing what she must do fills her with a sense of dread.

> Are you okay? I woke up and saw the news about your flight. I'm so glad you landed safely! I can't wait to see you if you're still up for coming to my hotel. Call me when you get this.

She waits until she gets to her car to respond. Leaning against her sedan, she flips the hood of her raincoat over her head, debating what to say. What Miguel said at the start of the flight replays in her mind. *Hard to see what's right in front of you sometimes.* After a moment, she types out a reply.

> I'm okay, thank you. But I can't come see you. I'm married and I can't do this. I'm sorry.

After sending the text, she loads her roller bag into her trunk. Her phone rings in her blazer pocket. She reaches for it, expecting it to be Joel. But it's Carter.

"Hey."

"Hey," he says. "I just saw the news. Was that your flight? Are you all right?"

"Yeah, I'm fine." She's surprised by the tears that spring to her eyes now that her adrenaline has worn off. She blinks them away and opens the driver's door.

Carter exhales into the phone. "Thank God. They reported you were having a mechanical issue, along with the storm. I was afraid . . . Are you on your way home?"

"I'm just leaving the airport."

"I'm at the hospital, but I'm going to see if someone can cover for me for the rest of the day. I want to be with you."

"You don't have to—"

"I want to."

His words cause a release of tension from her upper body along with fresh excitement at the thought of seeing him. She peers at the rain beating against her windshield. "Okay. I'd like that."

"Anna?"

"Carter?"

She smiles as she starts her car. "You go first."

"I love you."

Fresh tears blur her vision until she blinks them back. "I love you too."

CHAPTER FIFTY-FIVE

TINA

Tina stares out the Black Hawk's window as they fly low along the eastern shores of Seneca Lake. Moments ago, she spotted her parents' old cabin as they flew over the western edges of the narrow body of water. Now, they soar over the forested area she recognizes as Sampson State Park. She hiked this area with her parents a couple of times when she was in high school.

Her coffee rises to the back of her throat at the thought of the innocent baby being somewhere among these trees. She strains to spot any sort of movement within the forest, but it's too dense for her to see anything with her naked eye besides the thick foliage.

"We've got a heat signature!"

Tina turns from the window on her right toward the SWAT member seated on the other side of Castillo. He points to his laptop screen.

Tina leans into her supervisor to get a better look. A small reddish-orange blob centers the thermal image.

"It's moving!" the tactical agent announces.

"We need to get on the ground!" Castillo shouts.

"Roger." The pilot's voice comes over their headphones. "The Seneca Army Depot backs up against the state park. I'll set us down on their parking lot."

"Agent Harris," Castillo says into his mouthpiece, "have local authorities dispatched to the army depot. We're going to need some vehicles."

"Copy that."

As the chopper noses over, Tina closes her eyes, gripping a handle to her right as they get tossed about by the wind on their way down. She bounces in her seat when the Black Hawk's wheels hit the asphalt, and she opens her eyes.

As the door slides open, wind rushes inside the fuselage. Tina climbs out, followed by Castillo and a few of the SWAT team. The tactical agent with the laptop remains in his seat.

"What's the ETA on the local authorities?" Castillo yells to one of the SWAT agents.

Tina glances around the depot.

"Seneca PD dispatched two vehicles. One should be here in the next minute or two. The other is ten minutes out."

A patrol car marked "Seneca County Sheriff" pulls to a stop alongside the agents who have their heads down as the Black Hawk lifts back into the air.

"You two come with me!" Castillo points to Tina and a SWAT agent. "You guys take the next car," he shouts to the three other SWAT members on the ground. "We'll try to block him in."

Tina jogs after Castillo to the patrol car and climbs into the back beside the SWAT agent.

Castillo turns to the Seneca officer, who looks at him expectantly. Her hair is pulled into a ponytail at the base of her neck, and her eyes are serious.

"We spotted the heat signature of a person moving through the forest just east of Northlake Road," Castillo tells her.

She speeds out of the army depot and turns onto the two-lane highway before cutting into a road that leads to the state forest. They pass a small dirt road: PASCAL LANE. Tina almost hit a deer in this very spot one night, driving to her parents' place with Isabel in a car seat. She studies the forest out her side window. It's strange being in a place she knows so well, searching for a fugitive.

"We've regained a visual on the thermal activity. Suspect is moving slow, now on the west side of Northlake Road, heading toward the lake."

The voice that abruptly comes from the SWAT agent's radio in the seat next to her makes Tina jump.

"Roger," he says. "We're en route, heading north on Sampson State Park Road."

"We see you," the voice crackles through the radio. "You're approaching the suspect."

The officer steps on the gas.

"Suspect is now one hundred yards to your left."

"Stop!" Castillo orders.

The patrol car brakes to a halt. Castillo throws open the passenger door.

"Wait!" the radio crackles. "Suspect is moving north at increasing speed. He's getting into a vehicle on the passenger side . . . looks like a pickup truck. The truck is now moving north."

The Seneca officer reverses down the road. "There's an offshoot back here to a forest road," she says. "That must be what they're driving on."

"Head straight ahead!" Tina shouts. "I know that road. It meets up with this one farther north. Keep going and we'll run right into them."

The officer stops and looks to Castillo for approval.

He points out the windshield. "Go!"

She puts the car into drive and speeds up the road, thrusting Tina against the back of her seat. Tina stares out the side window, along with the SWAT member, until they pass a narrow dirt road on their left.

"That's it! Right here!"

The officer slams on the brakes as a black truck appears, rounding the corner of the dirt road. Everyone but Tina jumps out of the vehicle as the truck screeches to a stop a few feet from the patrol car.

Tina watches the three of them draw their weapons as Castillo orders the two men inside the truck to step out with their hands on their heads. The passenger door to the truck swings open. Tina registers the barrel of a pistol pointed at the car and ducks seconds before a loud blast echoes through the forest.

"Stop!" she screams. "The baby! Hold your fire!"

She hears Castillo shout something, but his voice is so faint she realizes he's away from the car. The sound of the Black Hawk helicopter grows steadily, filling the silence. The Seneca officer returns to the driver's seat and makes a call over the radio.

Tina slowly lifts her head to look at the truck sitting empty with both its doors open.

"Requesting backup on Northlake Road in Sampson State Park. Two armed suspects have fled their vehicle on foot. FBI is in pursuit." The officer's shouts into the car's microphone are almost drowned out by the rising thump-thump-thump of the Black Hawk's rotor blades hovering overhead.

Pulse pounding, Tina crawls out of the car, trying to avoid pressing her palms into the small shards of glass littered across the pavement from the shots fired. When she gets to her feet, she hears something like a squawk coming from inside the cab.

"Ma'am, I need you to stay back," the officer calls from behind her as Tina approaches the truck.

Liam, she thinks. *Please, God, let it be Liam.*

"Stop! I need to secure the vehicle."

Tina rounds the opened passenger door. She's aware of the Seneca officer rushing toward her in her periphery, but all Tina can focus on is the car seat in the middle of the truck bench. And the baby who looks to be asleep inside it.

Tina recognizes his thin blond waves from Makayla Rossi's Instagram. His eyes are closed, his jaw slack. Her heart plummets into her stomach, thinking of the gunshots fired moments before. *There's no way he could've slept through that.*

She's unsure whether the sharp gasp comes from her or the officer standing right behind her as Tina places her hand on the infant's chest, relieved to feel that he's warm to the touch.

"He's breathing," she announces after feeling the shallow rise and fall of his chest beneath her palm.

Tina unbuckles him from the seat and tries to rouse him awake. His eyelids flutter open before closing again. "But we need an ambulance. *Now!*"

CHAPTER FIFTY-SIX

JACK

At the sight of his wife, Jack jumps to his feet in the FBI conference room where he's been sitting across from Agent Pratt for the last half hour, recounting what happened at his condo. Makayla follows a dark-haired agent through the doorway. Her eyes are red, and the grief-stricken shock on her face matches his own.

"Have they found him?" she asks as Jack closes the space between them.

"Not yet." He envelops her in a hug.

A sob escapes her throat when he draws her against him.

"We'd like to ask you both a few more questions while we wait," Pratt says after a moment.

Jack lets go of Makayla, and they take seats across from Pratt.

"I'm Agent Ruiz," the female agent says to Jack.

Agent Ruiz sits next to Pratt as he slides a paper with six photos toward Makayla that Jack has already seen. "Can you confirm which of these men was on the flight? Keep in mind that their hairstyles or facial hair might be different."

Makayla looks between the six photos before she points to the one on the bottom-left corner. "His hair was shorter, but that's definitely him."

Agent Pratt appears satisfied with her choice. "His name is Conner Abrams. He was released from Otisville earlier this year after serving a sentence for third-degree robbery." The agent slides an enlarged driver's license photo beside the photo montage. "He used this driver's license to get through security. Had you ever seen him before today?"

Her mouth quivers as she shakes her head. "No."

"We're still working to identify the female parachuter, but we'll know soon. And we do know she was also traveling under a stolen ID."

"I think she befriended me online a few months ago, posing as another mom from my mother's group." Makayla gestures toward Agent Ruiz. "I told her on the way here."

Pratt looks at Jack. "Is this Cori, the friend whose contact information you sent me earlier?"

"Yes." Jack glances at his wife, reading the devastation on her face. He wishes he could comfort her but knows that nothing will. Unless they get Liam back—alive.

"Have you met her in person?" he asks Makayla.

"After she told me she was at our group's park day, I . . . I thought I had. But no, I don't think I did."

"Do you have her address?"

"No." Makayla presses her lips together. "But I told her all about my trip. My travel dates and that we were taking a nonstop flight." A tear slides down her cheek. "I never suspected anything, and I gave her everything she needed to know. It's my fault."

Jack takes her hand. "No, it's not."

"We'll need to see all the correspondence the two of you have had. Text messages, voicemails, online messaging. Everything."

"It's all on my phone."

As Makayla reaches into her pocket, Jack stares at Conner Abrams's photograph, feeling sick at the thought of Liam's fate being in this burly criminal's hands.

"I don't understand how this could've happened." He tears his eyes from the photo and looks at Pratt. "How did they even get an electric saw through security?"

"They disguised it as an electric shaver," Agent Ruiz says as Makayla extends her phone to Pratt. "We found it in the lavatory. They used a six-inch saw blade, which is the maximum length you can take through security. Then they attached it to an electric drill custom-made to look like a shaver. They even used the shaver outlet in the lavatory to power it. I'm guessing they packed it as two separate pieces to ensure it would pass through security."

"This was very well planned," she adds. "Our CSI team is still processing the plane, but it looks like the kidnappers wiped down the surfaces on their row so their fingerprints wouldn't be left behind. We would've expected several partial prints on the armrests and tray tables, but the only prints were on the armrests of the aisle seat." She looks at Makayla. "And we believe those will be yours. There were no prints on the electric saw or lavatory, either, so they probably wore gloves at that point, knowing they'd be leaving the tool behind."

A tall woman wearing a navy pantsuit appears in the conference room doorway.

"Sorry to interrupt," she says. "But they've ID'd the female parachuter." She moves toward the conference table, laying a paper in front of Ruiz.

Jack leans forward and sees another enlarged driver's license photo of a dark-haired woman.

"Her name is Raquel Cabral," the woman says. "She works as a nurse at the same hospital as Jemma Neilson, whose ID she stole from her locker and used to board the plane. The two of them look a lot alike."

Pratt's phone rings atop the table. "It's Castillo," he says.

The woman goes quiet, and every pair of eyes is on him as he takes the call.

"This is Pratt."

Jack watches the agent intently, trying to read his expression as Pratt listens to the other end of the call. Makayla squeezes his hand.

Jack strains to hear what's being said. The caller sounds male, but Jack can't make out the words. Pratt gets up from the table, turning his back to them as he moves toward the window.

Jack holds his breath.

"Okay. I'm coming up there. I'll let you know when I'm close."

Pratt lowers his phone. As the agent turns from the window, Jack steels himself for the worst news of his life.

"They found your son."

Makayla gasps. A ripple of fear shoots down Jack's spine.

"He appears to have been heavily sedated. But he's alive."

Makayla emits a whimper.

"He's being taken to the nearest hospital in Syracuse."

"Thank God." Jack wraps his arms around Makayla. He closes his eyes, and a tear escapes down his face. He kisses the top of her head.

He's alive. He's alive.

"How—" Jack clears his throat. "How did they find him?"

"Two men were stopped in a truck on a forest service road a few miles from where the woman's body was found. The men tried to escape on foot after firing at our agents, but they didn't get far. Liam was discovered in a car seat in the cab of the truck by one of our analysts. Both men are in custody. One has been ID'd as Conner Abrams, who's also being treated at the hospital for a broken leg."

"But Liam, he's okay?" Makayla asks.

"He's alive. He had no apparent injuries aside from being sedated, but we can find out more once he reaches the hospital."

Jack grips Makayla's hand and stands. "Which hospital?" His pulse quickens. It would take them over four hours to drive to Syracuse from the city. Liam needs them now.

"Syracuse General." He shoots a glance at Ruiz, the corner of his mouth upturning for a moment. "You can ride with us."

Ruiz is already up from her seat and leads them toward the door. "I'll drive."

CHAPTER FIFTY-SEVEN

JACK

Jack releases Makayla's hand in the back seat of the FBI's SUV when they pull into the Syracuse hospital parking lot. Jack and Makayla hardly spoke during the drive. The last two hours have felt like an eternity.

"We're here," Agent Pratt says. "Liam's abductor is here at the hospital with a broken leg. We're going to interview him before they take him to jail. We'll let you know when we have more information for you."

Makayla is already out of the SUV when it slows to a stop in front of the hospital's main entrance.

"Thanks," Jack says to the agent before jumping out behind her and following her through the automatic sliding doors.

Makayla stops a man in scrubs holding a large coffee who strides past them. "Excuse me! We're looking for our baby. He's been taken to the pediatric unit."

Jack's eyes fall to the large, bolded letters—*RN*—on the top of his name badge.

"That's on the fourth floor. Here." He motions down the hallway and continues walking. "I'll take you to the elevators."

They follow behind him in silence, and Jack wills the nurse to move faster as he watches him take a careful sip from his coffee. Next to him, Makayla seems wound up like a spring, still shaken from her ordeal, her body practically humming with nervous energy. They turn left down another hallway, and the nurse points to the elevator up ahead.

"There you go. Fourth floor," he repeats.

"Thank you," Makayla says.

She shoots Jack a look and quickens her pace. When she presses the button on the wall, the elevator doors open immediately. They exit on the fourth floor and rush toward a nurse's station straight ahead. Jack feels almost giddy with anticipation. A young woman wearing a Winnie-the-Pooh scrub top looks up from behind the desk.

"We're looking for our baby," Makayla breathes. "Liam Rossi. We're his parents."

"Oh, yes." She stands, turning to another woman behind the desk. "Can you call Dr. Manalo and tell him Liam Rossi's parents have arrived?"

"Sure." The older woman reaches for a phone.

The young woman meets Makayla's gaze. "I'm Liam's nurse, Kate. I'll take you to him." Kate smiles as she moves around the desk. "Your little skydiver is doing great," she says over her shoulder as they follow her down the hall.

The colorful walls are decorated with lit-up artwork of tropical fish and bright-colored sea life.

"Was Dr. Manalo able to get ahold of you?"

"Yes," Jack says. "He called us on our way here. He said Liam was sedated when he was found but still breathing on his own. And that they gave him Narcan in the ambulance."

"That's right," Kate says. "When the medics first assessed him, Liam's breathing rate and blood oxygen were low, but he responded immediately to the Narcan and became more alert. His blood pressure was also low, so they gave him some fluids through an IV. His vitals are now stable." Kate turns. "Did Dr. Manalo tell you we performed a CT scan?"

Makayla nods. "He said it was normal. No internal bleeding or trauma from the fall."

"That's right," Kate says as a man in light-blue hospital scrubs appears around a corner at the end of the hall. "Dr. Manalo, these are Liam Rossi's parents." She extends an arm toward Jack and Makayla.

"Nice to meet you." He nods at Makayla and then Jack. "Like I said over the phone, Liam's not showing any signs of neurological damage. We'll continue to monitor him, but he doesn't appear to have sustained any injuries. From the information we gathered from the flight, the parachuters jumped around fifteen thousand feet. I suspect his low breathing rate and blood pressure when they found him were more a result of his sedation than the jump from the plane."

The nurse flashes them a warm smile. "He's a very lucky little boy."

Jack's pulse quickens when the nurse slows in front of a room.

"Liam fell asleep about an hour ago, after I gave him a bottle." Kate turns before leading them into the room. "I can't imagine how scary all this must've been for you."

Dr. Manalo pauses, motioning for Jack and Makayla to go first.

Jack's heart throbs seeing Liam's sleeping face inside a large crib. The pacifier the hospital had given him falls from his mouth. Makayla catches it with a half laugh, half sob before she leans over the side and swoops him up. Thin cords stick out from the bottom of his blanket, attaching him to the cardiac monitor that hangs on the wall above the crib.

Liam stirs, but his eyes remain closed. Makayla draws him against her, cradling the back of his small head with her palm. Liam's eyes flutter open, and Jack kisses him on the cheek. Liam coos through the pacifier.

Makayla smiles down at him as fresh tears well in her eyes. Jack blinks away his own, knowing how different this night could've gone. He places a hand on Liam's back and leans his head against Makayla's, never more grateful for anything in his life.

CHAPTER
FIFTY-EIGHT

MAKAYLA

Makayla holds Liam in her lap, sitting beside Jack on the room's foldout couch. The weight of Liam's head on her forearm has made her hand numb, but she makes no effort to move him. Her gaze drifts out the window, settling on the tall patch of trees beyond the parking lot. She envisions the woman she knew as Jemma—and most likely Cori—suspended in the branches of a tree just like these, her head hanging flaccid from her broken neck. Makayla closes her eyes.

An image of Liam soaring toward the ground, strapped to his kidnapper's chest, overtakes her mind. On their way to the hospital, Agent Pratt informed them that a baby carrier had been found lying in the front seat of the truck where Liam was discovered by the upstate authorities. It must've been how the man was able to keep hold of Liam after jumping out of the plane. She thinks of Liam's head bobbing when they hit the ground. Even if it was a smooth landing, it still had to have been quite a jolt.

An involuntary shudder runs down her spine. The whole sequence of events feels unfathomable.

The few times she spoke with Cori over the phone, Cori sounded like she had an accent from upstate New York, where she said she had grown up. But it would've been easy enough to fake.

Being from Seattle, Makayla wasn't an expert at East Coast accents, but Jemma sounded like she was from Brooklyn or maybe Long Island. Now that she thinks about it, there was something familiar about Jemma's voice. The Brooklyn accent—and the trauma of Liam's abduction—kept her from noticing it at the time.

Makayla glances at her phone on the couch beside her. Despite her suspicions, she tried calling Cori on their way to the hospital, hoping Cori would answer so Makayla could ask her to come over—and prove her suspicions wrong. But Cori's phone went straight to voicemail. And since the last message Makayla received from Cori on the flight, before Liam's kidnappers jumped out of the plane, she hasn't sent her any more messages. She pictures Jemma sending the text, sitting a few rows behind her, smiling at Makayla's naivete while her baby was hidden in the woman's pet carrier. She's tempted to send Cori a text to see if she replies. But she knows she won't. Because there was never any Cori—only a scam to get rich by stealing Liam. And now she's dead.

A wave of guilt washes over her. She turns to Jack.

"This is all my fault."

Jack puts his hand on her knee. "No."

"I told Cori everything she needed to know about our trip. I gave her my flight number without realizing it, told her where I was sitting. I never even questioned that I didn't remember meeting her."

Jack squeezes her leg. "It's not your fault. How could you have known?"

She puts her hand on Jack's, allowing her guilt to be replaced with relief. Liam is *alive*. It all makes sense now that she knows he was sedated, the reason for him not making any noise throughout the flight.

Makayla turns to her husband as the questions she buried earlier resurface in her mind.

"I'm sorry about Sabrina."

Jack swallows. "Yeah, me too."

"But I still don't understand why she came to our condo. I could see Lionel coming over, but I thought you and Sabrina had a falling out years ago over her giving one of your accounts to someone else. Am I missing something between you and her?"

Jack doesn't answer immediately. Makayla studies him, steeling herself for what he seems so hesitant to tell her.

CHAPTER FIFTY-NINE

JACK

Makayla's knowing eyes search Jack's as she waits for his response. After he met Makayla, there was never anything between him and Sabrina. He should never have kissed Sabrina at the Christmas party, and he hates himself for his moment of weakness.

After the hell she went through last night, he doesn't want to give Makayla any more bad news. But he doesn't want to lie to her either.

He takes her hand. "No. You weren't missing anything—there was nothing going on between Sabrina and me." He should tell her another time, not today, but the words are out of his mouth before he can stop them. "She kissed me at the firm's Christmas party on the yacht ten years ago. I kissed her back, but only for a moment. I felt horrible afterward, even though it meant nothing."

Makayla pulls her hand out from his.

"I should've told you—I know. But you'd just lost your mother, and I . . . I didn't want to hurt you. And I didn't want you to worry about something that you didn't need to." He reaches for her hand again, and she lets him intertwine his fingers with hers. "I love you, Makayla. I've always loved you."

He glances at Liam. "Sabrina made another pass at me a few months after that, and I shot her down. That's why she gave my Goldstein account to someone else. I shouldn't have let her come up last night." He looks out the window at the parking lot below. "And now she's dead."

"That's not your fault." Makayla rubs her thumb against his forefinger. "Thank you for telling me."

Jack meets her eyes. "There's something else I need to tell you. About Lionel."

Makayla remains quiet as Jack tells her about the fraud and Lionel's threats—the thing he was so terrified of before going to bed, which has now paled in comparison to nearly losing their son. When he finishes telling her the story, it strikes him that Lionel is the one who ended up losing a child last night. By now, he's probably gotten the news that his daughter is dead.

Despite Lionel's betrayal, Jack's heart aches for the loss of his childhood best friend and his longtime father figure.

Makayla reaches for his hand as a knock sounds on the hospital room's door. Liam opens his eyes as Kate appears in the open doorway.

"There are three FBI agents here. And they're asking to speak with you."

CHAPTER SIXTY

MAKAYLA

Liam squirms on Makayla's lap, patting her forearm with his hand as he watches the FBI agents and analyst seated across from them. Agent Pratt introduced the analyst as Tina Farrar, adding that she was the one who found Liam in the kidnapper's truck. Jack shook the analyst's hand, and Makayla threw her arms around the woman's neck, thanking her. The two women held each other for a moment before they sat down.

Agent Ruiz flashes Liam a smile.

"What did the man who kidnapped our son tell you?" Jack asks them.

The agents suggested they speak in the pediatric floor's private consultation room, but Liam still needed to be attached to the monitor, and Makayla wasn't letting him out of her sight.

"He told us quite a lot." Agent Pratt leans forward, resting his elbows on his knees. "He knows we also have his getaway driver in custody and wanted to be the first to tell us everything."

"We still have to confirm his story," Ruiz adds. "But so far it seems to check out."

Pratt interlaces his fingers. "The deceased female parachuter, Raquel Cabral, was Conner Abrams's girlfriend." His gaze travels from Makayla to Jack. "According to him, Cabral was placed on leave by the hospital where she worked last spring while an investigation played out over

Cabral's suspected involvement in a patient's death. The hospital wasn't able to prove anything, and Cabral was later allowed to return to work. While she was on leave, she read your featured article in *Forbes*. Afraid she would lose her job—and possibly her health-care license—she was the one who came up with the plan to kidnap Liam after finding Makayla on social media, where she discovered Makayla was pregnant."

Makayla's breath catches in her throat as Pratt's eyes return to hers.

"She created a fake Facebook account and joined your Tribeca mother's group, posing as a new mom named Cori. When she discovered your mom was Lydia Banks, Cabral lied about her mother being Snow Browning, knowing it would create a welcome connection. After learning about your trip to Alaska, she told Abrams about her scheme, and he enlisted two of his fellow inmates from Otisville to orchestrate Liam's abduction. The getaway driver we arrested had done time for fraud and internet crime. More importantly, he has a brother who lives in Hong Kong who helped set up a bank account they thought would be untouchable."

Jack narrows his eyes. "I still don't understand how they got on the flight with stolen IDs. How were they planning to get away with it?"

Liam grasps Makayla's necklace and tugs, pulling her toward him. She works to pry the chain out of his little fingers.

"Cabral worked as a registered nurse at the same hospital as Jemma Neilson, whose ID she stole," Analyst Farrar says. "The two women look very similar."

Pratt nods. "Apparently, Cabral had been mistaken for Jemma Neilson once by a physician even though the two women worked on different units. According to Abrams, Cabral used her hospital ID to sneak into the locked break room on Jemma Neilson's floor. She took a photo of Neilson's driver's license. The man who broke into your condo has an associate who makes fake IDs, and he replicated the license, which Cabral switched during another shift." Pratt shifts in his seat. "Conner Abrams did the same thing while working at a couple of bars in the city. He waited until he found a regular who he could pass for and replicated his driver's license."

Liam wiggles beneath her arms when Makayla draws him closer. "Did they say how they sedated him on the flight?"

Ruiz nods. "At the start of the flight, Conner Abrams bumped into you on purpose. After monitoring your images on social media, they knew what kind of pacifier Liam used, so Cabral gave you back an identical one that had a slit cut through the teat, which was filled with a dose of oral morphine mixed with sucrose that Cabral obtained from the hospital where she worked."

Makayla runs her hand down the back of Liam's head, smoothing his hair. She recalls being surprised by how quickly he fell into a deep sleep on the flight. At the time, she'd been grateful—not at all suspicious.

"What if I hadn't gone to the bathroom?" She glances at Jack. "They couldn't have known I was going to do that."

"Abrams said they were counting on you either falling asleep or using the lavatory without him. They also had a plan for Cabral to distract you while Abrams snatched Liam if neither of those things happened."

"What about the flight attendant?" Makayla asks. "Derek. Has his body been found?"

She holds her breath as Pratt gives a slow shake of his head.

"Not yet," says Farrar. "It's dense forest area all around the Finger Lakes, so it's possible his body may never be recovered. But as you know, his fall would not have been survivable."

She does, but it doesn't stop the sob that escapes from her throat.

Jack wraps his arm around Makayla's shoulders. "What were they planning to do with Liam? If you hadn't have found him?"

The two agents exchange a glance before Pratt speaks. "Even though they were prepared to parachute out of the plane with Liam in the baby carrier, taking him with them was plan B. Abrams said if they had gotten the message from the man who broke into your condo that the funds were transferred, they would have left Liam in the dog carrier to be found after the plane landed. According to Abrams—and his driver—they were planning to return Liam once they got confirmation that the money was transferred."

Makayla straightens. "When the flight attendants searched their bags, didn't they see the baby carrier? That should've been cause for alarm." She inhales to the base of her lungs, trying to dispel the fury ignited by Britt's incompetent failure to check the pet carrier—and notice the couple had packed parachutes, not backpacks.

Agent Ruiz nods. "Yes. When I interviewed the attendant who searched their bags—and failed to check the pet carrier—she said she did see a small baby carrier inside one of their carry-ons. When she questioned them about it, they told her it was for their dog. Said she got tired on their long hikes."

Makayla turns toward the window. "She should've known better."

"I agree." Ruiz shrugs. "She admitted to not looking at it that closely and taking the couple's word for it. Said she felt uncomfortable having to search the passengers' bags. And having no children or pets of her own, she didn't know the difference between a chest pet carrier and a baby one."

Liam stirs on her lap, cooing when Analyst Farrar returns his smile. Now that Liam is safe, the sting of Cori's betrayal sets in. All these months, her trusted friend wasn't real. She used Makayla like a pawn. *And I played right into her hand.*

When it comes to friendships, she's usually guarded at first. But she was so quick to let Cori in. It could've cost Liam his life. A chill runs up the back of her neck.

Pratt looks at Jack. "Also, after what you told me about Rothman's fraud, we'll be launching a full investigation into the firm's accounts. So, if you're telling the truth and Rothman's lying, we'll find out."

"Good," Jack says, placing his hands over his knees.

"And the key card found on the man who broke into your condo was one of the building's master keys. One of the building's repairmen reported his key missing this morning. He must've stolen it after being let in the back entrance like he told you."

Makayla looks between the agents and Analyst Farrar. "What if the money had never come through?"

"Fortunately"—Pratt sits up straight—"you'll never have to know."

Makayla locks eyes with the analyst after she stands. "Thank you again for finding him." She smooths the top of Liam's hair. "I can't tell you how grateful I am."

"Just doing my job." The analyst smiles, her gaze traveling to Liam. "I'm glad we were able to. Now, I'm going home to hug my daughter and never let go."

CHAPTER SIXTY-ONE

JACK & MAKAYLA

Nine Months Later

"Smile!"

Jack moves his attention to his reflection on Makayla's phone as she holds it up to capture the three of them in their newly purchased SUV.

Jack smiles, and Makayla snaps the photo before he pulls away from their condo building, towing the U-Haul behind them containing her mother's baby grand.

"Who's excited for our move?"

"Me!" Makayla chirps.

"Ma ma!" Liam points to Makayla as she drops her phone into her purse.

Her Nikon camera sits between them on the center console, ready to capture the sights on their cross-country trip. After what happened, none of them were ready to get on a flight. He doubts Makayla ever will again.

They plan to take over three weeks to make the drive to Anchorage, stopping at several scenic sights along the way, starting with Niagara

Falls and the Great Lakes. As they pass a sign for the Financial District, Jack's thoughts drift to Lionel's arrest six months earlier after the FBI seized the firm's assets.

Jack can't help pitying the man, despite everything he did. His only daughter is dead, his wife of over forty years has left him, and he'll live out the rest of his days at a federal prison—alone and disgraced. Lionel pled guilty to his fraud charges and received a fifty-year prison sentence.

When he heard the news, Jack had been filled with relief at not having to testify against his longtime mentor. He hasn't seen Lionel since Sabrina's funeral. It was hard to hold a grudge after seeing the pain in Lionel's eyes. Despite Lionel's betrayal, Jack still feels the void of his absence in his life and chooses to remember the good times they shared.

They pass the Tribeca art gallery where Makayla's photography was featured last month.

He turns to his wife. "I'm so proud of you."

Makayla grins. "Thank you."

In the back seat, Liam giggles at the small, stuffed bunny in his lap. Jack takes Makayla's hand as they speed through the white-tiled walls of the Holland Tunnel beneath the Hudson River, relishing the time they'll have together on their way to Anchorage over the next three weeks.

Liam's kidnapping and Sabrina's death shook them. Even Jack's father has made an effort to see him more since it happened. He thinks of the hug his father enveloped him in last night when they said goodbye at his parents' home in Brooklyn. And his father's promise to visit them once they were settled in their new home.

He glances at his son in the back seat. Jack knows his relationship with his dad will probably never be what he would like it to be, or the bond he shared with Lionel. But if there's one thing he's learned from what happened last August, it's to make the most of the time he has.

◆ ◆ ◆

Makayla looks at her husband as they cruise beneath the Hudson River. She smiles, remembering the day two months ago when Jack broke the news.

"I got a job."

She'd been folding laundry when Jack blurted the words. She set down the pair of socks and braced herself for Jack to tell her he was starting at a new firm, knowing what this would mean. He would push himself to work all hours of the day and weekends to prove himself and work his way up to a senior account manager all over again.

Jack quit the firm after Lionel's arrest, and they put their condo on the market. Makayla would have no problem leaving it behind, but she feared Jack wouldn't stop until they were able to afford something similar.

Last month, photos she'd taken on her trip to Alaska had been featured at a Tribeca art gallery event. Afterward, she'd been blown away to learn that every photo had sold. Within a few days, the gallery asked to feature her photography again at their summer expo, their biggest event of the year. In the last few weeks, she'd been getting tenfold sales from her photography, which she advertised on her blog. While it helped with their finances, it wasn't enough to sustain the life they've been living.

"It's in Anchorage. I'd be a high school economics teacher."

Makayla spun around. From his high chair, Liam looked between his parents before plopping a Cheerio into his mouth.

"I thought we could get a house near your dad," Jack said. "With a big yard."

Makayla stared at her husband and realized he was serious.

"Liam can grow up hiking and spending more time outdoors. You could do your photography. I could be home every night. Off every summer." Jack stepped toward her as Liam watched them in silence.

"We could have the life you want. And that I want too. The money won't be the same but—"

Makayla threw her arms around his neck. "I don't care about the money." She let go of Jack and turned to her son. "What do you think, Liam? You want to move to Alaska? Have a yard and see your dad—and grandpa—all the time?"

Liam cooed, a Cheerio spilling from his mouth when his toothless smile reached his eyes.

Jack put his hands on the sides of Makayla's waist. "How about you?"

"I'm going to pack right now."

Jack laughed as Makayla marched into their bedroom.

Now, she runs her hand down the back of Jack's head as they emerge from the Holland Tunnel in New Jersey. Above them, a plane descends toward Newark Airport in the clear morning sky. Makayla suppresses a shudder, imagining Liam free-falling out of their aircraft—strapped to his abductor's chest. And Derek, who'd gone out without a parachute, giving his life while trying to save Liam. Three days after his fall, Derek's body was discovered by a couple of hikers on the shore of Cayuga Lake. A medical examiner determined the flight attendant was killed instantly upon impact with the water, and his body was likely submerged for two to three days before floating to the surface.

It's taken months of therapy for her to deal with the guilt she felt for Derek's death—and Liam's abduction. Part of her will always feel responsible for what happened to the flight attendant, but she's come to accept his death as an accident.

After attending his memorial service, she stayed in touch with Derek's mother, who received a substantial death benefit from the airline. It covered all her medical bills, including the experimental cancer treatment Derek was working so hard to help pay for. She's now in full remission. Although Makayla knows nothing will ever fill the void of losing her son.

She averts her gaze from the plane and leans back in her seat, seeing the reflection of Manhattan moving away from them in her rearview mirror across the Hudson River. She stares at the city's skyline shrinking in the distance as they speed along the interstate, thinking the packed-in skyscrapers have never looked more beautiful than they do right now.

Acknowledgments

To my agent, Jill Marsal, I'm incredibly grateful for your support and advice in helping me craft this story from the early stages.

I am beyond grateful to the team at Thomas & Mercer for making this all happen. To my editors, Jessica Tribble Wells and Kevin Smith, you are a joy to work with. Thank you for your brilliant insight, which allowed me to take this story to the next level.

To Leslie Lutz, thank you for your tireless efforts in working through the plot with me in numerous stages of this manuscript.

Thank you to Nancy Brown for your eagle eye, and to Traci Finlay for your guidance in my early draft.

Detective Rolf Norton, thank you for kindly answering my questions once again and helping me make this story as procedurally accurate as possible.

Thank you to retired FBI Special Agent Jerri Williams for speaking with me and sharing your knowledge regarding the FBI's role in this scenario. Any errors are entirely my own.

To Ty Kelly of Pelo Blanco Photography, thank you for taking the time to educate me on exposure and conveying emotion through photography.

To my parents, thank you for always supporting me. Dad, thank you for helping me bring authenticity to all the cockpit scenes in this story.

Cary, thanks for being my paramedic consultant.

Elise and Anders, thank you for cheering me on and for your excitement over my writing. You are my world.

To Jack Lawson and Keira Henson, thanks for all you do behind the scenes.

There are no words to express my gratitude to the readers, bookstagrammers, and bloggers whose support makes all this possible. Thank you, thank you, thank you.

ABOUT THE AUTHOR

Photo © 2021 Brittney Kluse Photography

Audrey J. Cole is a *USA Today* bestselling author of eleven novels. She resides in the Pacific Northwest with her two children. Before she began writing full time, Cole worked as a neonatal intensive care nurse for eleven years. She's also a pilot's daughter.

Want to hear about Audrey's next release and get free bonus content to her books? Visit her website at www.audreyjcole.com.